PEN

ARU

A journalist for over seventeen years, Pinki Virani was born in Mumbai in 1959. Educated at Mumbai, Pune and Mussoorie, she did her Masters in Journalism from Columbia University in USA under the aegis of the Fondation Aga Khan scholarship. Following an internship at a mainline London newspaper, she reported extensively on the race riots in Britain before returning to a career in journalism in India. She launched a city magazine, edited a city paper, and reported from all over the country as special correspondent for a national weekly.

Currently, she is working on her second book. Pinki Virani is married to a fellow journalist and lives in Mumbai.

# Aruna's Story

## The True Account of a Rape and its Aftermath

## Pinki Virani

PENGUIN BOOKS

Penguin Books India (P) Ltd., 11 Community Centre, Panchsheel Park, New Delhi 110 017, India
Penguin Books Ltd., 27 Wrights Lane, London W8 5TZ, UK
Penguin Books USA Inc., 375 Hudson Street, New York, New York 10014, USA
Penguin Books Australia Ltd., Ringwood, Victoria, Australia
Penguin Books Canada Ltd., 10 Alcorn Avenue, Suite 300, Toronto, Ontario, MAV 3B2, Canada
Penguin Books (NZ) Ltd., 182-190 Wairau Road, Auckland, 10, New Zealand

First published in Viking by Penguin Books India (P) Ltd. 1998
First published by Penguin Books India 1999

10 9 8 7 6 5 4 3 2 1

Typeset in *Garamond* by SÜRYA, New Delhi

Part of the royalties from this book will go towards looking after Aruna Shanbaug during her
lifetime and to a charity in her name thereafter.

*For Roshanara, and for all mothers
who are the guiding light in their
daughters' world*

# Contents

Author's Note       ix

Into the Twilight Zone       1

Out of Konkan Land       85

Towards an Elusive Mukti       191

# Author's Note

I had begun work on another book, not completely non-fiction like this one, when this assignment came. I was hesitant. As a journalist I report on events in order to fulfil people's right to know. To write an entire book, would I be exploiting Aruna Shanbaug's condition?

I have kept in touch with Aruna for a long time. When I was telling Bachi Karkaria, Senior Editor, *The Times of India*, about Aruna, she suggested I write 1,400 words for *The Sunday Times*. The response was staggering. Perfect strangers found out my phone number (this is not easy since it's not listed under my name) to tell me they would pray for Aruna's release; most of them were women. The dean and KEM Hospital were flooded with letters and calls, from as far away as Mizoram. Subsequently the hospital began receiving letters from readers of regional papers (my copy had been lifted and used without credit to either *The Times* or me), in Hindi, Marathi, Gujarati, Kannada, Tamil, Malyalam and Telugu. Later, when a friend returned from a Dubai holiday she told me about a nurse who had been raped in a hospital a little before her marriage, who suffered brain damage as a result and who is still suffering in the same hospital. She had read a 'special report from India', a no-credit rewrite of my article in one of the Middle Eastern English dailies, had cut it and mailed it to her sister in Canada.

Indians everywhere would be interested in reading Aruna's story, the publishers said. An incentive to write 75,000 words. But where would I get the details from, her personal life, her past, addresses of a family long gone, even the police file which was twenty-five years old? I asked KEM if they could locate her personnel file, year 1966. They voiced their doubts. They found it. I took this as a good sign even though I knew the rest of the research would be at enormous cost, mentally, physically and financially. Very slowly, but surely, lost files began reappearing; people provided their time and assistance because it was Aruna's story. Things which I thought would be near impossible to find out—several sources have died since 1973, mostly of old age—became known to me concretely through other sources I never realized existed. Doctors gave freely of their time, patiently explaining medical terms, wondering aloud why their medical community had done no case-study on staff nurse Aruna Shanbaug.

In the course of my investigation I discovered how exactly Aruna had been raped. I also discovered, to my shock, that the rapist did not serve a sentence for it. This is when I decided that Aruna's real story had to be told.

Thank you for buying this book. Half of the royalties from the sale of it are going towards making Aruna Shanbaug's remaining life as comfortable as possible. When she dies, the cheques will be sent in her name to a charitable women's organization which educates young girls in nursing.

Never before in my life have so many people been so directly responsible for my being indebted on behalf of a woman who has no idea that this has been written. I am grateful to all those who have been named in this book starting with Dr Pragnya Pai, including those whose names have been changed on their request. I also appreciate the assistance provided to me by the Bombay police, working and retired, starting with officers T.K. Chowdhary, K. Subrahmanyam, S.P.S. Yadav and V. Balachandran.

And then there is deep gratitude to two men who have been my pillars as I wrote this. V. Shankar Aiyar and David Davidar, thank you.

# Into the Twilight Zone

His eyes glittering in the dark, the man waits. He touches the dog chain, it is there. Wanting to be used. Its metal links feel cold to his fingers, but cruelly comforting. He has been seeing himself doing this for a long, long time.

Today he had wrapped the dog chain around his own neck thinking it to be her slender waist. Her white, milk-white waist with its delicate curves. In the middle of which is her perfectly round, tiny belly button. He has seen it shining through her sari before.

Her, with only the dog chain on her. Around her waist. Resting on her curves, caressing her navel. Above which rise and fall those small round, creamy breasts. Often he has imagined them filling his palms perfectly. Her light-brown nipples tautening in his cupped palms as she stands there, berating him in front of everybody. He would tighten his palms, squeezing the nipples sharply. She would walk away.

Not this time.

She will be here soon. He touches it again, the lengthy dog chain under his bush shirt, looped loosely around his waist on the top of his khaki half-pants. And waits.

Above him, at ground level, the world goes about its business. Double-decker buses brimming with people roar past, taxis toot impatiently ignoring the 'Hospital—No Horns' signage. In the cluster of buildings which constitute the KEM Hospital, doctors heal the ailing and ease the pain of the dying. Nurses bustle about, filling patient-charts and syringes.

She thinks she's going to marry her doctor. After he has done with her, it remains to be seen if her doctor does marry her.

But he isn't the sort who harms a woman, least of all someone as fragile as her. He had seen himself scooping up her bare body in his arms like that of a new bride, when she announced her marriage. She had felt like a lush feather rubbing against his chest.

By then she had been asking for it.

He has no doubt he will overpower her easily. He is well built, his arms can be like steel bands, his wife knows this. He flexes, blue-green veins stand out in relief under his name tattooed on his right forearm. No one will come to her aid either, even if she screams loudly. She will not be heard from this huge, cold tomb filled with dead files and discarded furniture.

Holding it up, he will swing one end of the dog chain in front of her. Those eyes which have looked at him with contempt, will fill with fear. That mouth which has belittled him, time and again in front of people, will beg for mercy. He will undress the bride, slowly, as she implores him to let her go. He will take her once, that's all, she will learn her lesson from it forever.

A key against the main door. It swings open. He moves a little more into the darkness.

She is surprised to find the door unlocked, he can see that. She closes it behind her, locks it with her key and clasping a freshly laundered sari packet walks towards her office down the end of the corridor. The evening, like the winter-morning, has settled in with a chill. Down here it feels a few degrees cooler. She stops abruptly, goes back to the main door to recheck it, and draws an additional bolt. Quickly she walks to her duty room, unlocks the door which swings inwards. She enters the office, lightly pushes the door behind her, it swings back, stops mid-way.

He silently adjusts his position in the dark to watch her through the gap. A shaft of light escapes the door, she has turned on the switch within. Keys click against the wooden cupboard inside where she keeps her clothes and handbag. A scrape of furniture, she crosses his line of vision to unlock the door of the inner room. It is a room meant for experimental surgeries on dogs, she has used it to change into her uniform for the last twenty-seven days. She has removed her nurse's cap, her jet-black shoulder-length hair is free of its pinned confines. She has already removed her blue belt, with her left hand she's unhooking the buttons of her uniform, with her right she's unlocking the dog surgery door.

Out of his line of vision, back into it, with her sari and petticoat on her arm. She goes into the darkness of the dog surgery, leaving the door open. He hears efficient rustles, she is out quickly, adjusting her sari pleats, running her hand over her blouse to smooth down the swiftly-tied fabric. She crosses over to the desk.

Now.

He pads to the door, pushes it open. The hinges creak ever so slightly in the silence. She looks up, straight at him. Why is there no fear on her face? She is standing at the desk, her brown handbag open in front of her, a small cane change purse open in her hands. She sets down the small purse on the table, her hands are shaking slightly, he is happy to see that. She blinks, squares her shoulders, looks at him, says nothing.

Now he will see that fear.

He reaches under his shirt, and pulls out the dog chain.

She swallows. He magnifies the sound of its rattle as he trails the dog chain on the desk in front of her. Her eyes follow the chain, she swallows again, moves back from the desk between them. Her chest heaves slightly, her eyes never leave the chain.

Now he is angry. She is not even afraid, he is going to have to make her cry so that she begs for his mercy.

He breaches the distance between them in four swift steps, slaps her hard on her left cheek. She falls against the wooden cupboard behind her, regains her balance, flies at him with her hands outstretched. He drops the dog chain, grasps both her wrists, squeezes them tight, pulls her towards him and presses his mouth down on her lips. She moves her mouth, bites him sharply on his left cheek. He has her wrists in a vice-like grip, he's holding her hard against himself, she bites where she can. Once, twice, thrice at different places on his left cheek.

He holds both her wrists in his left hand, with the back of his right he slaps her on her right cheek. She sags. He shoves her down on the desk with her back to the wood, clenches her ankles between his, straddles her thighs, leans over and rips open her blouse. She reaches out to push him, her fingernails claw at his neck.

He grasps her wrists in his left hand again, yanks her forward from the desk towards himself, swoops down on her, his mouth on hers and bites her on her lower lip drawing blood. While biting her lower lip he pulls up her bra. Then he throws her against the desk, yanks up her sari and petticoat, and starts to pull down her panties. She is menstruating. He withdraws his hand. She draws her legs in, kicks him in his midriff, makes to run. He grabs her from behind, knocks her to the floor, picks up the dog chain and wraps it around her neck. She feels the cold metal against her windpipe, tries to flee, he yanks her back with the chain, pushes her towards the dog surgery, she falls into the darkness.

She has fallen on her knees and the back of her hands. The dog chain is around her neck, he tightens it. She chokes, he twists the chain, she gags, fluids flow from her mouth and nose, her head lolls. He pushes away crumpled fabric, pulls down her panties, she is bleeding heavily.

He holds the ends of the chain in one hand, keeps up the pressure, unbuttons himself, feels for her other opening.

With the dog chain pulling at her throat, he rides her in the darkness.

There is another rush of blood, there is vomit and spit between her cheek and the cold floor.

He unwinds the dog chain from around her neck before he leaves, loops it back around his waist. He also takes her gold chain with its pendant from around her neck. From her limp hand he unclasps her wristwatch. He pulls her panties back in place.

He looks into her handbag and finds only a few small notes which he pockets. He picks up the rani-coloured silk sari, which she sent him to get just this afternoon from the laundry, it will look nice on his wife.

He closes the dog surgery door and the main door soundlessly behind him as he leaves.

Time: Between 4.50 and 5.40 p.m. Date: The 27th of November, 1973. Place: A hospital basement in the bowels of Bombay.

7.10 a.m. 28 November 1973. It is distinctly nippy. Twenty-six-year-old Inder

Gulamashi Bait Walmiki rubs his palms against each other and hastens his steps towards his workplace. Like yesterday he is late for work, 'kya karneka, what to do, it's cold'. He is on what used to be called Hospital Avenue, even though the three hospitals in the neighbourhood were never actually on the same road. A children's hospital, a general hospital and KEM were placed in a far-flung triangular formation to each other, built as they were at different times, out of philanthropy. KEM stands for The King Edward VII Memorial Hospital and was built, someone had told Inder in the hospital, during the angrez ka zamaana, British times, by Indians. It had been impressed upon Inder that this was an enormous achievement in those difficult days. The Indians had named the hospital after the angrez rajah to keep him happy so that he would keep giving money to run the hospital. Inder was glad they had so outwitted the rajah, or else he would not have had his job in KEM today.

Inder's father came for work to Bombay from Hoshiyalpur village near Bulandshahr in Uttar Pradesh. He was hired as a sweeper at the KEM, he soon sent for his family from the village and set them up in a hut resting against one of the outside hospital walls. Inder was a child when he played on Hospital Avenue, on the pavements, with his elder brother. It was a foregone conclusion that both sons would follow in their father's footsteps in two of the three hospitals surrounding their shack.

Inder reaches the hospital's Cardiovascular Thoracic Centre, across the road from the grand old stone edifice of KEM. The CVTC is a comparatively new building, a six-storeyed structure with the out-patient department and x-ray on the ground floor, the facility laboratory on the first, and the thoracic surgery operation theatre and general ward number 31 on the second. Inder has to get the keys from ward

31 to unlock the doors in the basement of the building. The basement has junk in it. It is supposed to be the experimental cardiovascular dog surgery laboratory with an attached nurses duty room. Heart surgeons have not started using this lab as yet, they continue working in the original dog lab on the terrace of the old building. But nurses are assigned to this lab, so they report in the basement and then go to the terrace. Inder's duty is in both the buildings. He has to clean the steps leading to the basement, then the big corridor in the basement, the nurses duty room, the dog surgery room, and after returning the key to ward 31 he crosses the road to continue work in the dog lab. But first he runs up to the second floor, ward 31, to get the basement keys.

7.20 a.m. Sadashiv Mahadeo Dalvi, security guard, reports slightly late for duty too, on the other side of the road in the stone building opposite CVTC. He has been on day shift for several months now, he prefers it even if it's cold in the mornings like right now and he feels a bit lazy to get up. Dalvi clocks in, puts on his uniform's cap, picks up his duty danda, feels the weight of this baton in his hand, flicks the danda into the air; this is what he always does when he reports on duty. A pre-work flex, it feels right. This morning the danda does not fall back into his waiting, outstretched palm. 'Tujhi aayi la!', an impossible imprecation bursts from him in Marathi, since no baton can have a mother. The offending danda hits the floor and clatters down the stone steps. Sweeper Sohanlal Bhartha Walmiki, entering the building, picks it up and hands it over to him. Dalvi is mildly surprised. 'You are supposed to report at seven o'clock but I have yet to see you come in before eight on any morning,' he tells Sohanlal. 'Why on time today?' Sohanlal mumbles something about there being too many soiled clothes to wash from yesterday's operations in the dog lab.

Thirty-four-year-old Dalvi starts his first security round of the day, tapping his danda rhythmically on the floor as he walks. Other security men might sit around on a stool all day, not he. He likes his job at KEM, on the days he can put errant visitors firmly in their place he even enjoys his job here. At the end of the day he does feel a bit sick himself, he even smells like it sometimes, ulti saarkha, vomity. But there is job security here, and free medicine for himself and his family. True, it is free for all of Bombay and even those coming from outside, but the doctors and nurses are most helpful to the staff. Holding a permanent job is a good thing, not like these sweepers who are 'tempoorwari'. They are strange these latrine washers, they announce their jobs by adding Walmiki to their names.

Tapping importantly, checking doors, Dalvi reaches the second floor and sees Sohanlal sitting on the steps leading to the terrace with a long dog chain in his hand. Dalvi raises his danda, waggles it up and down, the question in this movement being apparent. Sohanlal shakes his head, returns to the terrace, comes back without the dog chain and walks down the stairs with Dalvi to cross the road. 'CVTC basement,' he says, 'cleaning duty.'

$7$.45 a.m. Inder is looking towards the duty room door in the basement, it is slightly open. He is not sure of what he should do. The light is on in that room. Suppose he goes in there and the Sisters are changing their clothes? Obviously someone is in there, the basement's main door was unlocked when he came down with the keys from ward 31, perhaps one of the Sisters arrived very early today. But by now she should have come out of the duty room, he has been sweeping and swabbing the basement for the last twenty minutes. He is certain it is only one of the nurses who can be in there, there is no third key. Maybe there is only one Sister in there, the other one may be on leave like yesterday, but why so long inside? Inder is worried now, should he knock on the open duty room door? He does, the door swings open a little more, but there is no response.

A sound from the main door. Inder is relieved to see Sohanlal at the end of the corridor, entering the basement. Sohanlal comes from a village called Dadupur, which is also in Bulandshahr district, Inder's native place. He is a little hot-headed, says things he should not but he is young and has come only three years back to Bombay, he will learn. Inder quickly explains his concern to Sohanlal who says, 'We will go inside.' They slowly push open the door completely. Nobody. A big purse, some other things lying on the table but nobody in the duty room. The dog surgery door is closed. Inder looks at Sohanlal, walks up, knocks on it. No response. He knocks again, louder, 'Sister! Nurseji!' He cocks his head for any sound. Silence within.

Inder tries the knob, finds the dog surgery door unlocked, swings it open.

The light from the duty room falls on a naked leg stretched out on the floor of the dog surgery. Two naked legs, a sari with its petticoat rolled up, on it inky blackness which looks like blood . . . Inder slams the door shut.

'What is there, let me see.' Sohanlal is behind him, trying to open the door. Inder shakes his head, don't touch that door. He grabs Sohanlal by the arm, come on we have to call somebody.

11

$8$.25 a.m. Sister Sulochana Beechi, forty-six, has just finished setting up her table at the CVTC out-patient department on the ground floor of the building. She is in charge of the OPD, her duty will run till 4.30 p.m. Soon the crowding will start, more and more people suffer from heart problems in Bombay. It's not so much the Indian diet, it is the amount people eat, that too non-stop. However, Indian women seem to have stronger hearts although they cope with much more, there are more men to be seen in the CVTC OPD. Sister Beechi's thoughts come to a halt as a panting sweeper, followed by another one, run up to her duty desk.

'Sister, Sister, there is a problem downstairs in the basement.'

'What problem?'

'I don't know. There's a nurse who is not coming out from the dog surgery.'

'Which nurse is not coming out from the dog surgery?'

'I don't know, but she is not coming out.'

'Why not? Did you look to see?'

'She's sleeping inside, or lying down.'

'What? Why didn't you look properly?'

'She . . . she . . . I think she might not be wearing any clothes, so I did not want to see.'

'Come on!'

Sister Beechi hurries down the basement stairs, almost runs down the corridor, bursts into the duty room, looks around. On one corner of the duty table is an open brown handbag; a small cane change purse lies next to it. There is a glass almirah with surgical instruments, and an open wooden cupboard with a key in its keyhole. Partially obscured by the open cupboard door is a red chappal. The other red chappal is halfway across the duty room, pointing towards the dog's operation theatre. Sister Beechi looks at Inder, he gestures towards the door.

She pushes it open. It is dark in there. 'Is there a light here?' Inder nods, puts his hand inside, on the other side of the door jamb and flicks on the switch.

A low 'Hey Bhagwaan!' from Sister Beechi.

There's a young, small-boned, fair woman crouched over the floor. She is face down, her forehead touching the floor, her hair tangled and covering her face. Her elbows and the back of her hands touch the floor, the rest of her body isn't completely in contact with the ground till her knees, calves and ankles. She is on all fours. Her brown sari is bunched up near her waist along with her petticoat which has rolled up with it. Her legs are bare and slightly apart. There is blood everywhere, on her clothes, on her skin, on the ground. Her panties are soaking with blood, a rivulet of it runs down her inner thigh to form a small pool on the floor beneath.

The woman grunts.

Sister Beechi's hand flies to her mouth, 'Hey Bhagwaan!' She turns, sweeper Sohanlal wants to know who the woman is. She pushes out the sweepers from the room, bangs the door shut, screams at the sweepers that they should quickly bring a stretcher and runs up to the OPD. Staff nurses Chinamma and Amod Kutti have reported on duty at the OPD. 'Hurry,' she instructs them, 'go down quickly to the dog surgery with the first-aid kit.' From the door of the OPD she sees Dr Uday Gadgil, near the lift, on his way to ward nine. She runs up to him, 'Doctor, please come immediately, there is an emergency in the basement.' He follows her, they both break into a run.

**8**.40 a.m. Dr Gadgil gently turns the woman over. Her eyes are wide open. Her hair is matted with blood, vomit and mucus. There is blood on her face, from her nose, her mouth. Her lower lip is hideously swollen. Dr Gadgil swiftly does a check. 'Rush her to the Casualty, I will phone them from upstairs that she will need intensive care immediately. Also inform neurosurgery to reach the Casualty rightaway.' Sister Beechi's lips move silently, she has begun praying, as she recognizes the unfortunate woman: staff nurse Aruna Shanbaug.

There is a hiss, a sharp intake of breath as the other nurses recognize staff nurse Aruna Shanbaug. Sweepers Inder and Sohanlal place her on the stretcher. Sister Beechi leans forward and covers Aruna's exposed breasts and body with a sheet. She finds herself holding her breath as she watches the sweepers run across the by now busy road with the stretcher, dodging the morning traffic with its buses, taxis, cars and curious humans. Still praying she moves to the phone in the OPD and telephones matron Belimal. Sister Premila Kushe answers the phone. 'Staff nurse Aruna Shanbaug has been attacked in the basement, she's being carried to the Casualty. Something has gone terribly wrong for that child.' She puts the receiver down on its cradle to find tears in her eyes.

**9**.00 a.m. Matron Belimal and Sister Premila Kushe rush towards the Casualty. Aruna is being carried into it on a stretcher. Her eyes are wide open but unseeing. Matron Belimal runs towards the stretcher, lapsing subconsciously into Konkani, 'Daiva, daiva, oh God!' She gently touches Aruna's puffed cheek, Sister Kushe rubs Aruna's hands in her own, she is ice cold to the touch. Matron Belimal strokes her hair, 'Aruna, Aruna, kithan zaale Aruna?'

Aruna attempts to focus, her eyes follow the direction of matron Belimal's voice, tears well up in them, and flow. They run down her cheeks, she tries to speak, raises her head slightly, gasps with the effort. Sister Kushe strokes Aruna's hands, matron Belimal soothes her brow, 'Aruna maaka saang, kithan zaale? Tell me, what happened?' Aruna responds, again makes an attempt to speak, but only produces a low feral grunt.

Matron Belimal moves the sheet covering her slightly away from her face and neck to help her speak. Her eyes fall on the lesions around Aruna's neck. Her voice breaks, 'Sister Kushe look, somebody has tried to strangle this girl. Oh God, oh God, why her?'

Aruna's eyes seek out matron Belimal, they dart in her swollen bloodied face. Matron talks to her in a low voice assuring her that all will be well, and not to worry. Her eyes try to hold the matron's. Those tears, they just will not stop their silent course. Through their wetness, with her untold story locked within them, her eyes roll back to show their whites.

Aruna Shanbaug's spirit has kept her injured body conscious through a long, cold, pain-wracked night, all by itself. A full fifteen and a half hours of strong will.

Now, just when she needs it the most, her flesh is turning weak, letting her down.

Her God let her down yesterday.

S weepers Inder and Sohanlal rush to the dog lab on the terrace to tell the others about what has happened to their department in charge, staff nurse Aruna Shanbaug.

Technician Sambhaji Jethegaonkar listens to Inder telling

him how he found her in the morning, how somebody has tried to strangle her. He looks at Sohanlal standing behind Inder, stares at him for what seems like a long time. The sweeper leaves the lab and goes down the stairs.

Sweeper Udayvir meets him on the second floor landing. 'Where are you going Sohanlal?'

'To the diet department.'

'For what?'

'The dogs' food, what else?'

'She's told you not to do it, why are you unnecessarily making her angry again? She will shout at you in front of everybody.'

'She won't be saying anything for a very long time.'

'What? Why?'

'Ask Inder.'

Upstairs in the dog lab technician Jethegaonkar does not feel quite right. He is shocked, upset and angry. He has a suspicion. He picks up the phone and speaks to Dr G.B. Parulkar in a low voice.

Dr Parulkar, in turn, telephones the dean, Dr C.K. Deshpande. 'Is it bad? I mean, are the injuries only external? Has she been, uh, harmed in other ways as well?'

'It does not look good, sir. Actually, it all looks quite bad. I'm not sure how all the other nurses are going to react. There are likely to be repercussions. It would be wise, I think, to immediately inform the police. The faster the arrest, the less damage to the institution and its people, especially the nurses.'

Dean Deshpande instructs KEM's security officer Sisodia to telephone the police. 'Just tell them a nurse has been attacked, there might be a robbery involved.'

For the police, a quick list of the external injuries on staff nurse Aruna Shanbaug, Hindu female, age twenty-five years, height five feet, weight 104 pounds:

Contusion on the neck. Contusion right knee. Abrasion right hand dorsum. Contusion right hand dorsum. Injury with teeth marks lower lip with oedema of lip. Contusion left cheek. Contusion right cheek. Multiple semi-circular abrasions left side of neck near sterno-clavicular joint. Multiple linear abrasions right side and front of neck. Contusion right side of neck, front of neck and left side of neck. Contusion right wrist, contusion left wrist, both anterior laterally. Contusion with oedema two inches around anterior superior spine bilaterally. Contusion right thigh medially. Contusion with oedema both knees. Contusion left scapula. Contusion left side chest posteriorly.

The gynaecologist's report:

Hymen intact, admits two fingers easily. No vaginal tear.

Missing from Aruna's person as pointed out by her friend Sister Prema Pai:

One wristwatch, one gold chain with a pendant. Estimated cost for police: Rs 500.

9.30 a.m. Aruna is a hair's breath away from death. The vigorous treatment is immediately intensified, a phalanx of doctors and nurses prevent that last bit of life from leaving her body.

Dr Homi M. Dastur enters the Casualty. Among the finest neurosurgeons in the country, he quickly asks a few questions about the treatment administered, and in what condition the patient was brought in. The patient was brought in bleeding from the ears, nose and throat. She was groaning, vomiting slightly, yes she had convulsions. She could not recognize anyone or answer any questions. She went into spasms periodically.

Dr Dastur extends his hand to the soles of Aruna's feet. In an upward movement, he strokes the side of each foot. A normal person's reflex is for the big toe to move down. Aruna's toes go up. Plantars extensors. It means damage to the cortex, or damage anywhere from the brain along the conducting fibres all the way down to the spinal cord. Shown on a patient's chart as two arrows pointing upwards next to the word plantars.

Completing the rest of an extremely thorough examination, Dr Dastur checks the drugs administered, adds some, advises cervical spine and skull x-rays which he wants to see as soon as they are ready. He writes on the file:

Patient is semi-conscious. Responds very briskly to pain. Moves all limbs in response to pain, upper limbs better than lower. But no spontaneous movement except for smacking of lips. No facial asymmetry. Pupils normal. Plantars extensors. Apart from injuries noted she has a left parietal contusion. Bladder distension, needs catheterisation.

Impression:

Brain stem contusion injury with associated cervical cord injury.

**10**.15 a.m. Bhoiwada police station. A well-maintained ground plus one structure with a solid wooden staircase, long flanking balconies, a tiny tended-to garden with a bench. This should have been a big, happy family's house, children jumping up and down the wooden staircase with satisfying thuds, a puppy playing in the garden, grandpa sunning on the bench. Maybe it was, the Bhoiwada police station is a Raj-time construction. The cells behind the building have been built later.

The telephone jangles. Sub-inspector Sohoni has just joined the police force. He answers the phone. It's from KEM Hospital, security manager Sisodia on the line. Somebody has tried to rob a nurse and has attacked her. SI Sohoni starts taking down the details. What injuries? Is she in a position to give a statement? Any suspects? Place of offence? Do not allow anyone into the place of offence till the police arrives. Yes, the police will be there very soon. Please tell the dean to wait in his office.

Sub-inspector Sohoni informs the police inspector of Bhoiwada, Chandrashekhar D. Deo, about the telephone call along with the details. The inspector despatches sub-inspector Laxman Naik to KEM who takes some constables with him.

**10**.30 a.m. Word is spreading like wild fire. Nurses are converging at matron Belimal's office. A barrage of questions, a flood of concern, collective rage.

'What exactly has happened to staff nurse Aruna Shanbaug? She has been raped, hasn't she?'

'Oh my God, really?'

'They will not tell us even if she has, they will hide it.'

'Yes, they will cover it up.'

'Who has done this, it has to be an insider.'

'Of course, otherwise how could he go into the basement?'

'As though that is a problem! We all know how the security is mismanaged in this place.'

'What was security doing all that time? I have heard she was in the basement from yesterday evening.'

'And no one from security went to check whether the basement door was locked?'

'Her things must have been stolen.'

'Sister Pai says her wristwatch and gold chain are not there.'

'You all are bothered about a wristwatch and a gold chain! She has been brutally attacked.'

'Has she really been raped?'

'We all will be, very soon, if the dean does not take appropriate action.'

'What action! We have been asking them for tube-lights instead of those dim bulbs in most of the outside corridors for so long. No one has listened. We should all unite and go on a strike to teach them a lesson.'

'Will a strike stop the security guards from sitting around in the nights, smoking beedis and then going to sleep?'

'Where was the guard when she was attacked? What time was she raped?'

Matron Belimal interjects, 'We must stop using that word. Let us not forget she is to be married soon.'

'And will he marry her now?'

'Suppose it was him alone who did this to her? Maybe he changed his mind about marrying her.'

Matron Belimal speaks firmly, 'Enough of this nonsense.'

'Does he know? Has anyone told him?'

'Has anyone told her family?'

Matron nods, 'I have just sent someone to inform her sister in BDD chawls.'

'Matron, what will happen to Aruna Shanbaug? Will she become okay?'

'I don't know my child, I wish I did. Only God knows.'

**10**.45 a.m. Insistent knocking on the door. Sister Usha Samant is fast asleep in her room in the nurses quarters. She has the double-room to herself since her room-mate Aruna Shanbaug became non-residential at the beginning of this month; another nurse has not been assigned the other bed as yet. Usha is happy to have the room to herself so that she can sleep at will.

The knocking persists, now accompanied by a female voice in Marathi.

'Usha! Usha! Uth ga.'

'Kaay aahe? I'm sleeping, I have done night duty.'

'Usha, Aruna has been attacked in CVTC.'

Usha turns sharply on her bed, in the direction of the door. 'What?'

'Aruna Shanbaug, your room-mate. She has been raped. The police have been informed.'

Usha bolts upright in her bed. She is about to spring out of it to open the door, she stops herself. Aruna has been raped, she has been attacked, but by whom? Could it be that sweeper? Aruna had told her he was being very arrogant, that like an animal he did not even leave the dogs' food. She must have threatened him with something which had angered him. Should she tell this to the dean? But the police had been informed. The dean would tell her to talk to the police.

She does not want to talk to the police. If she tries to help them, they will harass her, they will keep calling her to the court. And supposing it is not that sweeper, they will question him on her suspicion. He could really do something to her after that. But supposing it is the sweeper? It does not matter. If he is arrested on her suspicion, he will make her life miserable after he is released. He will not have to go around looking for her to find her, she will be right here working in this hospital.

Aruna has already been raped, the harm is already done. What is the point now? Usha lies back on the bed.

'Go away, I am sleeping.'

**11**.00 a.m. Tubes, needles, bottles and vials of intravenous medicine, machines connected to a frail, pale, beaten-up body on which an additional battery of tests has just been conducted. Her head has been shaved bald for some of them. The doctor conducting his physical examination on her is frowning, he looks up as the dean arrives. He then quickly looks at the already thick file of notations to see if the gynaecologist has checked what he suspects. He speaks to the dean in a low voice for some time. The dean listens, asks no questions, shakes his head in the negative.

**12**.00 noon. Aruna Shanbaug's sister, Shantabai Vasudeo Nayak, is sitting on a chair in the dean's office being questioned by the police. With her is her 18-year-old daughter Savitri.

'The victim did not return home last night, were you not worried?'

'She normally comes home by 6.00-6.30 in the evening. At 7.00 p.m. I heard on the radio that children had been food-poisoned in their school in Mahim and that they were being taken to KEM. I thought she might be busy with that.'

'But she did not work in that department.'

'She did not tell us she was not working in any particular department.'

'Anyway, she did not come home at all in the night. Did you not worry later?'

'I thought she might have gone to sleep in the nurse's hostel itself since it got so late.'

'Did she often do that?'

'From the time she came to Bombay, seven years back,

she had been staying in the nurses hostel. She shifted to my house only on the first of this month.'

'Why, any problem in the hostel?'

'No. She came because she wanted to save money for her fiancé's dawakhaana.'

'If he is setting up a clinic, he must be a doctor. Please give us his name and address.'

The sister hesitates, then speaks softly in Bombay-Hindi, 'Hum ko nai malum woh kaunse doctor key saath phirti thi.'

'How can you not know the name of her fiancé? Especially when you knew she was saving money for his clinic?'

'She told us only that much.'

'Okay, we will come back to that later. Tell me if there is anything else missing apart from the gold chain and watch.'

'There was a pendant on the chain.'

'Can you describe the chain, locket and watch?'

The daughter speaks, 'She had her initials put in on the back of her watch. A.S.'

The mother, 'I only had the chain made for her, I have the receipt. The pendant was my daughter's, she had borrowed it to wear. It had tiny gold beads at the bottom of this shape.' She draws a hexagon in the air.

'What make was the watch?'

'We do not know.'

'Did she buy it herself, when and from where?'

The daughter, 'Her brother gave it to her when she started nursing. That is, my mother's brother.'

'Where is he?'

'Shimoga.'

'Where?'

'Shimoga, in Karnataka.'

'Any other gents in your family?'

'Kaayku? For what?'

23

'For this case.'

'No.'

'Please call her brother from Shimoga.'

The dean enters his office, seats himself behind his vast desk. He addresses Shantabai Nayak, 'Urgent telegram bhejo.'

1.20 p.m. Dr Sundeep Sardesai closes his books in his room on the KEM campus, takes off his spectacles and rubs his eyes. His MD examinations are barely two weeks away, there is still a bit of the syllabus to revise, though he has paced his studies quite well. His breaks have only been for meals, and that snatch of time with Aruna. He smiles to himself. That woman, she is like a child at some moments. But enough, he's meeting her at 4.00 this evening. Now down to lunch in the canteen and back to these books.

Some of the doctors stop eating and stare at Sundeep as he enters the canteen. At another table a lady nudges a man and gestures with her chin towards him. He is oblivious, he sits at a table with his stainless steel thali and begins eating methodically, chewing rhythmically. He is almost through his meal when a fellow MD-student walks up to his table hesitantly, 'Hello Sundeep, you're okay?'

He is mildly surprised, 'I'm fine.'

'Uh, uh, okay. Let me know if you need anything.'

Sundeep spoons some vegetable into his mouth. 'Need anything? For what?'

'Uh, nothing in particular, just . . . Anyway I have to go, bye.'

The friend turns to leave, changes his mind. 'Yaar, we all know that you are a calm sort of fellow. But how can you be so cool at a time like this?'

'It is difficult yes, but why should the exam make me, or you, hysterical?'

The friend stares at him with horror on his face. 'Sundeep, no one has told you? Your wife . . . uh . . . fiancée . . . oh hell . . . yesterday evening staff nurse Aruna Shanbaug was badly beaten up in the CVTC. He even tried to strangle her and, uh, uh . . . there is a suspected uh . . . you better see the dean.'

'How is she now?'

'Not good. But she has very strong will power. She was found only this morning, by then anyone else in her place would be uh . . . you want me to come with you to the Casualty?'

Sundeep shakes his head, 'It's okay, thanks. You carry on.' He looks down at his plate, there are the last spoons of dal-rice left. He eats them slowly, he's thinking of September when he received his first big blow, this is the second shock within sixty days. The spoon scrapes the empty thali, Sundeep pushes it away, gets up from the table and walks slowly, as if in a daze, towards the rear of the main hospital building. The dean should be in his bungalow.

He is. He looks carefully at the young doctor, sits him down on the sofa and asks for a cup of tea, with extra sugar, from the kitchen. He does not speak until Sundeep has had a few sips.

'Dr Sardesai, you have heard?'

'Why didn't anybody come and tell me in the morning?'

'Ah yes, maybe they were looking for you?'

'Looking for me? I was in my RMO quarters, studying. No one came to find me.'

'Dr Sardesai, you are here now. It is for the best you were not around when the police were questioning everybody.'

'I don't understand.'

'She is badly injured, there is a suspect but the police have to complete their investigations in their own way. Why should you have to spend a lot of your time being questioned by them when you have the most important examination of your life in two weeks?'

'Has she been . . . raped?'

'Yes.'

Sundeep stands up, the cup still in his hand, 'I have to go and see her, I have to see what I can do to help her. I should have been there in the morning.'

The dean takes the cup from Sundeep's fingers and sets it on a low table near the sofa. 'Son, the best doctors in the business have examined her, don't worry about the treatment. Tell me, have you met anyone from her family, her sister in Bombay perhaps?'

'No, never.'

'You never met anybody from her family?'

'She never really spoke about her family, I got the impression she did not want to. So I never bothered. In any case, it did not matter. But, yes, I do know her cousins.'

The dean replies, 'I ask from the medico-legal point of view. If we have to run any other tests on staff nurse Shanbaug we need the written permission of an immediate relative of hers.'

Sundeep shakes his head in bewilderment. 'I will give the permission and sign the forms, she is to be my wife soon.'

The dean pats him on his shoulder, 'Sit down. Have another cup of hot tea with me. This one has turned cold. She will be shifted to neurosurgery in a short while, under Dr Dastur. You can see her there. By then the police will also have left the premises. So tell me how are the preparations for your MD exams, what are you specializing in? What are your plans for the immediate future?'

The dean is trying to tell him something, Sundeep understands this. But what? And why won't he just say what he thinks he should in so many words instead of beating around the bush? Sundeep exhales, concentrates on marshalling his thought processes into their normally streamlined channels. No point getting all worked up over a fait accompli, it is best he maintain his equilibrium and cross each bridge only when he reaches it.

1.50 p.m. A crowd outside the matron's office. Raised voices, knots of angry nurses.

'This is not good. It can happen to any of us tomorrow.'

'What are they going to do about what has happened to Aruna Shanbaug?'

'I have confirmed that she was raped.'

'How can you say that with one hundred per cent certainty, Prema. Aruna is in a coma, only when she comes out of it will we know exactly what happened.'

'That is right. Besides, I went and saw the gynaecologist's report after Aruna's initial examination. It specifically says hymen intact.'

'It was not that kind of a rape.'

'What rubbish are you talking Prema? What other kind is there?'

Sister Prema Pai hesitates, then speaks because she knows only the nurses will pay attention. 'I will not name him, I spoke to another doctor who also examined her. He told me about it. He also told some higher-ups who ignored what he said. She was raped . . . the other way.' Sister Pai starts weeping.

Shocked silence, a few nurses comfort Prema. There is a whisper, 'You mean, the way the dogs do it?'

'No, that's unbelievable!'

Another voice asks, 'Prema, has she been examined completely for what you are saying has been done to her?'

Prema shakes her head, 'The doctor was very thorough in examining Aruna. He was medically convinced so he said he wanted to confirm one hundred per cent what he suspected and put down his findings on paper. Permission was not granted.'

'But why?'

There is another voice, 'Because the case is bad enough the way it is, the higher-ups don't want it to look even worse.'

'Look? This is not about how anything looks. This is about us, human beings, women, professional nurses. It is about our safety. Tomorrow if something happens to another one of us, even the police will not be called because of how it will look?'

'Possible. There might be another kind of cover-up at that time. I think we will have to look after ourselves, to make sure we are safe and unharmed.'

'But how, and what can we do now about Aruna's rape?'

'We will have to wait till Aruna herself speaks. Meanwhile we should immediately go on strike.'

'Strike? Like how the mill workers go on strike? But we are nurses!'

'Yes, let us go on strike. Let the authorities understand how serious this entire situation has become.'

'But we have no written proof that Aruna was raped. Suppose they ignore us?'

'They cannot. They know the truth. They know we know the truth.'

'Yes, let us go on strike. We need to press for security for ourselves.'

'That is right. We have to look after our own interests too. There should not be another Aruna.'

Within the hour the nurses' strike is total.

Perhaps this is the first time since India attained independence that nurses have struck work, there are no records to suggest otherwise, nor memory. Certainly, this is the first time in KEM's illustrious history that there is any kind of strike.

Sister Shashikala Vaaran looks into the future, 'Everything changes after this. Nurses henceforward will stop thinking of their jobs as anything beyond their shifts.'

$2$.20 p.m. Bhoiwada police station. The official complaint book is opened to start the file on the Aruna Shanbaug case.

'Complainant's name?'

'No complainant.'

'How can there be a complaint without a complainant? No complainant, no complaint, no case.'

'Nobody wants to be a complainant in KEM.'

'Not even the family?'

'They are saying it happened in the hospital so KEM must take all responsibility. The hospital is saying it is run by the Bombay Municipal Corporation (BMC) so permission will have to be got from the municipal commisioner which will take time. Basically nobody wants to come to court or get involved even though it is such a serious case.'

'Hey asa lok manjhe police kaay karnaar? Really, how can the police be effective when citizens are like this? Put down sub-inspector Laxman Naik's name as complainant. Any suspects? Have people at least given their statements honestly?'

'People are being questioned, statements are also being taken down. We should have a very clear picture on the suspect by this evening.'

2.50 p.m. Dr Dastur scans the skull and cervical spine x-rays. Nothing more than he expected to see. He instructs that the x-rays be repeated later in the day. Dr Dastur orders a cervical collar for Aruna's neck and she is shifted out of the Casualty to ward 33, under his care.

Notes made by the nurses monitoring their colleague, staff nurse Aruna Shanbaug:

The spine x-ray shows congenital fusion between C6 and 7.

Painful stimulation produces groaning, which was not present in the morning.

Has spontaneous gnashing of teeth.

Lower limbs move less.

3.30 p.m. Patient unconscious. Does not obey commands. Plantars up.

Blinks when pupillary reaction checked.

Blinks on touching eyelashes.

Spasticity of lower limbs persists.

Vital functions normal.

Dr Sundeep Sardesai stands at the bedside of his wife-to-be in ward 33, neurosurgery, looking at her. The attending nurses have moved away discreetly.

He smiles. She is going to hate it when she gets up and sees her reflection in the mirror. It's not that she is vain but

Aruna is happy that she's a pretty woman. She is going to be utterly distraught when she sees they have made her bald. Actually she has a very interesting skull shape. Sundeep's eyes travel over the shape of her skull and come to rest on her closed eyes.

He leans forward and gently, softly, like he would put his lips to a butterfly's wing, kisses her eyelids. 'Rest,' he whispers, 'I'll come back later.'

**5**.00 p.m. Dr Sardesai is back, looking ashen. He realizes he had gone into denial earlier. He realizes there's no point pretending that he can study while Aruna is unconscious. He realizes that this is the very ward where she had been on night duty and he had proposed marriage to her. He realizes that when he kissed her eyelids he was kissing her for the first time since they met. He realizes he is crying right now.

Dr Sundeep Sardesai pulls up a stool at Aruna's bedside, sits on it, takes her limp left hand in his and draws it across his face. 'Did you feel that,' he whispers to her in Konkani, 'you have just made me cry. Do good Goud Saraswat Brahmin girls make their husbands cry like this, shame on you Aruna Shanbaug. Now I expect you, I command you as your husband to open your eyes.' He talks to her for over forty minutes, pausing every now and then as if hearing her answers.

**6**.30 p.m. Patient unconscious. No response to commands.

Plantars up.

Being fed by Ryle's tube.

Chewing movements of jaws and gnashing of teeth.
Lower limbs spastic.

$7$.00 p.m. Crime reporters of Bombay's daily morning newspapers start using the phone quite forcefully around this time. They collect, they collate, they speak to their sources in the police, they call up police control room to find out if there has been anything out of the usual, 'Kaay vishesh?'

Today is a little different. The BMC beat boys have heard from an opposition corporator that there has been a total strike by the nurses in KEM protesting against a rape of their colleague. The BMC reporters inform the crime reporters and everyone is on the phone checking it out. They speak with doctors, nurses, unions, other BMC managed hospitals, the BMC commissioner, the chief minister's secretary. KEM's dean does not come on the line.

The picture which emerges is printed the next morning in the English and language papers. Some use it at the bottom of their front page, some lead with it on their City page. There has been an attempt to murder a nurse, Aruna Shanbaug, twenty-five, at the King Edward VII Memorial Hospital, for reasons as yet unknown. The Bhoiwada police are investigating. Hospital sources do not officially deny a rape of the assaulted nurse. However nurses of KEM have embarked on a three-day strike for reasons which include additional security and better working conditions. Nurses from other hospitals are scheduled to join them for a token half-day's strike in expression of their solidarity. The municipal commissioner is expected to be summoned by the chief minister for questioning in this connection. The assaulted nurse is reported to be in a coma.

7.30 p.m. The left side of Aruna's swollen mouth twitches. A few seconds later there is a spontaneous jerking of all four limbs, more the arms than the legs.

8.30 p.m. Twitching movements continue. Dr Sunil Pandya, assistant to Dr Dastur, is informed. He comes into ward 33 immediately, checks, readjusts the medication.

9.30 p.m. Dr Sundeep Sardesai comes after dinner and sees Aruna's face twitching. He checks her medical charts, pulls up the stool and chats with her for another forty minutes. His voice is hoarse, he laughs as he tells her 'Normally you are the one who talks so much to me', and wishes her good night.

10.00 p.m. The Bhoiwada police have completed the recording of all the statements. Aruna's colleagues in the dog lab have been most forthcoming, they have spoken to the police about their suspicion, how she tried to stop the man from stealing the dogs' food. They have heard of her being strangulated, they think he used the dog chain from the kennels on the terrace. The chain is missing, so is he, he was there in the morning though. But his father is here in the hospital, he got his son this job of a temporary sweeper. He is a mukkadam, sweeper in charge, he has been with KEM for long, due for retirement shortly. His name is

Bhartha Dhekolia Walmiki, he's a good man. No, we have not told him that we are speaking to the police about his son, but word has gone around and the ward boys, sweepers and everybody are talking about it . Some of them are saying that the security chief himself did it, but there will be a cover-up and the police will catch some poor man.

Inder Gulamashi Bait Walmiki, sweeper: 'A few months back the attendant in the dog lab, Laxman, went on leave. Sister Aruna Shanbaug told Sohanlal to do Laxman's work. He resented it. She reported him. He told me he would take revenge by molesting her. I never took it seriously. Later when another altercation took place Sohanlal again repeated his threat of molesting her.'

Sahadeo Sitaram Parab, security guard: 'I am on duty from 3.00 p.m. to 11.00 p.m. every day on the ground floor of CVTC. No work is conducted downstairs, nobody goes into the basement after 5.00 p.m. Between 4.00 p.m. and 6.00 p.m. are the visiting hours in the CVTC's wards and there are always a lot of people. So security moves away from the ground floor exit which goes to the basement, begins its rounds and moves closer towards the entrance of the building. I saw sweeper Sohanlal Bhartha Walmiki come up from the basement and leave the building at 5.40 p.m. yesterday, 27 November 1973.'

Jaisinh Vithoo Jadhav, custodian: 'They have to come to my office at 7.00 a.m. every day to report for work, Sohanlal comes late every day. Some months back staff nurse Aruna Shanbaug complained about his work and said he was very arrogant. One hour later I went and rebuked him in her presence. He assured us of better conduct. After a few weeks staff nurse Shanbaug phoned me again. The next day when Sohanlal came to report for work, I warned him again. Then, during the day when Sister Shanbaug was present, I went to the dog lab again and spoke to him in front of everybody. I told him I was sacking him right there and then. He begged of us, he pleaded so much that staff nurse Shanbaug said to give him a final warning and let him stay.'

Sambhaji Sitaram Jethegaonkar, technician: 'I work in the dog lab. Sohanlal is not regular, sometimes he has come to work even at 8.30 a.m. when his duty is supposed to start at 7.00 a.m. I have warned him often. His duties include cleaning the kennels, then the lab itself, washing the clothes used in the operations and disposal of dead dogs. He also used to get food for the dogs from the diet department. He is a man of quarrelsome nature and used to grumble a great deal when work was entrusted to him. He would refuse to do the work so the other sweepers Inder and Udayvir would do it.'

Udayvir Channaram Walmiki, sweeper: 'Yesterday, on 27 November 1973, I reported on duty at 7.00 a.m. From 7.00 a.m. to 11.00 a.m. I cleaned the bathrooms on the second floor. In the afternoon I went on duty to the dog lab and assisted the doctors on the operation. When I was cleaning the bloodstained clothes of the operation Sohanlal came and told me he would spend one month's salary to sleep with staff nurse Aruna Shanbaug. I told him nurses are like our sisters and, anyway, we have to work under them.'

Bhartha Dhekolia Walmiki, mukkadam: 'My son Sohanlal has taken his wife to Poona since her mother is very sick. They left this afternoon, 28 November 1973. I know where her family lives in Poona and am willing to take the police there.'

Bhoiwada's police inspector C.D. Deo looks at his watch and calls for sub-inspector Ramchandra Narayan Wayadande. 'Take the suspect's father with you and leave for Poona right away. If the suspect is there pick him up on the spot, bring him back immediately. Put him into the lock-up, we will question him first thing tomorrow morning.'

**10**.30 p.m. Aruna's eyeballs roll to the right. The nurses on duty turn her head slowly, bring her eyeballs back to the left, they swing back to the right. Then her limbs move, without any jerks, more the arms than the legs. The nurses pat her briskly, no facial response. Plantars extensors.

**11**.15 p.m. A new drip has to be started, the existing vein will not do. The nurse pricks the needle in a fresh spot for the intravenous, Aruna reacts briskly, then settles down for the night.

**2**.00 a.m. 29 November, 1973. SI Wayadande, a constable from the Bhoiwada police station and Bhartha Dhekolia have reached the outskirts of Poona, Dapodi. At the famed College of Military Engineering's gate, the vehicle turns into the campus and drives right through to the rear of the CME, to an area called Bhopkel. There is an open ground followed by a cluster of huts. Bhartha Dhekolia enters one of them, in a little while he brings out Sohanlal.

SI Wayadande looks hard at the accused. Somehow—perhaps because of all that he had managed to do to that nurse—he had expected him to be taller and broader. Sohanlal is stockily-built, but his eyes glittering in his dark, impassive face provide a glimpse of the savage beast within. Wayadande mentally notes, once again, that a man's size has nothing to do with his capacity for evil. He reaches for the handcuffs.

People come out from the other huts to see what the noise is about. Sohanlal's very young wife, Vimala, stands at the door of her parents' hut, looking at the police through the ghoonghat partially covering her face. SI Wayadande puts Sohanlal Bhartha Walmiki into the waiting vehicle and heads back to Bombay.

**6**.00 a.m. Dr Sundeep Sardesai has come to say good morning to his fiancée. He wishes her, she groans. He checks her vital functions, they are normal. He pulls up the stool, takes her hand in his and tells her he can't stay for long, now that she's getting better they should both remember that they should not violate the visiting hours too much. Of course the dean has given him permission to come and spend time with her whenever he wants but as a doctor and a nurse of KEM they should exercise a bit more discipline in the future. 'I am sure you agree, if you do not you will tell me, you always do.'

**6**.10 a.m. Aruna's level of consciousness shows a definitive improvement. Spontaneous movements start in her upper limbs, lower limbs too. She flexes her knees and hips, makes grunting noises while doing so. Sundeep keeps talking to her, asking her questions. She attempts to answer. The nurses check her eyes and make a note. Pupils equal, reacting briskly to light. No conjugate deviation of eyes.

**9**.00 a.m. The morning papers have been read, reactions begin.

The dean's phone rings off the hook. KEM's telephone lines get jammed with calls from Bombayites wanting to know if Aruna has come out of her coma, some offer blood, most want to know if she has her family around her. People turn up at the gates wanting to see her, they are shooed away by heightened security.

Politicians come to talk to the nurses about selflessness and Florence Nightingale. They point out that if the strike continues nurses from other hospitals are scheduled to start their sympathetic strike shortly. Surely the nurses of KEM do not want to be held responsible for unattended, ailing patients all over the city? The KEM nurses are very clear in their stand, they have announced a three-day strike and three days it will be. There is only one patient they will look after in these three days and that is staff nurse Aruna Shanbaug. Nurses from other hospitals are joining them with a token strike of only half a day, which is good to draw attention to their working conditions as well. Do the politicians want to be held responsible if what happened to staff nurse Aruna Shanbaug happens to another Sister anywhere in the city? Meanwhile KEM might like to hire new, capable security guards, instruct the ward boys to speak to the nurses with respect and install tube-lights everywhere in and around the hospital.

**11**.00 a.m. Dr Dastur checks Aruna's condition. She is semi-comatose. He applies some painful stimuli. She responds to the pain. He checks her toes, plantars up. Her pupils are normal but her eyeballs keep rolling up and down. No lateral conjugate deviation. Dr Dastur asks if a second set of x-rays were taken yesterday, they were, they are handed over to him. He checks them, instructs the orthopaedic unit to take a look at the neck x-rays. 'We should do an EEG now,' he says.

EEG stands for electroencephalogram, the patient's head doesn't need to be shaved for this, gel is applied, eight to sixteen electrodes are attached and the brain's wave pattern is recorded. The nurse informs Dr Sardesai about the EEG, nobody else from Aruna's family is around even though these are visiting hours.

**11**.05 a.m. Bhoiwada police station. Sohanlal Bhartha Walmiki's questioning is complete. The officers look in the register to see what other charges have been made by the hospital other than 'attack on nurse with intention to rob'. None. No one has come forward—not one doctor, nurse or relative—to add attempt to rape or even outraging of modesty. Sohanlal Bhartha Walmiki is formally arrested for Attempt to Commit Murder and Robbery.

12.00 noon. Dr R.M. Bhansali from orthopaedics checks Aruna along with her x-rays. There is no evidence of a fracture or subluscation. The collar around Aruna's neck is discarded.

**12**.30 p.m. Taxi driver Shivram Ramchandra Meher lounges on the back seat of his vehicle at Dadar near Broadway. His is a Bombay-Poona-Bombay taxi, he is waiting for passengers. It has been a very dull morning, he has read the Marathi newspaper word by word already. He is just about to nod off on a pre-lunch nap when there is a volley of sharp tapping on the raised glass of his window. 'Aye saala, kaach tod . . .' The rest of the sentence dries up in his throat along with the intention of its delivery. Police. One officer, two constables. They want to go to Poona. Meher quickly gets out of the back-seat, dusts it and holds the door open for the officer.

He swiftly, efficiently, drives his vehicle through the traffic out of Bombay city till he reaches Chembur, the officer wants to know how long it will take to reach Poona. 'Depends upon the traffic on the ghats, saab. Also depends upon the truck traffic on the outskirts of Poona around the factories.'

'We want to go to Dapodi, CME.'

'Then that will cut down some of the time, saab.'

The policemen start talking among each other, Meher tunes in and out of their conversation depending upon the traffic he is negotiating and the state of the road. They reach Panvel where they stop for water. Meher suggests that they have something to eat a little further up in Khopoli, 'very good batata wadas there, saab'. At Khopoli Meher parks and shows them the restaurant. Each time he has brought customers here the restaurant owner has given him snacks and tea free. 'Come with us,' says the officer.

He is seated at the same table as the police. He alternates between feeling important and foolish. The next time he comes here the restaurant owner will give him lot of bhaav. But suppose the restaurant owner thinks he is being arrested? Meher looks around, the restaurant owner looks far too busy keeping up a steady flow of steaming batata wadas from his kitchen.

The officer asks him if he will have anything with his wadas. 'Chaay, saab.'

The snacks and tea are served, Meher does not follow his customary habit of pouring his tea into the saucer and slurping, so as to impress the police. The officer offers him a cigarette and tells him with a friendly smile that he will have to come to court if they find anything where they are going.

Meher almost drops his cup of tea. 'Kaayku?' He does not want to get involved and says so with some show of indignation in Bombay-Hindi, 'Arrey saab, apun ko koi lafde mein nai padneka hai.'

'Have you been listening to our conversation?'

He has, bits. 'No saab.'

'Okay I will explain. We are going to Dapodi to find some clothes which might have bloodstains on them. If we do you are a witness, in which case you will have to come to court to give gawaahi.'

Meher is dismayed, he should never have taken these passengers, he says this too, 'Kya saab, pehle bolta to doosra taxi mein mai-ich bithaata.'

'Abhi chhup baithta hai key nain? Kabhi se dimaag chaat raila hai. Shut up and eat your batata wada instead of my brain. Do you want another?'

Meher wants to tell them that he wants to go home and that they can go to hell. But then this is the police, they might make it happen the other way around. So might as well make the best of a bad situation. 'Murder case hai kya?'

'No.'

'But you are saying bloodstained clothes?'

'He tried to murder her.'

'Her?'

'Arrey baba, you read newspapers? You read this morning's papers about the nurse?'

'But saab, according to the paper, he has made an ekdum bhayankar haalat of her, worse than trying to murder her.'

'The law says there is an attempt to murder, after which there is a murder. There is no in-between. You either die or you do not.'

'But I read that the bichari nurse is stuck in between, neither living nor dead. The papers are also saying rape kiya?'

'There is no complaint from her side on it.'

'But she cannot even speak, she is in a coma, that's what I read.'

'Her family is there, the doctors are there, they have to come forward with a complaint and medical proof.'

'Ajeebach duniya hain,' Meher shakes his head at the ways of a strange world.

The drive to Dapodi resumes, they climb the Western Ghats, enter Khandala where it is green, cool and pleasant. The officer takes in a deep breath and sounds relaxed, 'It is so nice to get out of Bombay into such beautiful weather.'

Meher decides to press his case a bit. 'Saab, if you find anything and I have to come to court, dhandey ka time pe nai bulaaneka.'

The officer laughs, 'Even in the Hindi movies courts do not work at night. Courts function during office and business hours, so you will have to come dhandey key time pech. Don't worry so much, we will find you when the time comes.'

'This is exactly what I am worried about,' mutters Meher.

They reach the hut behind CME at 4.00 p.m. The police start their search, it does not take long. A small battered metal trunk in the corner reveals Sohanlal's wife's clothes, one khaki half-pant with bloodstains on it, one shirt with bloodstains towards its front bottom and a man's underwear with bloodstains on the front. All the three latter items of clothing look as though attempts have been made to wash off the bloodstains before putting them right at the bottom of the trunk.

The officer shows the three items of clothing to Vimala, Sohanlal's wife, sitting outside the hut with the ghoonghat over her face. She identifies them as her husband's clothing in a low, scared voice.

Back to Bombay with Meher gloomily contemplating kutcheri ka chukkers, the inevitable rounds of the courts in store for him now that he is part of this lafdaa.

$6$.00 p.m. Accused Sohanlal Bhartha Walmiki is sent for a medical check-up to the police surgeon of Bombay, C.A. Franklin. His report:

Three abrasions on the left cheek. Upper one crescentic with convexity up. Second one 1.5 cm to the left of the angle of the mouth. Third one midway between first and second. Second and third infected.

Abrasions to the left of Adam's apple on neck, several in 0.8 cm diameter. His own fingernails trimmed recently, not marks of his own scratching.

Abrasion on inner aspect of left elbow 0.4 cms in diameter.

Almost inconsequential injuries, no indication at all of the fight that a woman put up against bestiality. But this list can help in the courts to prove attempt to rape, this is clear. Except that those who should, and can, make the difference do not seem to want to notice.

$T$he next morning there are two long-distance calls, one from Bangalore. The wire services have picked up the Aruna Shanbaug story, sent it upcountry and to the South. Newspapers, English and regional, have used the story. The caller from Bangalore says she is 'praying for Aruna Shanbaug, please tell her'. There are flowers from people, some land in the dean's office wanting to see her. 'Do you think she is some kind of clown and this hospital is a circus?' he asks before having security throw them out.

Letters to the Editor start flowing in, expressing outrage, wanting to know what kind of security working women can expect anywhere else in the country when in a place like Bombay this can happen. A woman's life has been destroyed because of Rs 500, what does the BMC have to say about the running of its hospitals? A few angry editorials appear. The BMC decides that it needs to stem what appears to be a growing tide of dissatisfaction against its performance. Before its own administrative capabilities are questioned further the focus needs to be changed. A call is put through to the state government, from here a call goes to the police commissioner of Bombay. The case is to be transferred to the Crime Branch. 'But Bhoiwada has already arrested the suspect, his conviction is inevitable.' Just do it.

Sundeep spends more and more time at Aruna's bedside with Ramdas, her cousin. Ramdas's sister Nirmala, newly-wed, has been away in her husband's village. She rushes in and is beside herself with grief. 'What can I do? There must be something I can do to help her?' She is so overwrought that the nurse asks her to leave the ward for fear of distressing the patient. 'Come when you can, you live so far away in Borivli now,' says Sundeep to Nirmala. 'And now you have to take care of your new home. But do keep telephoning Ramdas, he will tell you the daily news. Come quickly when she opens her eyes, it will be wonderful.'

Nirmala wants to know if Aruna's brother has arrived, if her sister and nieces are spending adequate time at the hospital. Sundeep looks blank.

Meanwhile what of Aruna herself, what of that spirit? It

fights, it subsides, it rises again. She has convulsions and fits. She is administered enormous quantities of different types of medications. Her physical wounds hurt, taking their time to heal. She is in severe discomfort when passing stools, she cries out in pain through her semi-comatose state, each time she does so. She runs a continuous temperature. She gets all kinds of infections, urinary, chest, for these she is given more medicine. Throat suctions are done. She is subjected to constant tests. She is fed through the Ryle's tube, there's not one nurse in the hospital who isn't committed to putting her back on her feet again. She's still in a light coma. Occasionally there is the flicker of eyes resembling opening and closure movements.

Plantars extensors. This does not change.

3 December. The Aruna Shanbaug case is transferred to the Crime Branch. The file goes from the Bhoiwada police station to the Crime Branch office opposite Crawford Market, a stone building with a curving staircase. The investigating officers asked to handle the case are police inspector Vakatkar, assistant police inspector Tarte and sub-inspector Sahasrabudhe.

Sub-inspector Keshav Shridhar Sahasrabudhe voices the thought on everyone's mind. They have all read about the case in the papers, there have been telephonic discussions with the Bhoiwada police. 'They have given a medical report that there was no vaginal penetration. Why is there no medical report about whether there was any unnatural offence or not? If proved it will get him an additional ten years.'

'Perhaps because she is supposed to get married shortly.'

'Then why not at least 376 read with 511, Attempt to

Rape? If not that then 354, Outraging Modesty which is two years added to whatever sentence he gets?'

'God knows.'

'Even his own statement is not enough. We would definitely need a medical examination report and, of course, a complaint to that effect.'

'Look at who the complainant is. One of our people from Bhoiwada, her own people have not bothered. Okay now you stop bothering about this for five minutes and just help me put together these papers of the Godrej riots.'

SI Sahasrabudhe sets about sorting out the statements of the hundreds of people they had questioned at Vikhroli where their own officers had died in a crossfire between the rioting mobs of the Shiv Sena and Datta Samant's workers.

4 December. Assistant matron Durga Mehta arrives from her home town, Amreli in Gujarat. She comes straight from the station to KEM with her bags. Near the entrance she meets Sister Premila Kushe who enquires about her mother's health.

'She is vastly improved now. Being a nurse really helps at such a time.'

'This was her third paralytic stroke?'

'No, her fourth. She lost her speech again as well. But she has recovered from her paralysis and her speech is back. That is why I say being a nurse is a boon in your own home as well.'

'There might be some difference of opinion about that here.'

'Why do you say that? What's happened?'

'What hasn't? The nurses went on three-day strike because

of staff nurse Aruna Shanbaug. She was attacked, and some say raped, in the CVTC basement.'

'Oh God!'

Assistant matron Mehta quickly walks to matron Belimal's office, and is given the details. She sighs, 'I told her not to change there. Nurses should not change anywhere and everywhere. You want respect as a nurse you have to keep your dignity as a nurse.'

Matron Belimal nods. 'That's true for all women.'

Prema Pai is also present and asks matron, 'Now at least they will close down the CVTC dog surgery for good?'

Durga Mehta addresses the matron, 'I suppose there's no point discussing how nurses should not have changed there. The more we talk about it the more it means we could not control our own nurses. And there is definitely no point in now saying staff nurse Aruna Shanbaug did not obey orders properly. Well, I'll go and change and report for duty.'

Assistant matron Mehta leaves the office, Sister Pai is furious with her. She talks to matron Belimal in Konkani, 'How can she talk like that? Did Aruna ask for this in any way? How can it be implied that this would not have happened if Aruna had changed elsewhere? Who does that Durga Mehta think she is?'

'Would this have happened if Aruna had not changed in the basement alone? Would this have happened anywhere else in the hospital, or even in the city, to her? May be, may be not. As for who is Durga Mehta, she is the finest nurse this hospital can ever have. She feels very strongly for KEM. It makes me wish there were more Durga Mehtas in the nursing profession, especially now after Aruna's case.'

Sister Pai looks at matron Belimal for some time. When she speaks there are icicles in her voice, 'So this is what you elderly women are saying. That her sin was that she disobeyed orders. And that her punishment—I suppose you'll also think that this is from God—for that sin was the attack and the rape. In other words, if women do not behave themselves it is okay for them to be brutally beaten and raped.'

Matron Belimal shakes her head, speaks to Prema in Konkani, 'Really, how you carry on! There is no justification for what has been done to Aruna. My point is that women themselves have to be constantly careful, not just about their bodies but also their minds. This is how Indian women have always been, right down the centuries. Nowadays there is a lot of talk about equality between the two sexes, I see many articles encouraging women to be like men. I don't understand these articles. Why should women disturb their natural balance to become like men?'

The icicles deepen in Sister Pai's voice. 'Forgive me matron, but all this philosophy does not apply to Aruna. She came to Bombay to become a nurse, for a better life than the one she would have had being married to some village idiot. We now know it was that sweeper Sohanlal who did it. Why did he? Because she was the only one in that department, I repeat the only one, who was making the point about his stealing food from the mouths of dogs. Tell me, how was any natural balance being disturbed here, how was it even a matter of equality? She was just doing her job properly; it had nothing to do with her being a woman or a man.'

Matron Belimal sounded tired. 'I'm told she spoke with him very sharply too often.'

'So?'

'She could have just drawn the attention of the higher authorities to what he was doing and left it to them. Why get mixed up with the sweepers?'

'Matron what are you saying? She was his higher authority. It's true that Aruna had, sorry has, a sharp tongue. But she used her tongue to protect the interests of dumb animals and also the institution which paid her salary. She was being loyal when she spoke sharply. Well, whether she was punished for caring or speaking sharply is hardly to be discussed now. You said so yourself a few minutes back, nothing excuses what has been done to her.'

'Prema, I say this with the experience of an old woman and also that of a working woman since several years. We have to do our dharma; you can define dharma any way you like, a mere duty, a responsibility, religion, a conscience-call. And we have to look after ourselves while doing our dharma because there is no such thing as equality. Not between men and women, not between classes of people. These are balances, disturb them and you invite trouble. Haven't you heard this from childhood, in Hindi they even say chhotey logo key muh nahin lagna chahiye. Do you now understand what they mean when they say do not waste words, and your thoughts, on small people?'

Prema begins a sharp retort, the door of matron Belimal's office bursts open as a young nurse runs in. 'Matron, come quickly! Aruna has started screaming in her sleep.'

Notes from the patient-chart of staff nurse Aruna Shanbaug.

7 December. Level of consciousness slightly improved. Still screaming from time to time. Opens eyes and blinks frequently. But does not open eyes on calling out to her. Chest sounds moist on both sides. Suction throat every two-three hours.

8 December. Quiet with Largactil. Chest clear. No more pressure sores when opening bowels. Limbs being moved passively. Patient irritable. Intermittent oxygen is being given through humidifier.

9 December. Screams almost continuously. Needs to be sedated with Largactil 25 mg four times daily. No facial asymmetry. Plantars continue to be extensor. No bed sores. No convulsions or spasms. Being fed through Ryle's tube.

10 December. Quiet with Largactil 25 mg six-hourly. Has temperature.

11 December. Sedated with Largactil 25 mg six-hourly. No temperature.

12 December. EEG repeated. Midline echo obtained.

13 December. Screaming continuously. Grinding teeth, jaws in chewing movement, sucking reflex noted.

14 December. No change in condition.

15 December. No change in condition.

16 December. Continuously screaming.

17 December. Screaming continuously. Largactil and Calmpose injections have no effect. Gardenal injection 100 mg six-hourly. Slept for four hours with this.

18 December. Leaking by the side of the catheter persists. Bladder wash done. Neurologically the same. Continuous screaming, decorticate with sucking reflex and constant chewing movements. Plantars up. 9.00 p.m.: Patient quiet with Gardenal. Remains quiet for two-three hours after Gardenal injection. No fever. Leak by side of the catheter continues. Gynaecologist informed.

19 December. Quiet with Gardenal. Leak by the side of the catheter continues. No temperature. Neurologically still decorticate with chewing movements and sucking reflex. All four limbs markedly spastic.

**19** December, 2.00 p.m. Two panchaas for the panchnaama, CID officers and the accused Sohanlal Bhartha Walmiki sit in a vehicle outside the

Crime Branch office. They reach Dapodi a little before 6.00 p.m.

Vimala stands helplessly outside the hut, her ghoonghat covering her expression, as her handcuffed husband enters the hut with the police. She isn't as yet out of her teens. Her father Muktiar Bikram Bilar, a mukaddam like her father-in-law, is still at work. Her mother Birma is sick, lying inside in the hut, covered, medicated and asleep.

The police search silently around the huddled mass which is Birma. They locate a packet hidden in the tarpaulin roof, in the north-east corner of the hut. The outside of this small package is a dirty banian. Inside which is a plastic bag. Inside the plastic bag is one chain with a hexagon-shaped pendant and one watch, Tressa make, with A.S. carved on its stainless steel back.

The panchnaama is done.

The driver reverses the vehicle to return to Bombay. Everyone gets in, seating Sohanlal in the centre.

He has made no attempt to talk to Vimala. He has not even looked at her.

**22** December. Dr Sundeep Sardesai raises his right hand and slowly smooths Aruna's fevered brow. She is quiet, her chart shows the amount of drugs she is being soothed with. Gardenal. Largactil. Siquil. Calmpose. Her chart shows Dr Sardesai other facts which as a doctor he understands, which as a man who loves this woman he ignores.

He pulls up the stool, takes her hand in his, starts talking to her in a low voice. 'I'm sorry I wasn't here in the last few days. But you know I was giving my MD exams. I had a choice. I could spend time with you every day and give my exams alongside. Or I could just give my exams and see you after that. You will be happy to know that I have fared better than I expected. You will be happier to know that I've found a small place which I can rent as my consulting room. It is in Dadar, part of a nursing home. I'm starting work there next month as per our plans. By then my day attachments with two hospitals should also be worked out.'

Sundeep pauses, as if listening to what she has to say. He nods, 'Yes, yes. I know which other hospitals you want me to . . .' They talk for a long time. Sundeep shifts his position every now and then, to the left of her bed, to the right, as he speaks, checking her joints and reflexes. Later he speaks to the dean. 'Aruna has had no physical movement since three weeks. She is becoming rigid, she's developing a tightness of tendoactivities. Could we please start some posturing and physiotherapy?'

Timings are fixed for the physio sessions every day, Dr Sardesai is there for all of them.

Crime Branch assistant police inspector Yashwant Jabaji Tarte has been thinking about the conversation between sub-inspector Sahasrabudhe and his colleagues. He wonders if he could attempt to question the victim Aruna Shanbaug. Even if she whispers a few relevant words it would make an additional case against the accused. He telephones KEM, an appointment is set up for him with Dr Dastur.

'She showed some improvement in the first ten days,' Dr Dastur tells API Tarte. 'But subsequently she has not shown further recovery.'

'Can I try and speak to her?'

'Of course, but from the medical point of view she is still in a coma. Patients in a coma generally do not answer questions.'

'How long do you think she will remain unconscious, doctor?'

'I cannot give you an exact date, inspector. And even if I give you an estimated time I would not advise you to pin your case on it.'

'The case as it stands is signed, sealed and delivered. I'm just hoping I can get this girl complete justice. Therefore some indication of the time involved would help.'

'I see. Well, given her condition and the level of her progress I would say she is likely to take at least another three weeks to regain the kind of consciousness you would need for your questioning.'

'Okay doctor, thank you. Can I telephone you after three weeks? Can I also leave my number in your department just in case she comes out of her coma before that?'

'Of course. But I say this again inspector, do not pin your hopes. Her brain is not entirely functional anymore, her memory is likely to be affected.'

Part of the patient-chart of staff nurse Aruna Shanbaug.

December 23. She still screams every 5-10 minutes. No temperature today. Breathing comparatively quiet. Urinary leak considerably reduced. Chewing movements much less, so also the sucking reflex. Ampicillin, Luminal, Largactil, Calmpose continued.

December 25. Semi-comatose. Crying.

December 26. Irritable. Yelling. Catheter is blocked, so

also bulb. Bulb cannot be deflated. Urine is acidic, tendency to form crusts and block catheter. Catheter changed.

December 27. Urine comes out from side of catheter. No fistula. 9.00 p.m. Patient rowdy and restless. Cries loudly and incessantly. Dr Sunil Pandya informed. Advises Largactil 50 mg stat. Tab. Calmpose 10 mg stat.

December 28. Slight rise in blood pressure, 150/100. Pulse 120. Patient put in head high, full block position. Screams off and on. 8.30 p.m. Patient vomits.

29 December. Dr Dastur decides to do a carotid angiography on Aruna. He asks the nurse to get written permission from her immediate relatives when they visit. The signature on the release form would have to be that of a brother or sister, none of whom are seen regularly around Aruna's bed.

The carotid consists of two large arteries, one on each side of the head that carry blood to the head. The arteries divide into two. An external branch supplies blood to the neck, face and other external parts. And an internal branch supplies blood to the brain, eye and other internal parts. An angiography is an x-ray examination of a particular part of a body and its blood vessels following the intravenous injection of radiopaque fluid.

At the neck the carotid arteries run parallel to the windpipe.

When Sohanlal Bhartha Walmiki savagely tightened that dog chain around Aruna Shanbaug's neck he cut into her windpipe and deprived her brain of all-important oxygen. And in doing this he killed several of her brain cells.

As he kept twisting the dog chain around her slender neck, did Sohanlal also damage the carotid artery carrying blood to Aruna's brain? And how deep was the damage to the carotid artery? Would the damage be containable, could it be defrayed, by medication?

Questions to which the carotid angiography would have most of the answers. It is scheduled.

Aruna's relatives refuse to give their permission for a carotid angiography.

The procedure is clearly explained to them, they are requested to be present during the angiography, the benefits of the angiography are spelt out. The relatives refuse to sign.

The dean is informed. He says medico-legally they are bound to get that one signature.

The dean is equally cut-and-dried with Dr Sardesai who quietly implores that his signature be accepted on the form. Then, softening slightly when he sees Sundeep's obvious frustration, he adds, 'Son, please put yourself in my place. I cannot jeopardize the interests of my hospital in any way, especially when I know there can be legal trouble ahead with people trying to take advantage of an already impossible situation.'

The nurse on duty in neurosurgery speaks to Sister Pai about speaking to Aruna's brother and sister about the angiography. She contacts the sister who refuses, 'Ask my brother for permission. I cannot give it.'

Sister Pai points out that there are several other papers which need to be signed by them, normal formalities when a patient is checked in. 'Speak to my brother, I cannot sign any of them.' Sister Pai leaves a message with the sister for the brother urging him to contact the hospital immediately. He does not. She tries telephoning him at several places in the city, with no success. She personally visits the place he is supposed to have stayed at while in Bombay. A relative there tells her there is a message for her, 'He is leaving Bombay for ten days due to some family illness. He does not want the angiography or any other procedure done till he returns.'

The carotid angiography is cancelled.

It is never, ever, performed; no one appears to sign any papers at all.

30 December. Staff nurse Aruna Shanbaug, still in a semi-comatose state, starts laughing.

A long spell of laughter.

Then she screams.

Then she laughs again.

There is no registration of any of these emotions on her face.

31 December. Dr Sundeep Sardesai spends the last day of 1973 by the bedside of the woman who was to be his wife early in the new year.

He sits on the stool, holding her left hand in his, telling her about where they will go for their honeymoon.

She screams. He closes his eyes. 'Don't do that, please,' he whispers.

She laughs. He buries his face in her hand.

A new sheet for the new year on Aruna Shanbaug's file.

1 January 1974. Vomited twice after feeds.

2 January. No vomiting. Laughing spells absent. Spasticity in upper limbs markedly less. Passing urine well without a catheter. No temperature.

3 January. Patient removed Ryle's tube. Reintroduced.

4 January. Crying a lot. Moves all limbs spontaneously.

6 January. Had a large vomit this morning. Crying spells. No laughing spells. Turns in bed spontaneously.

10 January. Dr Dastur notes that the patient has upper brain stem injury.

19 January. No change in neurological status. Still tends to be in decorticated posture. Still screams. Largactil or Calmpose makes no difference. Unresponsive to verbal commands.

21 January. Seen by Dr Dastur. Patient keeps her eyes open but does not blink on menace. Cortical blindness following post-cerebral artery damage since pupils are reacting well. She does move her eyes in the direction of loud sounds.

23 January. Dr E.P.Bharucha assesses present condition and prognosis. Impression: Extensive upper brain stem injury with cortical blindness.

30 January. Fully conscious. Does not obey commands. Diarrhoea persists. Patient lies with eyes open and all four limbs flexed. Tries to look around. Cries.

One man. Plus a savage twist of one chain. And the thirty seconds for his sperm to release.

Equals one broken woman. With brain damage so irreversible that it does not even register images. And perfectly healthy pupils but blind for life.


T his is how it is, a life in the day of Dr Sundeep Sardesai.

Dr Sardesai is at KEM by 9.00 a.m. every single morning by which time Aruna has been bathed or sponged, powdered and settled in with fresh clothing on a tightly-made bed. Dr Sardesai opens the small locker near her bed where he has kept several packets of tiny black and red felt bindis. He chooses one and neatly sticks the dot on Aruna's forehead, slightly above her eyebrows, equidistant from her eyes. The first time he does this the nurse on duty clears her throat. The second day she breaks down and weeps. A week later matron Belimal comes to stand by him, watches him apply the tikka and pats him gently on the shoulder, 'God bless you son.' Every now and then an extra nurse is present at that precise moment when he looks up after opening the locker.

The physiotherapist arrives, Dr Sardesai assists, constantly murmuring words of encouragement to Aruna. Physio done, he talks to her for a while and leaves only to be back a little after teatime. With assistance from the nurses, he mobilizes her. He makes her sit up in bed, he makes her sit on a chair. He hoists her out of bed and makes her walk, it's a dragging movement actually. Sundeep and a nurse or one of his doctor friends on either side of Aruna, holding her up by her shoulders, bending over to get her to move her legs, left foot, right foot, she sags. They begin again, hold her up, guide her left foot, guide her right foot.

By 5.15 p.m. Sundeep is at his clinic at Dadar. He specializes in diabetes, he is getting really very good at his work. Patients crowd his waiting-room. At around 8.30 p.m., just before leaving his clinic, he calls KEM, gets the daily report on Aruna's food, medicine and behaviour. The report does not vary too much.

TPRN, which stands for Temperature Pressure Respiration Normal. She lies in bed with hands and feet flexed. Splints are being used to assist in keeping her limbs straight. Sometimes she goes into a foetal position. Cries loudly, weeps softly. Laughs manically. Alternates between laughing and crying. Also has spells of screaming which can last upto two hours.

Cannot see. Takes feeds by mouth. Eats when given, stops when apparently full. Depending upon moods responds to commands. Sticks out tongue for some doctors only. Difficult to control when restless as she becomes rowdy. Able to hold up her head on her own for short periods.

According to neurosurgery's instructions, Dr Sushila U. Sheth has started speech therapy with her.

A trial with Piracetam produced no beneficial effects. Mild thrombocytopenia with subcutaneous purpuric spots prompted discontinuation of all drugs except her anticonvulsants. Piracetam is said to accelerate recovery of functions in injured brains. Some centres abroad have reported satisfactory results.

Passes urine in the bed. Motions every second or third day without enema or purgative. Menses regular, last for three days.

Skin rash all over the body including webs of the hands. Suspected scabies. Medicated accordingly inclusive of ointment application.

Recognizes pain very well, unlike previously. Since she continues to keep all limbs, including knees, flexed, there are marked deformities at elbows and wrists. She cries when attempts are made to straighten these.

And thus Aruna dwells in her twilight zone.

Dean Deshpande is feeling extraordinarily uncomfortable. He is relieved that he invited matron Belimal for this meeting. Matron took his permission and brought along Sister Prema Pai. All of them are in his office talking to staff nurse Aruna Shanbaug's sister. The silence in between sentences is so deep that they can clearly hear the fan blades completing each rotation above their heads.

The dean clears his throat, 'So you do not know when your brother is expected again from Shimoga?'

'No.'

'Can you telephone him and find out?'

'We don't have a telephone.'

'You can book a trunk call from here, my office, and wait comfortably till they give you the line.'

'He doesn't have a phone.'

Matron Belimal speaks softly, 'Perhaps you would like to take Aruna home.'

'Why should I take her home?'

'She is your sister, isn't she?'

'You have done this to her in the hospital, now you want to get rid of her?'

'That is not correct. We are discharging our duties, and doing much more, towards her.'

'More than you are doing,' interjects Prema in Konkani. Matron shoots her a warning look.

The dean speaks. 'The issue here is that Aruna needs to be discharged because there is no point in keeping her in the hospital. She does not need any more medical treatment. We have to send her home now.'

'You know she doesn't have her home in Bombay. Her house is in Haldipur, Karnataka, where she has a sick mother.'

'I meant that you should take her home, to your house. Please take her home and doctors from here will come to your house regularly to check her up. Medicine, as and when required, will also be sent.'

'My kholi is too small, there is no place to keep her in such a cramped room. And how are we to feed her? We are poor people.'

The dean clears his throat. 'There will be a compensation amount which would take care of Aruna's expenses.'

'How much?'

'You want to take advantage of Aruna's situation to make money?' Sister Prema Pai is livid.

Her tone is flat, her sentences are clipped, delivered in blunt Bombay-Hindi. Aruna's sister says no, she is not taking any advantage. She's just baldly stating her case, she cannot afford any additional burden on her home, spacewise or financially. She's out of the house selling milk twice a day, she doesn't even have the time to nurse anyone. Her daughters are grown, they come to KEM with food for Aruna, soon they will get married and go away. This is all.

Matron Belimal asks if she has thought of any solution.

Aruna's sister frowns. 'It is your responsibility to look after her because this happened to her during her duty-time in your hospital because of one of your other employees.'

'Still, we have been sending you so many messages and only now have you come for this meeting. So you must have thought of something which would want to make you take Aruna home.' Matron Belimal is softly sarcastic.

The sister pauses and then speaks. 'Keep paying her monthly salary with bonus. Also, a bigger house in the BMC quarters near Worli Dairy. On a permanent basis.'

The dean's meeting with Aruna's brother turns out to be unscheduled, unpleasant and unsatisfactory.

He has given instructions that the moment Aruna's brother is seen by her bedside he should be informed, even if he is at home. He is called accordingly.

The dean wastes no time, walks quickly to ward 33, re-introduces himself, attempts an ice-breaker. 'So, you are here from Shimoga?'

'Yes.'

'You have come after quite some time.'

Silence.

'You plan on returning after some time, I'm sure.'

'No.'

'I see. Well, let me come straight to the point. Your sister has been a patient with us for ten months. We have, in keeping with KEM's tradition of free service, taken care of everything including the biggest of tests. However, money is not the issue, especially for our staff who have watched over their colleague day and night. You know the condition she was brought in. You can see the overall improvement in her since then.'

'When will she get properly better?'

'That cannot be said. The ultimate degree, and the quality, of recovery also cannot be predicted.'

Silence.

'Medically your sister does not need hospital care any more. We can discharge her as soon as you are free to take her home.'

'I do not live here.'

'I am well aware of that. But I also have to make you aware of the fact that a patient cannot live in a hospital forever.'

Silence.

'So, when do you plan on taking your sister from here?'

'Doctor, you know I live in Shimoga. How is it possible to take her over there?'

'You can make some arrangements for her in Bombay, some other relatives can take care of her, perhaps your sister who lives at BDD chawls.'

'If anyone was agreeable would I not make the arrangements?'

'Then you will have to think of taking her to Shimoga. We will make arrangements for her to reach there safely, a doctor, nurse and two helpers will travel with her in the train. There will also be a compensation amount which will be handed over to you after you have signed all the papers.'

There is anger in Aruna's brother's voice. 'This is not about compensation. I have recently left Bombay to restart my life in Shimoga. It is a partnership in a small Udipi on the Shimoga main road. My family prays for it to do well, but I can't say for sure right now whether I would have to shift again or not. Can you understand this?'

The dean says he can. He adds, 'In these 301 days I have understood quite a bit about human nature.'

This was conceived as the ideal spot, from here good government could emanate. One hundred and eighty degrees of visual pleasure. The Arabian Sea in the visible distance, a sprawling oval-shaped ground in the middle and this building, for the Government of Bombay on this side of the open grounds. The building was designed in consonance with the government's plans for Bombay, grand but containable, and construction commenced on 16 April 1867, with a sanctioned budget of Rs 12,80,731. The building was completed on 20 March 1874, at the total cost of Rs 12,60, 844. Bombayites, or indeed even the rest of the country, would be hard-pressed to find any other public—or perhaps even private—edifice built under budget inspite of taking several years.

It truly was a good way to work. Governance, in front of it the green of the Oval Maidan, on the other side the blue-green of the sea. A gentle sea breeze would ever so often waft over the Oval and bring into the building with it the sounds of the waves swishing, the definitive click of rubber against willow from cricket in the maidan. Among the lofty arches and the pillars, and the large wide-open windows and airy workplaces, the officials would govern one of the most precious stones in Her Majesty's crown.

The century-plus-old building lost its history along with its beauty and virtue when it was turned into the Sessions Court. Woodwork converted the wide verandas into clerical spaces crammed with desks, arches were boarded up and windows worked into the resultant rectangles, courtrooms were carved out of corridors, rusting steel cupboards were jammed against exquisite old-wood louvered doors, metal mesh attached to every window to keep out the birds. But pigeons have their own way of staking their claim to the high ceilings, they have entered the Sessions Court to stay. They perch on the lined up tube-lights to shit with impunity along the sides of the corridors. For this reason too advocates and their clients are mostly to be found talking in groups bang in the middle of the walking space.

Sohanlal Bhartha Walmiki's case is committed to this Sessions Court on 10 April 1974. The trial begins on 7 August 1974. He pleads Not Guilty. Thirty-eight people have been questioned for this case. Depositions begin. It is observed in the course of the proceedings that the accused 'followed her, surprised her while she was preparing to leave and dragged her to the operation theatre and tried to satisfy his lust. However, it appears that as Aruna was menstruating he was constrained.' Several other facts are also orally observed, but what is the use?

2 October 1973. The Sessions Court is working on the birthday of M.K. Gandhi, Father of the Nation, believer in human goodness and justice for all. The sentence is pronounced

on Sohanlal Bhartha Walmiki. He is held guilty of the
offences under sections 307 and 397 of the Indian Penal Code,
Attempt to Commit Murder and Robbery. He is sentenced to
suffer seven years rigorous imprisonment on each of the
counts. However, since he has no previous record of any
conviction his two sentences can run concurrently.
Additionally, he has been arrested on 28 November 1973 and
he is in detention till this day. This entire period shall be set
off against the term of imprisonment under section 428 of the
Criminal Procedure Code.

The date of Sohanlal Bhartha Walmiki's arrest should
actually be noted as 29 November. He was picked up on
29 November at 2.00 a.m. in Poona, officially arrested at
11.05 a.m. of the same day. By pure oversight he gets to spend
a day less in jail.

But then what is a day here or there for a man who is
going to be spending seven years less since his sentences run
concurrently? Another two years less because no one has
complained about Outraging of Modesty, never mind the
obvious Attempt to Rape? Or ten years less because no
Unnatural Offence has happened on paper? A total of how
many years less, not counting the fact that there is no set jail
term under the law for someone who kills human brain cells,
inflicts irreversible brain stem injury and leaves the victim
hopelessly alive?

**3** October 1974. Headlines
of the stories on the City & Suburb page of *The Times of
India*.

Two Suspects Held. Taxi Runs Into Crowd. 19 Held In
Two Riots. Bye Bye, Monsoon.

The bigger headline is above the smaller stories. Life
Term For Murder Of Architect.

The story under the headline: 'Found guilty of the murder of a civil engineer and architect Mr Minu Rustamji Karanjia, Dhobi Talao, Ansari Ahmed Imtiaz was sentenced to imprisonment for life by Mr Wani, additional sessions judge. Mr Karanjia's grand-nephew who was residing with him rang the bell on 5 October 1973, for half an hour but there was no response from his grand-uncle. The accused then opened the door and the grand-nephew found Mr Karanjia lying in a pool of blood with a bedsheet covering him. In his defence the accused said he had been brought to the flat for the purpose of "committing an unnatural offence". As he refused to oblige, Mr Karanjia had tried to assault him. In the struggle, the accused used a knife in self-defense. The judge disbelieved the defence and sentenced the accused.'

A sensational story with a twist, the reporter at the Sessions Court on 2 October correctly decided this to be of more interest to readers and covered it accordingly.

Of what interest a sweeper going in for six years, one month and twenty-six days, with every likelihood of him being released even earlier if he stays on good behaviour?

$A$ hand-written note from speech therapist Dr Sushila U. Sheth to Dr Sunil Pandya.

'I have examined Miss Shanbaug and assessed her for speech therapy. At present the patient has no speech except for occasional shouting. She is able to laugh which comes as a spell of uncontrolled laughter. She is able to swallow indicating a good control of muscles of deglutation. If given a command loudly she can show her tongue or close her eyes or raise her hand a little. This shows that she has some comprehension of spoken words. To a clapping sound she does not pay any attention or indicate that she has heard it. It's impossible to know if she observes any object shown to her. Under these circumstances it is very difficult to get any cooperation from her in the methods that we usually use for training aphasic patients. It is likely that she may be helped better if someone from her family spends more time with her than what they are doing at present. It will be best to talk to them personally about this. They can then be instructed to train her continuously for speech. I shall however continue to make attempts to train her which is an uphill task in the face of her physical and mental trauma.'

28 November 1974. The dean asks for a note from neurosurgery. He needs to forward it to the Bombay Municipal Corporation, questions are being raised there. Why should a patient occupy a hospital bed for 12 months when there are several other very ill people who could positively benefit from that space and care?

Dr Sunil Pandya has the note typed and despatched to the dean's office.

'Staff nurse Aruna Shanbaug was admitted on 28 November 1973. On examination she was found to have a number of external injuries and signs of injury to the brain stem. The superficial injuries soon healed. She improved over the next few months to a state where she could open her eyes and stare, swallow fluids and semi-solids and turn about in bed on her own. At times she appears to understand but this is difficult to confirm as there is hardly any meaningful response from her. She is unable to attend to any of her own needs. She has to be clothed, fed and changed. No communication is possible, she cannot make any need understood. She cries aloud and in a protracted manner when disturbed. Occasional spontaneous, and apparently irrational, outbursts of laughter are also noted. She has severe limb and trunk weakness and incoordination. She cannot sit on her own. Our physiotherapist is putting in a lot of effort to prevent joints stiffness and muscle wasting. Our speech therapist is trying her best to coax her to speak but with little success up to now. She has remained in this almost unchanged state after the initial improvement. These findings point to a severe brain stem disturbance along with involvement of the basal ganglia.'

Dr Pandya's note is read in the BMC. Only two questions are asked of KEM.

Can she get better?

The answer would have to fall in that grey area of medicine where hope optimistically triumphs over experience. The Guinness Book of Records is filled with such instances. There are cases in the world where people have got up from their coma to walk away from their beds and lead near normal lives. Of course, there are also several cases where people have stayed in a coma forever and died when they came to old age. However this case is different, she's no longer in a coma. Possibly she has the dubious distinction of being the only case of her kind in the world though this cannot be checked for obvious reasons. Part of her brain has died for what currently looks like forever. It's difficult to say, medical science progresses every single day, there might one day be a cure for her condition. As of right now, the answer is no.

The next question: has her family abandoned her?

Ever since they have been asked to take her home they have hardly been coming to the hospital. The nurses told them they needed to come regularly to talk to Aruna in their mother tongue, Konkani, as this would help enormously in her speech therapy and also improve her general level of consciousness. Studies have proved that brain injury recovery is benefitted from friends and family speaking constantly and comfortingly to the patients about their immediate environment. Aruna's family members reply that the reason they come less to the hospital is because they are being 'harassed' to take her home. They are passing the entire blame on to the hospital. Some in the family are trying to secure as many benefits as possible in the name of rights. Only after securing these rights will they think of taking on the responsibility, that is their attitude. Here it can be safely surmised that the family is presently in the process of abandoning her forever.

There is a meeting at the BMC, a decision is taken, the dean is informed. Move her to the convalescent home in that far-flung suburb of Bombay.

The convalescent home is a place where there is no medical intervention bar heavy drugging for patients in severe pain. Death lurks in the corridors here, spitefully refusing to enter the wards while terminally-ill patients wait within. Not unlike some of Mother Teresa's homes where the dying are comforted till death claims them. Sometimes this takes months, the lucky ones have been released in weeks.

Arrangements are made to shift staff nurse Aruna Shanbaug to the convalescent home. The nurses come to hear of this move, they march up to the matron's office for confirmation.

'It is not what anyone among us wants,' she says with enormous sadness. 'We are doing so much for her, it is frustrating to see no improvement. Perhaps it is time to let her go, leave her to her fate. I have been thinking, are we wrong in taking such good care of her that even if she wants to, she cannot die? She has nothing left to live for, we may not want to admit this but it is the truth God has willed for her.' Matron's voice has sunk to a hoarse whisper, tears glimmer in her eyes. 'When I do my pooja everyday I ask God, why her? Can there ever be a crime committed by anyone in this life, or the past one, to merit such a terrible punishment? There can be no other woman in this world who suffers the way Aruna does. Yes, perhaps it is time for us to allow nature to take its own course.'

Matron's spoken thoughts are drowned in a flurry of furious voices. 'Anyway we have no choice in the matter, these are orders from the BMC.'

'But we should object, they cannot do this to her.'

'Who will object? The BMC will ask them to take her home with them.'

'But she will get bed sores there, nobody will keep turning her around the way we do.'

'She will die there.'

'That is the whole idea, that she should die.'

'But why? Who is the BMC to decide that she should die? If God wanted her to die she would have stopped breathing in the CVTC basement.'

'Who is the BMC to decide where she should die? When her time comes, let her go peacefully and happily right here from KEM.'

'Who does the municipal commissioner think he is? Who is paying his salary? And who is paying for all those useless corporators to sit around filling their pockets in the BMC? The same people who are paying ours, the people of Bombay, through their taxes. These BMC fellows are worrying about Rs 500 being spent on Aruna, what about the thousands they spend on themselves for no benefit at all to the city?'

The staff nurses of The King Edward VII Memorial Hospital spontaneously, collectively, strike work immediately.

Three hours later they are informed by the BMC, through the dean, that their colleague Aruna Shanbaug will continue to remain a patient in their hospital. The nurses may please resume their duties.

Some think she ought to live. Some think she is better off dead. Her family does not think of her anymore as a living, feeling, human being.

She came from the South to seek her future. The man who loved her came from the West. The one who lusted came from the North.

One unfortunate woman at the centre of them all. How many conflicts, yet, must find expression in her?


She wasn't like this at all earlier, in fact she was so particular about not discussing her colleagues. But now there are times, the nurses feel, that Aruna actually enjoys gossip.

When they collect at her bed to change her sheets or bathe her or just take a small break around her, they chat. About other nurses, the senior ones who think no end of themselves, the junior ones who just don't know their jobs, the doctors, the dean. Names flow freely, instances are recounted, inferences drawn; in short, solid bouts of good gossip. And Aruna seems to listen, an attentiveness comes over her blank face, she quietens down, she seems to start enjoying what she's listening to. The expression is one of a child listening to a new, non-threatening story.

'So what are you'll trying to teach her now?' Dr G.H. Tilve enters ward 33. He is the head of the department of medicine and is constantly being requested by the nurses to come and check staff nurse Aruna Shanbaug. A cough, a leaking nose, a loose tummy, a small rash, scratches on the sole, the last one turned out to be from Aruna's long toenails which had not been cut in a while.

Dr Tilve checks her temperature, pressure, respiration, eyes, tongue, a quick over-all physical. 'She is perfectly normal,' he says. 'What is the matter, why did you call me?'

The two nurses present look at each other sheepishly, one of them speaks up with guilt in her voice, 'She has developed a rash above and below her eyebrows. Also on her upper lip and chin.'

Dr Tilve looks, so she has, though it is just an angry reddening, as if the skin had been plucked, and not a rash. 'When did this happen?'

The nurses hesitate, the other speaks this time. 'A little while back. Soon after we threaded her eyebrows. They had not been done ever since she came, and they were looking so bad, so we thought . . . there's no problem, is there doctor?'

Dr Tilve laughs heartily. 'What are you going to do next?'

'We have to take her for her bath now. No problem putting water on her face, with that redness on it?'

'No, no it's okay, just make sure the water is lukewarm. And what soap and shampoo is being used today?'

The nurses blush. 'Doctor, you're making fun of us!'

Dr Tilve laughs again. 'Of course not. It's well known in the hospital that the nurses try out all the new soaps, shampoos and powders in the market on their colleague.'

'She liked good things Dr Tilve, she still does.'

'Why not, why not. Here, let me give you a hand, you are taking her for a bath right now?'

Dr Tilve assists the nurses in transferring Aruna on to the gurney and leaves the ward smiling. The nurses ask the student nurses in the ward to help wheel her to the bathroom. Chatting among themselves, a minor gossip session, they start the fairly long and cumbersome procedure of bathing Aruna. She is thoroughly sponged every day; baths, including the head, are twice a week.

They undress her, there is a knock on the bathroom door. There is an urgent telephone call for one of the nurses from her home. She takes off the huge rubber apron, hastily pulls on her watch, stockings and shoes and says she'll send a student nurse from the ward. The student nurse arrives looking scared. She has never bathed a patient before, and this one is like handling almost dead weight. The other nurse slowly, patiently, teaches her the ropes. She gently pulls back Aruna's fingers to wash her palms, Aruna yelps in pain. She deflexes her elbows to wash the insides, it hurts Aruna again.

Each time Aruna shouts in pain the student nurse jumps back in alarm. The nurse laughs, 'Don't worry, it's not your fault. Her joints have become too rigid. Also she has become very sensitive to the touch of strangers. That is why we do not even allow ward boys to lift her from the bed, she starts shouting like anything when their fingers touch her.'

The student nurse swallows. 'I heard she was raped. Is she getting frightened because men are touching her?'

'Most of the doctors who examine her are men. Her fiancé—you will see him when he comes now, in time for her physiotherapy—is a man. But yes, she has been used to them for some time now and she does react more badly to the touch of a strange male than of a female. But then again, this might be because they are ward boys and their hands are rough. Here, just give me that soap for a minute. Have you finished soaping her completely, okay let's turn her around, gently, make sure the soapy water doesn't go into her eyes and mouth . . . careful, careful, oh God catch her!'

4 December 1974. Patient had a fall while being given a bath this morning. Two scalp injuries. One near occiput and

the other just above it. The lower one is a haematoma. The upper one is a lacerated wound. One stitch given.

**30** September 1975. The medical records officer of KEM, M.A. Shitole, sends a typed memo to neurosurgery that the municipal commissioner of the BMC has asked for a brief, but comprehensive, note on the likelihood of Aruna Shanbaug's recovery. The municipal commissioner wishes to study the note before putting it up in the forthcoming all-corporator meeting.

Dr R.D. Nagpal, assistant neurosurgeon, replies: 'Miss Shanbaug has shown no improvement. She is entirely dependent. She needs to be fed, clothed, bathed and cleaned. She is unable to comprehend, talk or walk. She has no chance of further recovery.'

15 December 1975. Shitole sends another typed memo to neurosurgery. 'Will you please submit the latest report on the condition of staff nurse Aruna Shanbaug. This is on the agenda of the dean's meeting fixed with the municipal commissioner on Tuesday, 16 December 1975.'

Dr S.K. Pandya, neurosurgeon, replies: 'Thank you for your note dated this morning. There is no change in the staff nurse's condition since our last report. May we please put up, once again, our request for her transfer to a convalescent area where her needs can be attended to? She now needs no neurosurgical attention. If she is shifted elsewhere, one more bed will become available to patients in need of surgery.'

This is the ward in which she has nursed patients, helped them get better so that they could go home to their families. It was not too long ago, but it doesn't seem like that anymore to anyone, perhaps not even to her. In the last twenty-four months staff nurse Aruna Shanbaug has herself occupied a bed in this ward, now there is no more healing to be sought here. She is shifted to a room attached to ward 4. The room is an unused one, identified and cleared for her—under the hawk-eyed supervision of several nurses—of its cobwebs and cupboards containing ancient files.

By and by the BMC will send a note asking why a private room is being occupied by one patient for such a long period of time.

The dean will reply that the room is not really a private one, it has just become so. Anyway there is no alternative since all her relatives have left her quite some time back, it would be accurate to say that they have vanished. The King Edward VII Memorial Hospital is now her only family.

The BMC will want to know if any official letters have been sent to her blood relatives. An address will be pulled out from Aruna's employment file, the one her brother entered when he was in Bombay, of the Udipi he worked in. A letter will be sent, it will come back unopened, 'addressee not known'. Nurse Prema Pai will be requested to procure the address of the sister at BDD chawls, a letter will be sent there. No response. A telegram will follow. It will be ignored. Another letter will be addressed to the brother and sent at the sister's address, who knows what will happen to it.

Eventually there will be a telephone call to the dean from the BMC. Think of shifting her to that convalescent home where she did not go the last time.

The dean will sigh and ask, 'Do you want another strike on your hands?'

Here the matter will rest, uneasily, for a little more time.

**25** December 1976. The dean of KEM, Dr Deshpande, is beside himself with rage. He has never, ever, felt so angry; at least his secretary has never seen him this livid. Neither has the matron nor the nurses accompanying her. They have no idea how to pacify him since they do not know what the problem is. The Sisters came into his office following an annual custom, to discuss the budget of the annual get-together for the staff nurses. The budget has yet to vary but this gives the nurses a chance to drop not-so-gentle hints about other matters which need the dean's attention and intervention. So far no one has been able to say anything, the dean has been raving and ranting, about what is unclear.

The secretary remarks on it to Dr Tilve who has just come into the ante-room and asked to see the dean for a minute. 'This might not be a good time to ask for anything.'

'I do not want to ask for anything,' points out Dr Tilve tersely, stressing on the word ask. 'Please buzz the dean that I'm coming into his office.'

'Dr Tilve,' says the dean when he sees him at the door, 'come in, please come in. I couldn't talk about this with these ladies being present. Dr Tilve you come in and tell me why people are so disgusting. Not people, some men. Just look at this man and his warped mind, I could kill him. In fact now that you are here, let us send for this man right away and bash him up.'

'Yes of course, why not,' Dr Tilve's voice is soothing. 'But why do you want to beat him up?'

'This animal has written me a letter, and he says what was done to her before should be done to her again!'

'Ah, I see,' Dr Tilve's voice soothes some more. 'And who might he be referring to?'

'Why our staff nurse Aruna Shanbaug of course.'

'Of course.'

'I'm going to send the peon right now to this fellow's house and ask him to come to my office right now since he's "willing to volunteer for this good cause". Then you and I can thrash him together.'

'If you don't mind my asking, Dr Deshpande, where does this man live? How do you know this letter is from Bombay?'

'Oh I don't know. Let me see, one minute.' The dean picks up a single sheet of paper from his desk and glances at it. 'Damnit! He hasn't given his address, such scum never do.'

'May I see the letter?'

Dr Tilve quickly scans the letter. The man writes that he read the article on Aruna Shanbaug who is neither alive nor dead because of what was done to her. In his opinion if she is raped and strangled again, the shock will make her come out of it and cure her. He could do the needful since it's for her ultimate benefit. Dr Tilve passes the letter on to matron.

'What article is this man talking about?'

'I think I know,' says matron a trifle hesitantly. About a month back a journalist from a Hindi magazine came and said he wanted to do an article on Aruna as it was now three years since she went into a coma. I told him she was not in a coma but he was quite insistent. We gave him the details, but we never said anything about the rape. I should have realized that the article had appeared when two-three people telephoned about her health and some people came wanting to see her.'

'Were her relatives among them?'

'I don't know, Dr Deshpande. We only know what the brother and sister look like. A few months back someone visited and did say she was her cousin from Borivli but then people will say anything to get their own way. I don't give any of the visitors permission to see Aruna.'

'This is it. Matron, I as dean forbid you or anyone else in this hospital from allowing any outsider to see staff nurse Aruna Shanbaug. This includes journalists, the vultures! They don't know how to fill space so they come to write about a defenceless, defeated woman. Henceforward no journalists to be spoken to, let them come to the dean's office and we will deal with them. Don't they realize the more they write about her the more publicity she gets and the more people come to see her as though she is some medical freak? And think of this, has not that journalist given this evil man who has written this letter an evil idea?'

'I'm sorry Dr Deshpande, this will not happen again.'

The dean suddenly softens, tears up the single sheet into little bits and throws it into the waste-paper basket near his foot. 'There, that's where this man belongs. Matron, there is another reason why we should ensure that she shouldn't get written about. Suppose the BMC people read it and get on to us again? As it is I'm having a tough time keeping her hidden from their gaze. Each time they remember her, I have to work very hard to deflect their attention to other pressing matters of the hospital.'

Everyone murmurs their agreement.

The dean orders tea and biscuits for everyone.

Dr Sundeep Sardesai is slightly late today, he arrives to find that Aruna's physiotherapy has been abandoned for the day. She was uncooperative, she was shouting angrily. Now she is irate.

'Any why this bad behaviour?' he asks her in Konkani as he leans over the locker to pull out the little packet of tikkas. 'Because I am a bit late? That's silly, you know it. People should not cut off their pretty noses to spite their faces.' He chooses a black bindi, like your mood he tells her, and dots it onto her forehead.

She has been alternating between irritable and irascible

since the past few days. As the nurses have been putting it to him—'patient moody', 'patient moody', 'patient rowdy'. Dr Sardesai fishes out a small diary from his breast pocket, under his white doctor's coat, and flips a few pages. 'No wonder you are behaving badly,' he tells her, 'you are pre-menstrual. Actually your periods should have come three days back. Well, we will monitor you for the next few days and then decide.'

He walks around the bed talking to her. She turns her head around in unsteady confusion on the pillow, seeking the source of his voice, her eyes darting in frustration in her face. He pulls up the stool and sits by her bedside. He continues talking to her, she stops her head movement, while her eyes continue to dart, and listens, where is he? Dr Sardesai almost breaks down and weeps, he keeps forgetting the fact that she is blind. He clears his throat and takes her twitching hand in his, telling her about his clinic, his hospital list which has grown, his patients, some of their idiosyncracies.

He does not tell her where he has been this morning, to a temple on the outskirts of Bombay where he had organized a special pooja for her recovery. The place is said to be very powerful, ask and ye shall receive. He has been asking for her recovery at innumerable places of worship, conducting poojas, chanting mantras, everything, anything. Much against his own grain he has even been consulting several astrologers, her cousin Ramdas has been accompanying him everywhere. Together, but without it letting it be known to the other, they have been careening between wild hope and utter despair.

She has turned her face to him, her eyes are closed, but around her mouth with its still-pink lips hovers what he thinks is a smile. She has slipped into a child-like nap.

On his way out he meets Dr Tilve in the corridor, wishes him. Dr Tilve returns his greeting warmly, young Dr Sardesai

79

was his student. 'How is everything doctor?'

'Very fine, thank you doctor.'

'No complaint, I hope, about how we are looking after Aruna?'

'No, no, not at all. In fact she smiled at me today.'

It is Dr Tilve's turn to clear his throat.

T he dean's worst fears materialize sooner than he thinks, within six days of his tea and biscuits with the nurses.

There has been a change of guard at several levels in the BMC, new brooms start pretending to sweep clean. Some officers are assigned to study how wastage in all the BMC run hospitals can be cut down, their report is expected on the last day of the end of the year. The officers have been zealous, staff nurse Aruna Shanbaug is an asterisk at the end of their report.

On the second day of 1977 the dean is informed telephonically that she should be shifted to the convalescent home. As soon as possible.

For the dean this is déjà vu. 'The nurses, her colleagues, will go on strike again.' He has actually begun enjoying this little trump-card.

'Let them.'

The dean bolts upright in his chair. 'What!'

'In our studied opinion she will not enjoy the same kind of support from the nurses the way she did earlier. The younger nurses don't know her at all, they might even be resenting the extra work they have to do for her. Some of her batchmates might also have left the hospital after getting married. All this adds up to at least thirty per cent less strength than earlier. Those who strike now will receive show-cause notices, several steps will be taken. They will not be allowed to hold the hospital to ransom for one patient. Please make the necessary arrangements, Aruna Shanbaug should be out of KEM by the end of this month.'

Dean Deshpande spends some time thinking about all the pros and cons. In mid-January he instructs his secretary to make three calls for him. One to the convalescent home, they must keep a bed for Aruna from the first of February. The other to Dr Sundeep Sardesai located at one of the several hospitals he is associated with, the dean would like him to come over to his residence at a time suitable to Dr Sardesai in the next forty-eight hours. The third call is an internal one, to matron who comes to his office right away. The dean tells her about his conversation with the BMC. 'This time they are serious, very serious. Nurses who oppose will get themselves into trouble.'

'But why are they being so inhuman, what difference can one bed make in a hospital which has over a thousand of them?'

The dean gives a small, helpless shrug.

'What should I tell the Sisters?'

'The truth, what else?'

When matron reaches her office nurse Prema Pai takes one look at her expression and knows what is about to happen. She also understands that this time they are powerless to resist.

The dean's subsequent meeting with Dr Sundeep Sardesai is no less disquieting for him.

'I think you have guessed why I wanted to see you, Dr Sardesai.'

'Yes Dr Deshpande, the BMC is shifting her to the convalescent home. It is kind of you to personally tell me this, I appreciate it.'

'I'm sorry son, I have tried.'

'I know. I understand the pressure, I have been under a lot of pressure too from my family and friends.'

'To get married?'

Dr Sardesai shakes his head slightly. 'My friends say what kind of a stupid doctor are you, you know it's irreversible brain damage, she can never get well. They are not even waiting for my go-ahead anymore, my doctor friends have begun looking for a suitable girl for me. My family has been looking anyway.'

'That means your family knows about Aruna, what did you tell them?'

'Nothing, what is there to say. They do not know about her, I would have told them only after settling into my clinic, a little before the wedding. I suppose now they never will know.'

'You have been very brave through it all, you have stood by her unselfishly all these years. It takes a truly decent human being to do this.'

Dr Sardesai shakes his head again but says nothing.

A small hesitation before the dean asks, 'You don't have to answer this if you don't want to, but whenever I have seen you I have wondered about this. You are such a good doctor, how could you . . . I mean, I know you care deeply for her but as a medical man surely you must have understood there was no hope?'

There is an emptiness in his voice as he replies, 'I banked on that one per cent chance of a miracle. I knew within the first six months that she would never recover.'

'You are a genuinely good man Dr Sardesai.'

His eyes are bleak. 'Am I? I was to marry this woman, spend my life with her. She was trying to save money for my clinic, for our life together. Now I am about to leave her to

82

die, that too a death which will not be pleasant or comfortable, I know this. If I am such a good man should I not be taking her home?'

Although Dr Rajesh Parikh is a student at the medical college attached to KEM, his feelings for the institution run much deeper. His father, Dr Mahendra Parikh, is professor of obstetrics at KEM, Parikh junior has almost been nurtured on the campus. He has a fairly good idea of what he's going to specialize in, KEM is a part of his dreams, future plans and commitment. Dr Rajesh Parikh thinks about them, in between classes, as he takes a stroll down the stone corridors of the hospital.

He really has no business being here he realizes with a start, he is near ward 4, in front of that nurse's special room. He has heard about her, every medical student is told her story in their first year itself. He should not be going in, he tells himself. He parts the curtain, the door is slightly ajar. He steps in gingerly, stands on the other side of the door, feeling like a reluctant invader. He does not really know what he expects to find.

The curtains are drawn across the only window. When his eyes adjust to the gloom, he sees a small twisted body lying on a crumpled bed. The head is bent to one side on the dented pillow, the eyes are open. He holds his breath, he does not want to disturb her, he does not want her to panic if she senses him in any way. The body moves, the knees rise at angles, the hands flex at the elbows and the wrists, the fingers clench, the head moves restlessly on the pillow, it lolls alarmingly, the eyes look straight at him.

He knows she is cortically blind. She is still looking at

him. This makes him curse himself under his breath, he has no right to be standing here almost exploiting the fact that she cannot see.

She laughs. Long, sustained, rising, mirthless laughter.

He's still holding his breath, he exhales. He waits till the spell subsides, somehow he feels he should not be walking out at such a time. She stops laughing as suddenly as she had started, mid-note, as if someone has abruptly turned off a radio. He whispers 'I'm sorry' and leaves the room.

Behind him, from the room, is heard the sound of a woman weeping; heartbroken, heartbreaking.

# Out of Konkan Land

The National Highway 17 starts from Kanyakumari, Cape Comorin as it is sometimes called in harkback. It's a magical point on India's southernmost tip, here the Arabian Sea and the Bay of Bengal pour into each other. The highway ribbons its way through five states on the country's western coast: Tamil Nadu, Kerala, Karnataka, Goa and Maharashtra to conjoin the NH 4 at Panvel and be relentlessly drawn into Bombay. In hugging the western coastline, the drive from Kanyakumari on the NH 17 provides a happy sort of highway hypnosis. The sea, always the shimmering sea on the left, edged with sand in several stunning shades of singed sun and sienna; and all around the hundreds of wondrous greens in coconut trees and cashew plantations, bunches of about-to-burst-into-bright-yellow banana clusters and stalks of rice swishing dreamily in a gentle sea breeze. God's own country.

So the Shanbaug ancestors thought when they decided to dock at several inlets on the west coast. Centuries ago—and no one can pinpoint exactly which one because it is all interconnected with the argument on whether the Aryans came to India or actually went from here—several Goud Saraswat Brahmins began moving out from their dwellings. The geography in and around Bengal was called Goud Desh then, and these were Brahmins living by the river Saraswati;

ergo Goud Saraswat Brahmins or as they are best known, GSBs. Their land was ravaged by a drought and the rishis had to permit these vegetarians to eat fish, but then the river began drying up and so the migration had to happen.

Some deep, collective instinct in the community's psyche warned against only farming in the future, commerce was thus their logical choice. And so some GSBs wound up trading as far as Kashmir and Afghanistan, with some deciding to let the rivers be their guide. They cut across the country and examined possibilities which the trading post of Kutch offered. Using the South Pole as their guide and the stars above these migrants mastered the art of trading by, and through, the sea. Veteran political commentator M.V. Kamath, himself a GSB, swears that there still stands a prominently painted arrow pointing towards the South Pole in Kutch.

The Shanbaug clan among the GSBs did not enjoy Kutch much and set sail once again with their gods and their women and their children, to reach Goa. Here the ruling Portuguese could insist upon their religious conversion and so the now somewhat weary Shanbaugs were off once again with the stars above as their guide after crossing seas, mountains and deserts in search of somewhere to set anchor. They went downstream to North and South Kanara to dock at whatever looked like a welcoming river mouth. And to the village of Haldipur where one section of them were to return to being landlord farmers.

The GSBs who had opted for trading had opened accounts with the Vijayanagar empire, with the Bijapur kingdom, with the Arabs, with the Whites and had slowly moved to Bombay to continue with their generations of trading from a port town where they could enjoy similar weather and fish. Fish curry-rice, to be precise. A standing joke among GSBs is that Yama, the lord of death, once decided to visit Bombay and saw a hugely successful GSB who was selling spices and silks across the seven seas. 'You,' said Yama, 'I'm taking you back with me. We leave at eight tonight.' The GSB burst into copious tears. 'Behave yourself,' thundered Yama, 'a man like you should have no fear of death.' 'Oh no, lord,' protested the GSB, 'it is not the dying, it is the timing. Can't we leave after dinner? There's fish curry-rice tonight.'

The GSBs of Bombay also assisted their farmer kinsfolk in selling their goods when they came in from the villages. Every March these farmers from the west coast would get on to their manjis, the specially built boats piled high with their produce—rice, ginger, pepper, coconut, coir, cardamom—and set sail for Bombay. But how to feed so many guests turning up all at once? And they could not eat out just anywhere, with food cooked by just anyone, they were Brahmins! For a way out the GSBs looked towards the cooks who fed thousands during marriages and festivals in their temple-complex muths in Udipi. And thus came into being the Udipis of Bombay, churning out hundreds of idlis-dosas-vadas everyday along with piping-hot, almost home-made sambar.

With more business came organized banking, the GSBs set up their own institution. Even more employment opportunities opened up. The GSB youth began trickling in from the villages in Kanara and Goa where the sizes of families had far outstripped the capacity of their land to feed them. Those who dug in never went back, and assisted more brothers and cousins and relatives in leaving their villages to make Bombay the city of their destiny.

Like Yeshwant Laxman Shanbaug, a yejaman to the hilt in Haldipur, a landlord who lived in a huge house he had ordered built with teak pillars and hand-polished flooring. There was rice in the fields and there were coconuts on his trees with enough fish in the nearby Badgani river. But

89

Yeshwant knew he had to look ahead. He reached Bombay and started an Udipi, the Hindu Vishranti Gruh near Agripada police station. Soon enough several young rural GSB males had apprenticed at the Hindu Vishranti Gruh as cooks, managers, cashiers, accountants, buyers-suppliers, waiters and dish-washers. Yeshwant Laxman Shanbaug was only upholding the time-honoured tradition of his ancestors.

$B$ut not all ancestors spawn resilient branches on the family tree. There are invariably those offspring with weak intellect. Tell them destiny is according to thought, and they will quickly prefer to find fate as a comforting word. Aruna Ramchandra Shanbaug understood this very early on in her childhood. All she had to do was compare her uncle Yeshwant's house across the bramble-hedge and her family's to keep the lesson alive in her mind.

'Amma,' she said to her mother one evening while fixing the wick to light the oil lamp, 'I'm going to Bombay.'

Sitabai Ramchandra Shanbaug was a simple woman, some in Haldipur even thought her stupid. Which was unfair since it was two of her six sons who were of shadowed mind. But her last-born, Aruna, did tend to fluster her with her often unexpected remarks. So Sitabai sought time. 'We will wait for Balakrishna.'

'Then what will happen?'

Sitabai was always at a loss when posed a question. And Aruna being difficult was always a problem compounded. Her voice shook a bit as she replied, 'Then you and your brother can decide.'

'What is there to decide further? I'm going to Bombay. I will work there.'

This was all too much for Sitabai. She abandoned her attempt at grinding rice and udad dal for tomorrow's idli-vada. Her body drooped against the wall as she said in a low voice, 'Balakrishna told me the last time that proposals had started coming for you. You are so fair and beautiful. Why won't you marry like your two sisters? You have never been outside Haldipur and now you want to go directly to Bombay. No woman from this village has ever stepped outside for a job.' By Sitabai's standards these were a lot of words and she was beginning to feel slightly weak. Still, she tried once more with a daughter who often spoke like a stranger. 'Balakrishna is your brother, from the time your appa is gone he looks after us, surely he will do what is best?'

'Can't I also know what is best for me? And why must you make everything into a woman-women thing? I want to do good work, not serve idli-vadas in an Udipi, so how does this become a men-women business?'

Sitabai was now exhausted. Why did Aruna question everything? Why couldn't she just be accepting the way all women were? 'Daiva kartiree . . . for God's sake. Please finish this grinding. I am very tired today.'

Aruna watched her mother slowly retreating into the inner room. Sita married to Ram. This should have been an idyllic union, according to the holy books. Aruna shook her head and sat at the big, circular stone mortar, firmly grasped the bulbous stone pestle with both her palms. This was the part she hated, the grinding and the relentlessness of the sound of the grinding. Grind, she thought, as she expertly flicked a bit of the wet dough into position, grind, grind, grind. Get married and get ground into domesticity. Like Sitabai and her nine children. Why had her mother had nine children, and her last of all when least expected so late in the day? Other women did not have so many children, it means

91

there were ways of keeping your family small and happy. She had asked her mother this once and the reply was what she always got, and the word her father had always used. Fate.

Aruna shifted position on her haunches, consolidated the semi-solid dough and began giving it one last, good grind so that it rose well by the morning. This word fate, how everyone used it to explain away everything. Before she was born they had a partnership in a shop selling grains and everyday spices, mirchi-masala, right here near this house in which she was born, on the main road. Then they had to make the road broader and call it National Highway 17—the milestone said NH 17—so they knocked off their shop. But the government gave them money in exchange, so why didn't her appa collect it from his partner? Fate.

What happened to their fields? Fate.

Why did appa die during the outbreak of dysentery in Haldipur? Fate.

Aruna giggled. Thirty days away, in March, were her final, eleventh class exams, for her matric degree. She had not even started studying for it. If she didn't fare too well in the matric, she would tell them all it was fate.

The next morning dawned clear and bright, and as crisp as the vadas deep-frying in the pan. Aruna loved the combination. One soft, white, steamed idli, staying like a mini-cloud on your tongue before melting away. And then one big bite, clear into the centre-hole of the small crisp brown vada. Sometimes she bit right through a tiny piece of coconut nestled in the vada next to the chopped, fresh green chili. She liked that a lot too. But there was nothing to beat the smell and sight of fish curry cooking. It bubbled gently in the pan as it brewed in its own juices, delivering all that it promised on hot, boiled rice, each cooked grain distinct from the other. The coconut had to be ground very, very fine though for the curry, otherwise it tasted all lumpy.

Ayyo, coconut! Amma had asked her to go and call Anjaiah to get a fresh coconut off the tree for the chutney. She had asked her to do it yesterday too and she had forgotten. Today there wasn't much likelihood of finding Anjaiah. It was jatra day and Anjaiah would already be dead drunk somewhere on arrack. Amma would look disturbed again. No chutney with idli-vada was a sin for all good housewives, wasn't it! But what Aruna could not undertand is that if you used coconut in all your cooking everyday and if you owned coconut trees and they stood right there in your backyard then why did you have to call a man from outside to give you your own fruit? Why couldn't the Shanbaug men just learn to climb trees like all other men in the village? She was told often that landlords had to keep their dignity. What landlord! No land, only lord.

'Aruna. Aruna?'

Amma. Aruna slipped out of the hedge and swiftly crossed the few feet to the edge of NH 17. Out of sheer instinct she looked to the right, where the road two hours up went to Karwar and another two hours later reached Panjim in Goa, and an overnight bus journey from there would take her to Bombay. People had proper addresses in Bombay. Block, building, road, like that. In Haldipur there were no streets so there were no names. Just as well because during the monsoon they would turn into rivers of mud, the way all of Haldipur did.

But this had to be said, Haldipur really came alive during mid-February at jatra time. It was as if the 4,000-odd population overnight decided to collectively shake off their stupor and step out of their stultifying lives. The women would dress in their shiniest saris, they would oil and braid the hair of their daughters tightly with specially-chosen coloured ribbons. Then men would bare their chests to stand on the NH 17 in double-file with two lengths of thick, running rope held firmly in their palms. The rath from the Gopinatha Venkataramana temple on the other side of the NH 17 would now be pulled, gaily festooned with flowers, redolent with the smell of camphor, priests would chant mantras and the bare-chested men would tug at the ropes of the temple's chariot.

Chants would be heard from men and women alike with childish trebles adding to the festivities.

'Gopinathaaaaa. Venkataramanaaaaa. Go-pi-na-tha, Ven-kata-rama-na.'

The wheels on the ancient hand-carved, all-wood, mountainous rath bearing the gods of Haldipur would protest and then slowly turn. The men would tug some more and the wheels would complete a full circle. Creakily majestic, the rath would go down a bit on the NH 17. Traffic on the highway would slow down—Anjaiah and the other drunks would ensure it did by standing in the middle of the road and throwing coloured powders on the passing vehicles—to notice that there was, indeed, life on the side of a national highway. So what if no one had heard of a village called Haldipur.

And so what if it did not have electricity and no train station, and buses stopped only on request. It had tradition, so there.

T he jatra also brought with it Haldipur's annual film screening. A huge, billowy, slightly mouldy-smelling tent would come up on the village's largest flat and open space. In the front would be the screen and bang in the middle of the tent would be the projector, occupying pride of place. Somewhere beyond the tent would be the generator, guttering, coughing, spluttering into the dialogues on screen. Tickets were standardized, multiples of annas rising every year to much grumbling, and entrance was through a small curtain-like opening which would flap the mould right up your nostrils. Free seating. Most of the children crowded importantly around the foot of the table bearing the projector.

The film had to be a Hindi one, no other language would do on such an important festival day. It didn't really matter if it wasn't the latest-latest one from Bombay, that could always be seen next year. But there had to be tears for the women and fights for the men and buffoonery for the children and the hero and heroine in the movie had to be instantly recognizable to all in the audience. Before the film could start, drinking goli-soda was important. The vendor would use his finger to push down the marble blocking the neck of the bottle, the soda would bubble upwards, out of the bottle, down the chins of near-ecstatic, inexperienced drinkers while the goli-soda vendor used an eight-anna coin to run chimes against his lined-up bottles. With all criteria fulfilled and the sun down on the horizon, the show would begin.

Aruna would find most of the movies with rural themes ridiculous. They show you happy villages with bustling buxom belles, she thought, or hamlets bedraggled with poverty. They have never come to Haldipur, this nowhere place. It was not even on the map of India, she had checked this with the geography master who had not seen the point of the question.

Actually Aruna went to the movies for the songs. She loved them, she would sit outside her house facing the NH 17 only so that she could catch that rush of music from some passing vehicles. When she reached Bombay she would get herself a radio and listen to it night and day because over there you could just put on a switch and there would be electricity. This she had decided upon long before she had decided what she wanted to do in Bombay.

The film would wind its way to its usually melodramatic climax with several stops in between. The projector would stop whirring, mid-dialogue; the generator would conk out; the film would unspool from the projector on some delighted child below who would promptly try to wrap the celluloid garland-like around his neck; the reel would finish and on the screen would be inverted numbers madly rushing past each other. The audience would boo and cheer and jeer, and a good time would be had by all.

Humming a song from the film, Aruna raced home in the velvet night. She was not afraid, she was grown up, all of seventeen years, and what is there to worry in your own village anyway. In the dark she could be mistaken for a well-built child with her five feet height, fine-boned and lithe body, and hair neatly sectioned into two fat braids. Ducking in through a hole in the bramble hedge Aruna paused. She heard voices inside, with the lone oil-lamp casting a weak shadow on the wall with its feeble flicker.

'I have left the Udipi. I have got another job in the Kamala Mills dyeing department, they will pay Rs 200 every month. Few other benefits are also there.'

Balakrishna. Oh good, now she could discuss her plans with him. He would have to locate that doctor relative of theirs in Bombay to find out which place to apply to and then to get all the forms for her. She hoped amma would not say anything.

Amma did in her customary low voice, sounding more wounded than ever.

Aruna sat outside the house, leaned against its wall and looked at the stars. It was truly a lovely night. This was her last jatra in Haldipur, she would remember it.

Balakrishna's voice rose several octaves. 'She is getting nice proposals. One boy is nearby in Kumta. They don't even want too much dowry. Will she be happy here or in Bombay? It is such a wicked city. And what will she do in Bombay, where will she live? My own position there is so uncertain.'

Aruna spoke for herself clearly, firmly, from the other side of the wall. 'I will be a burden to none. I will earn even while I learn and I will be staying in a hostel. I am becoming a nurse.'

Stunned silence within. The dry scrape of scuttling leaves near the water-well. A racing truck on the NH 17 leaves behind receding music in its wake.

T he high-ceilinged hush imploded with a sudden blast of Marathi film songs from the surrounding labour area of Parel. It entered the examination room stridently and insistently. Mill people must be like this only in Bombay, thought Aruna, not a care that this is a hospital and patients could get disturbed. She filled in her name neatly on the examination answer sheet, slightly pressing the point of the pen she had borrowed from Balakrishna. Blue ink blotted on the sheet. Ayyo-yo-yo, should she ask for another answer sheet? But supposing they cut marks for wastage of paper?

Aruna closed her eyes and waited with her eyes closed for the question paper to be distributed. She was a little tense. All the answers would have to be in English, admittedly not her strongest language. Third class in English in her matric. Third class in General Science also. Best marks in Kannada but that did not count here. She prayed. She didn't trouble God too often, but this was urgent. Aruna sent up a one-liner, 'Daiva, please help me become a nurse in this hospital.'

'This' was the King Edward VII Memorial Hospital attached to the Seth Gordhandas Sunderdas Medical College. The former came to be abbreviated as KEM and the latter GS Medical. But no alphabets could have been said with more pride than on the day Aruna was giving her written nursing test, 15 February 1966. Exactly forty years after its conception KEM was continuing to prove to be among the finest hospitals in the country, people were talking about it being the best— and the biggest—in all of Asia. And GS Medical was sending out dedicated young doctors. There was still a commitment to this place, the same kind of fervour when it was founded during India's freedom struggle.

The British would not appoint Indians to important posts at the only medical institution then in Bombay, Grant Medical College. Dr K.N. Bahadurji, Sir Pherozshah Mehta, Sir Narayan Chandavarkar and Sir Chimanlal Setalvad came together to exert their not inconsiderable goodwill. Sir Pherozshah set the ball in motion in 1907. The government of Bombay maintained the hospitals and the Bombay Municipal Corporation (BMC) paid for the police force in the city. Sir Pherozshah had this reversed.

It took another four years and the demise of King Edward VII for matters to move further. In 1911, the BMC was informed that 'a hospital in the northern part of the Island would form a most fitting memorial to his late majesty'. A free site measuring 50,000 square yards was granted in the textile mills and labour area of Parel, the market value of which was then estimated to be Rs 5,00,000. Substantial monies would also be paid in installments towards the construction of the hospital, starting with Rs 5,75,000.

Now the time was right. The trustees of the estate of the late Seth Gordhandas Sunderdas—including Dr Bahadurji and

Sirs Pherozshah, Narayan and Chimanlal—offered government loan notes of Rs 14,50,000 at 3.5 per cent to the BMC for endowing a medical college. Their conditions were that the college must be attached to KEM, that it should be affiliated to the University of Bombay, that the BMC must ever afterwards maintain the college like the hospital and that the professors and teachers at the college must be Indians. The BMC accepted with alacrity.

The total cost of the hospital was now estimated at Rs 25,27,699 and that of the college at Rs 13,64,574. The year was 1917 and money began pouring in when Indians heard of their own medical college with a hospital attached. Rs 1,20,655 came from Sir Currimbhoy Ebrahim, Rs 1,00,000 from Purshottam Mangaldas Nathubhoy in memory of his wife Bai Lilavati, Rs 50,000 from the estate of Dr Habib Ismail Jan Mohammed, Rs 17,000 in the name of Dr Cawas Lalkaka. Smaller donations came in the mail, through stuffed brown-paper bags and fistfuls of cash delivered by hand. Indians, Bombayites specially, wanted every brick to be their own.

Mr W.A. Pite, architect of the King's College Hospital in London, was invited to comment on the plans drawn up by Mr George Wittet. He suggested small alterations. Make pavilion-like wards with a separate but connected pavilion to house the matron and nurses. Also, provide for extensions on the hospital building. Mr Pite's advice was sound. Mr Wittet altered the plans and the government sold, at a very nominal price, to the BMC two more plots of land to the north and the south of the original site. Construction of the college was handed over to the Tata Engineering Company.

In 1924, the BMC passed this resolution: 'That the medical staff employed in the King Edward VII Memorial Hospital should consist of properly qualified independent Indian

Gentlemen not in actual Government Service.' The college opened in the next year with forty-six students, six of whom were women; it was designed to cater to 300 with a hostel for a third of them. The hospital was opened to patients in 1926; it could accommodate 304 beds with provision for expansion to 400 without overcrowding. Dr Jeevraj Mehta—an MD, FRCP from England, denied employment at Grant Medical—was appointed dean.

It was a heady time for all. For Indians, by Indians, organized through the foreigners, with them even paying for some of it during their own rule. Joseph Baptista, president of the BMC, captured the essence of the times in his speech: that the two institutions had cost Rs 77,00,000 and were expected to spend Rs 6,00,000 annually but 'we have bought all that gold can buy for our hospital'. He added, 'Besides, we have got what gold cannot buy but what civic patriotism alone can give; the services of a number of men and women animated by an ardent enthusiasm for the work they have undertaken.'

Enthusiasm wasn't the word to associate with Aruna Shanbaug for the examination she was undertaking right then in that hall with so much hallowed history. She stared at the question paper and it faced her insolently, throwing up queries about which she did not have a clue.

Who is the pioneer of modern nursing? To get thirty grams of calcium, how much solution is to be taken, if 120 grams of calcium is dissolved in four ounces of water? What is the instrument for measuring temperature called? What is the date 30 January 1948, associated with?

Ah, she knew this one, they stood for two minutes silence

on every thirtieth of January at her Rural Education Society High School in Haldipur. She wrote: 'Died of Ghandi'.

Then there were the fill-in-the-blanks. Tashkent is a city in ____. What did this have to do with nursing, but anyway she knew the answer. Pakistan.

Nirmala was waiting outside for her in the garden patch near the Casualty. 'So,' she asked, and waited for Aruna's reply.

'So nothing.'

'Going to fail or what?'

'There is still the personal interview in the afternoon. And even if I fail I will re-apply for the next batch in six months.'

'Good, then for six months you also sit at home with me. We will sit around and do faaltugiri together.'

Aruna smiled. These Bombay people used such strange words, almost as if it wasn't Hindi. Khaali peeli bom kayku maarta hai. She had seen a policeman yell this at a handcuffed man as he was dragging him into the Agripada police station when she had gone to see her uncle's Hindu Vishranti Gruh. Uncle Yeshwant had a nice family. Theirs was not a very big house in Agripada but it was filled with a lot of laughter, and warmth. Uncle's wife was Vatsalabai but Aruna had already taken to calling her amma, just the way her children Nirmala and Ramdas did.

Ramdas was younger than her by four-five years, it was nice to have someone like a kid brother. And Nimma, as she had nicknamed her, was like an elder sister, protective and guiding. Nimma had been accompanying Aruna for all her work to KEM and back. It helped that Nimma had finished her matric and was happily faaltu. Nimma had also taken her to Chowpatty, the sea had a very different colour in Bombay. As though it was sad. The sea also sounded exhausted.

The mill siren set up its wail every morning at eight. Aruna looked at her watch, Bombay was so time-to-time. The siren ceased exactly as the seconds hand on her watch completed its rotation at twelve. Balakrishna had given her the wristwatch, a round Tressa with a gold dial and a black, nylon strap. It was the first watch in her life and Aruna felt very proud of it. She felt professional. She would soon have to go to the utensil shops on the other side of KEM, where all the mill labour lived, and get A.S. engraved on the stainless steel back of her watch, the way they put their names on all their vessels. Best way of keeping track of your own things in the nurses hostel.

Aruna Shanbaug had scraped through the written test by the skin of her evenly-shaped, pearly-white, pretty teeth. Seventeen and a half out of fifty. The orals had been alright and the physical had revealed that she was very slightly myopic. But she would rather be dead first than wear spectacles, that too for such a small number which she did not even know she had. For the four months of training she would receive a monthly stipend of forty rupees plus an allowance of fifteen rupees for uniform and three rupees for the dhobi with free boarding and lodging. She would have to work for a minimum of one year after training. If she stayed in the hostel as staff nurse they would cut boarding and lodging directly from her salary.

Meanwhile, for her training period, she would have to provide for herself six white saris, blouses and petticoats, twelve white coats—length twelve inches from the ground, two pairs white shoes, six pairs white stockings, one umbrella, one rain coat, two bedspreads, one woollen blanket, one pair surgical scissors, one clinical thermometer and one wristwatch with a seconds hand. So much for four months! Aruna knocked the list down to half and then further quartered some of the items. Cheaper to wash fatafat on a daily basis while having her bath, like she did in Haldipur.

Books. *Practical Nursing Book* by W.T. Gordon Pugh, *Anatomy & Physiology for Nurses* by Dr K.S. Mhaskar, *Dictionary for Nurses* by Lois Oakes, four exercise books of 200 pages each. She had picked up the books at much less cost, second-hand, from Lakhanis in Girgaon and he had said he would take them back at the end of her training if they remained in good condition. She bought only two exercise books; what could there be so much to write about when you had to absorb it all, to practise it day after day.

Sister-tutor Premila Kushe, anatomy teacher, had noticed her keenness to learn. 'Aruna Shanbaug's concentration is one hundred per cent,' she noted. Sister-tutor Kusum Upadhyay was also struck by Aruna's sincerity. 'Student-nurse Shanbaug,' she observed earlier on in the course, 'why do you lean forward like that on your desk all the time with your eyes screwed-up? If you cannot hear or see properly from behind, please come and sit in the front row.' Better to speak the truth. Aruna rose, 'My English is a problem.'

'Where are you from?'

'Haldipur, Karwar district.'

'So you understand only Kannada fluently? But Karwar is on the Konkan coastline so you should know Konkani also.'

'I do. I can follow the English also, but most of the technical sentences . . .'

'Alright sit down. I'll explain some of the points again in Marathi. You should be able to follow since it is quite similar to Konkani.'

$S$taff nurse Aruna Shanbaug stood on a chair and looked at her reflection, in parts, on a small mirror in the nurses quarters. She giggled. She looked a bit strange in the white uniform, the dress made her look like a little girl, like the Bombay children going to school. Also, it was a bit airy around the knees and upwards. And those long white socks, Aruna dissolved into a flood of giggles. Good thing she had slim legs or they would look like the white banding the forest department put around the fat trees on NH 17.

Bells rang from the temple near the nurses quarters. Aruna quickly jumped off the chair and did a namaskar in its direction.

'You do that every morning and evening when the bells chime because it reminds you of your village?' observed her batchmate through training and room-mate Usha Samant.

'I do it, ashtey,' she added succinctly in Kannada. 'Do you want to contribute half the money with me in buying a full-length mirror for our room?'

'They might not like us hammering nails in the wall. Will they let us put it up?'

'Let's find out, you never know anything in life until you ask. Anyway we don't have to put it up, we can always rest it against the wall.'

'I might not be able to afford it if the mirror costs too much.'

'You find out the cost. I'll get the permission to bring it in from matron. If you can't afford it, you can use it anyway and not feel bad about doing so.'

Usha flushed. Aruna just said anything jhatkarke, her tongue really tore into you at times. But she was good-hearted, Usha knew this, they had spent quite a lot of time together. She had been to Aruna's uncle's house in Agripada with her on more than one occasion. Next month, for the Independence Day holiday, she was taking Aruna to her village near Poona. Usha found herself feeling unusually philosophical. Perhaps Aruna had been a shy child in her village, here she probably felt obliged to sound sharp and direct like the city was supposed to be. What outsiders thought of Bombay, what they became here thinking they couldn't just remain themselves. Tsk.

Aruna hummed under her breath and peeped into the small mirror. She straightened the stiff boat-like cap on her head. She tucked in her hair tightly behind her ears. The Bombay water had made her hair even more curly. Luckily the polluted mill air all around her had not touched her skin which remained clear and soft. Aruna squared her shoulders. The uniform looked much smarter without a slouch. A straight back suggested authority. At the end of this month she'd get her first salary, she was going to buy a nice Philips radio, latest model. She would get permission from matron for it along with the mirror.

Nirmala was horrified. Sometimes she felt Aruna was too smart for her own good. 'From where is this, now?' she demanded to know.

'From where is what?'

'This sudden jhatka to go abroad.' Nirmala frequently peppered her Konkani with Bombay-Hindi.

'It's not sudden. It's not a jhatka. And the way you are going on, as though I am like all those silly people who somehow or the other want to settle down abroad.'

'Then what?'

'Nimma, I want to study further, take a proper degree in nursing.'

'After that?'

'I'll study, see the world a little. Then I'll come back and get a senior posting in nursing with my foreign degree.'

'Then?'

'Nodanna,' Aruna declared in Kannada, 'we shall see.'

'You don't want to get married or what?'

'Nimma, just because you have finished your matric and are waiting and waiting in your house for some fellow to walk in and take you to his house to do the same work doesn't mean all women should be like you.'

Nirmala bit her lip, Aruna and her muh futt ways, this style of speaking was one day going to get her into trouble. Nevertheless she persisted. 'Okay so you'll become an educated madam running a big hospital with one thousand nurses under you. But do you, or do you not, want to get married?'

'If I meet someone nice and educated, of course.'

'Then if you get married you will have to have children?'

'Who says? Sometimes men don't want children.'

'Such men do not marry. And you better not tell any man that you don't really like children, otherwise nobody will marry you.'

'So if a man and I decide that okay, we can marry each other, when we discuss children should I not be truthful with the man I am going to spend the rest of my life with?'

'Ayyo rama-rama-rama. Aruna you are simply too much. All I'm saying is what is the need to sound like a bindaas Bombay chhokri when men prefer women who don't sound like the 9.47 Dadar Fast?' Nirmala was referring to Bombay's local trains which run on Fast and Slow timings; South Bombay residents who do not have to use the local trains refer to their existence and schedule derogatorily. She sighed and added, 'Anyway you will quietly do exactly what you want the way you always do. Thinking-thinking and planning in your mind all the time! When did you decide to study abroad?'

'How long have I been at KEM, Nimma? You have to give me credit for talking to people, reading the English papers and going to the library.'

'Achcha so you will go abroad and then you will come back and then you will marry and have children. Then you will have to give up work no, to look after the children?'

'Which times do you live in? This is 1969, I don't think you realize it. So many women in India are going to work on a full-time basis now. There is no need to feel bad about working, and there is no need to feel bad about working and looking after your home at the same time either.'

Nirmala realized, for the nth time, there was no getting past Aruna. Still, she had to articulate the thought that had just occurred to her. 'But what is the need for women to take on men's jobs also? Men don't do women's work, do they? See, there is a nice balance. Women look after the home, men go to work. It is different if the money is very badly needed. Otherwise why should women do double gadha majuri?'

'How can you ever think that women who earn their own money are doing double the work-load of a donkey? Such women are respected by everybody, including men.'

'You mean our fathers don't respect our mothers?'

Aruna's voice turned cold. 'Do they?'

Nirmala gave up. She signalled to the waiter for the bill. These had become regular, welcome outings. On pre-designated Fridays they met at the Mahalakshmi mandir at Haji Ali and on Tuesdays at the Siddhi Vinayaka in Prabhadevi. After which they had a quick filter-coffee at the closest Udipi. The timings depended upon Aruna's workshifts. She had done night duty yesterday, no sleep at all, but still looked fresh as a daisy. 'Okay, so where all are you going to apply? For your foreign studies, I mean?'

'I already have. To England of course, they have the best

further studies. I have given your address on the application forms.'

'How will you pay for it all?'

'I have started saving for the air-ticket. For the rest, where ever I have applied I have asked for a scholarship.'

'They give, just like that? So much money?'

Aruna laughed. 'Nimma, you are so naïve at times. You know the pujari . . .'

'Which pujari?'

'Arre baba I met a big, learned pujari who came from the north somewhere at Prema Pai's house.'

'That Prema Pai, I did not like her when you introduced us at KEM. She is jealous of your looks.'

'Do you want to hear the rest?'

'Achcha, tell-tell.'

'The pujari said I had a sau mein ek patrika. Those were his exact words, that I had a rare horoscope. He said I would be a success. I would live long and I would go abroad.'

'How do you know that pujari is not talking rubbish, especially since he was at that Prema's house?'

'It does not matter. I know that I will become known in my field.'

There was someone else from the KEM staff nurses going abroad that year for further studies. She had achieved all that Aruna aspired to and had become a role-model for girls in her substantial Gujarati community. Senior assistant matron Durga Mehta had secured a fellowship in the administration course at the Royal College of Nursing and was scheduled to leave within a few days. Senior assistant matron Mehta was making her last rounds of the wards at KEM thinking she would really miss the place while she was away. Nurses who saw her coming immediately straightened up on duty, nudged their colleagues, hissed 'Durga!' and then pretended to look nonchalantly attentive to their tasks on hand.

Senior assistant matron Mehta resisted the urge to chuckle. She was aware of her formidable reputation as a disciplinarian. She knew the nurses equated her name with the goddess Durga who spared none. She did not mind, a little bit of fear of authority kept matters in check. Even when out of uniform, Durga Mehta never dressed in a manner which detracted from her authority. The sari pleats would be knife-sharp with safety-pins tactically, and discretely, holding the fabric in place. The mid-riff never showed through. The pallav crossed an impeccably stitched blouse with precise pleat upon precise pleat held together with an exquisite antique broach at the left shoulder.

Sister Mehta reached ward 4 and saw nurse Placida D'Silva changing the linen on a patient's bed. The patient, a woman in her mid-thirties with a sallow skin, sat on a stool and watched the young nurse make the bed as if it was the last time this would happen in her life. Probably. KEM was a free hospital, several poor people found their way to it for treatment. They were rarely the sort who had a bed at home, or crisp clean linen.

Sister D'Silva felt someone's eyes on her, looked around, saw Durga Mehta and promptly dropped the pillow. The patient leaned forward, picked it up, clutched its softness against her bony chest and rested her chin on it, all the while her eyes never losing sight of the movements of Sister D'Silva making her bed. With two pairs of eyes now on her, Sister D'Silva was not going to get this bed made correctly. Senior assistant matron Mehta walked up to the bed and checked the patient's chart dangling at the end of it. She nodded at the patient and asked, 'Koi khaas takleef?' The patient searched her mind for some special sort of complaint, came up with none and so said, almost woebegone, 'Kal humko discharge karne wala.'

Durga Mehta gestured that she expected Sister D'Silva to move back a bit. With one swift motion she pulled off the bedsheet and with another—now using two hands—from the foot of the bed, she tucked one side in neatly under the mattress. She walked to the opposite end, pulled the bedsheet and wrapped it, with its tightness, around that side of the mattress. The mattress turned slightly concave under the pressure and then settled neatly on the bed frame. The long sides received similar treatment. Edges were firmly and methodically tucked in, what is more they stayed there at the four corners. 'This method, as you should know, is called Hospital Corners,' said senior assistant matron Durga Mehta to staff nurse Placida D'Silva. The patient jumped, pillow et al, on the luxury of the smooth bed with what sounded like a small whoop of happiness.

Staff nurse Aruna Shanbaug rushed into ward 4. 'What is it, Sister Shanbaug?' asked senior assistant matron Mehta loud enough to be heard ten beds down and with enough steel in her voice to stop anyone in their tracks. Aruna came forward slowly and wished her warily, 'Good afternoon, Sister Mehta.' She threw a warm smile towards Placida D'Silva and widened her eyes for a second in mock fear. Sister D'Silva quickly looked down to hide the laughter in her eyes. 'You seem to be off-duty,' observed Sister Mehta taking in Aruna's sleeveless blouse and sunshine-yellow sari. 'Then why are you here in this ward?'

'My room-mate is on duty in this ward just now. I wanted to ask her something.'

'Wards are not meant for nurses to stand around and chat in. Patients recuperate here. Could it not wait till your room-mate went off-duty?'

Aruna shuffled and quickly looked around the ward for her room-mate. Placida D'Silva found herself staring at Aruna's bare forearms, her delicate frame, her glowing skin and thinking, 'My! She's so pretty.' Placida had seen Aruna getting into a taxi the other day outside the hospital's main gate. She had been wearing a dark-green, mid-knee, straight, tight skirt with a loose shirt-like blouse tucked neatly into the waistband. She looked smart, really smart. Unlike these other 'vernies' who could not even carry off their uniforms properly, thought the convent-educated, Bombay-born Placida. No wonder there were doctors running after her. The nurse's grapevine had informed Placida that there were at least two, with names, who made quite a few rounds of those wards in which Sister Shanbaug was on duty. One of them was a real Romeo. The junior doctors joked that he had already specialized in cardiology. But imagine having doctors wanting to get your attention! Like those doctor-nurse romances in the Mills & Boons.

'Sorry Sister Mehta but I need to ask my room-mate for our room key.'

'Where is yours?'

'I left it behind in the room this morning in my hurry.'

'You often do that?'

Aruna sounded offended. 'Of course not. I am very careful. This is the first, and last, time.'

Senior assistant matron Durga Mehta nodded her permission and proceeded on her rounds with her thoughts. If she were inclined towards colloquialism—which she was not, she was very careful with her words—Durga Mehta would call Aruna Shanbaug a chatak chandni. It is among the several Bombay words which defy translation. A mix of

Hindi and Gujarati with the first word intentionally mispronounced,—a chatko is what you would get if you touched a live-wire. Chandni is the moonlight—used, obviously, for women and meant to be only vaguely derisory while sounding complimentary. Sister Shanbaug is so casual, thought Sister Mehta, but so competent. There is no denying her adaptability, her facility with medical instruments and her capacity to absorb practical knowledge.

Sister Mehta turned the corner of the quadrangle. She was looking forward to the course in administration. It was always nice to learn something new about your own profession. It would also recharge her batteries. It would make coming back to KEM even more pleasurable. Durga Mehta had started as student-nurse in 1951 and was as much a part of KEM as its first dean, her uncle Dr Jeevraj Mehta who went on to become the first chief minister of Gujarat. How different the two brothers were, Jeevraj and her father Jagjeevandas Mehta, and yet how similar. Service for the country ran in their family's blood. Her father chose the grassroots social worker route and gave up everything—he had been a wealthy textile merchant—to join Mahatma Gandhi's freedom movement. Life subsequently had always been simple but honourable.

Durga Mehta would have become a doctor like her uncle, indeed he expected it of her. But she wanted to be self-dependent, for her MBBS education she would have had to place a monetary strain on her father. She had also heard Sardar Vallabhbhai Patel's moving speech on how women could contribute to the freedom struggle, and after it continue to serve the country by tending to its ill and weary. Her uncle had later told her of an incident which made her glad she had chosen nursing.

Whenever he would be touring peri-urban and rural

Gujarat, the people would turn to her uncle and ask for hospitals. Fine, he would say, I will give you the four walls and the doctors. Will you make your daughters the nurses? The people would shy away. But when articles began to appear about Dr Jeevraj Mehta's own niece becoming the first nurse in the entire Gujarati community, it made a lot of difference to their perception. The men of Gujarat grew less sceptical about their daughters training as nurses.

Dr Jeevraj Mehta remained the first dean of KEM till August 1942 before plunging headlong into the freedom movement. But he always spoke of KEM as a part of his own being. 'I was fortunate enough to have as my colleagues on the hospital and medical staff individuals of the highest capability and deepest integrity. There was a great sense of pride in the staff members. Seniormost physicians and surgeons insisted on teaching the junior batches as they felt the clinical training imparted to these youngsters at the start of their careers was of paramount importance in laying a good foundation. My colleagues cheerfully worked for eighteen to twenty hours at a stretch. KEM was the first teaching medical institute in the country entirely staffed by Indians. The eyes of the British officers were focussed on us. We wanted to make them realize what independent Indian doctors could do without them, nay inspite of them.'

Sister Mehta's father had added, in his quiet thoughtful manner, 'The British will leave, we will be independent India. Then we will have to prove that we should not let ourselves down as a nation. This, I suspect, will turn out to be our toughest task.'

Sister Usha Samant had a headache. The songs from the blasted radio were going right into her brain and echoing there. This was all just too much, she had taken enough. 'Aruna, please shut down the radio.'

Humming the song, Aruna turned down the volume on the radio.

'I said turn it off.'

Aruna turned the volume down even further.

'In which language do you want me to tell you to stop the noise?'

Aruna continued humming and working on her embroidery. She had started with pillow-covers for her bed, graduated to fine embroidery on her sari blouses and was now engrossed in completing the border of a six-yard sari for Nirmala.

'Didn't you hear me?'

Aruna and her maddening humming. Usha swung her feet off the narrow bed, reached across to the other side of the small room and was about to touch the radio when Aruna's hand shot out and grasped her wrist. 'Don't you dare touch my things without my permission. Do I touch anything that belongs to you?'

Usha wrenched her wrist out of Aruna's grasp, sat on her bed and rubbed it. 'You have become unbearable.'

Aruna looked up from her embroidery. 'Your problem is elsewhere, you are taking it out on me.'

'May be, but you are also creating a nuisance in the room.'

'Oh really, like how?'

'Your radio. You turn it on the moment you enter the room and it is on even when you have gone down the corridor for your bath. The radio is off only when you lock it in your cupboard before leaving for work or going out.'

'That is all, na?'

'Lately you have started dipping your saris for starching in that slippery kanji which you store in buckets in the room.'

'What's your problem with that?'

'Whenever I come back from my night-shift I find one kanji-bucket in the room. I almost fell over it this morning.'

'Okay, I will keep the bucket under my bed.'

'But why must you keep the bucket in the room? Why can't you just keep it in the bathroom, where all the other nurses soak their clothes?'

'Because that is where all the other nurses soak their clothes.'

'Why must you keep soaking your saris in kanji?'

Aruna bit off the red skein of thread with her teeth and proceeded to thread a green one through the needle.

'Aruna, please switch off the radio, it is driving me mad.'

'I keep kanji-fying my saris because they are cotton ones which I buy at Dadar for thirteen rupees each. If I do not use the kanji they will not stiffen-up after ironing and will be useless. I will look limp when wearing them.'

A thought struck Usha. 'Where do you get the kanji from, and enough for a full sari?'

'Why, you want some for yours?'

'Shut the radio. I want to sleep.'

'I request the staff-canteen cook for some whenever I want it. I tell him in the morning. Then he drains off the starch from some of the rice for our dinner and keeps it aside for me to collect in the night.'

'But it's almost three-fourths of the bucket and quite heavy. The canteen is so far away from our quarters. You are so delicate. How do you manage to get it up till here in the room?'

Aruna leaned sideways and turned off the radio on the small writing desk. 'You catch up on your sleep. You always have a headache when you come from night-shift.'

'If you don't tell me I'll tell matron I want to change my room.'

'So go.'

'Tell me otherwise I'll never talk to you again.'

'The cook carries the bucket up to the room late after dinner.'

'This is unbelievable. Oh I see, that is why buckets come only when I am on night duty so that I won't object to some man coming into my room.'

'He does not come into the room, he leaves the bucket at the door. He's an old man.'

'Young or old, you know men are not allowed into the nurses quarters. If matron comes to know she will have you thrown out. By the way, why does this old man do it for you? How can you be so sure he won't harm you?'

'I give him a small tip. He's my jaatwaala. Your own people can never hurt you, they help you.'

'I swear you people come from outside Maharashtra and just break all our rules. All you people from outside, why don't you stay where you all are and help each other there? What is the need to crowd Bombay?'

Aruna leaned over and flicked on her radio.

Doctor Sundeep Sardesai had also come to Bombay from 'outside'. He had left his home and fields to study medicine at KEM. Home was ancestral property with rolling fields abutting the NH 17 in Margao, Goa. Dr Sardesai's ancestors were the GSBs who settled down in Goa for trading with Portugal, through the ruling Portuguese, and a spot of farming. Dr Sardesai did not think of home often. He knew it was there for him whenever he wanted to visit, no point cluttering your emotions. He had come to Bombay in the early sixties to become a doctor, which he had. Now he had to complete his MD by the end of 1973, a mere three years away, which he would. He hadn't as yet decided what he would specialize in. This made him slightly uncomfortable.

As would be evident by now, Dr Sardesai was a man who lived a very ordered life: things had to be thought out well in advance, meticulously planned and only then executed in detail. Dr Sardesai was going to complete his MD, settle comfortably into his practice and then purchase his own flat. This was not a part of his plan but by that time Dr Sardesai would be a terrific catch for the girls in his community. Lookswise too Dr Sardesai passed muster. Yes, shorter than the average Indian male height of five feet eight inches, but that was neither here nor there. Dr Sardesai was already a good doctor, the senior nurses had noticed this and commented upon it to each other with some satisfaction. Sister Premila Kushe added that his bedside manner was very sincere. 'Patients and their relatives have so many queries,' she said in the nurses staff room. 'But Dr Sardesai bends over their beds and answers them all with patience.' Do doctors with good bedside manners make for patient parents, wondered Sister Placida D'Silva while she listened to the conversation among her seniors. If they are patient with their patients do they make for better fathers and husbands? Then Dr Sardesai's wife would be very lucky.

Marriage was not even the last item on Dr Sardesai's immediate three-year agenda. There were timings for everything, including marriage. His would be only after he purchased his own flat. Now this would take some doing as flats were so expensive in Bombay. Before that he would have to put down, he was sure, a huge deposit on some room for his private consultancy in the evenings. There was a lot to achieve single-handedly and soon, so it was best that he kept his wits about him, the way he had managed till now. Eat sensibly, sleep soundly, exercise a bit, choose your company carefully. Bombay was a city where you could easily get side-tracked if you let yourself be led.

Now look at staff nurse Shanbaug here in front of him in the ward. How focussed she is. They had been working for six months in the same ward and he had been observing her. She was really very good at her work. She was gently practical with patients, she found their veins with the minimum of fuss for IVs, her injections appeared to be painless. The surname on her name-tag told him she was a GSB, her accent suggested she came from the Karwar belt. He wondered if there were many other progressive girls like her in her village. He doubted it.

Dr Sardesai watched staff nurse Shanbaug expertly complete a lumbar puncture on a child-patient. Generally it was doctors who did the lumbar punctures, but it was acknowledged by all that staff nurse Aruna Shanbaug was really very good at them. The child's mother looked utterly distraught that a needle was going to be stuck into her son's thin back. Staff nurse Shanbaug mildly told the mother that her tension was transmitting itself to her child. She then turned the boy around on his tummy and relieved him of his fear by telling him about what she was doing in a soft, story-like tone.

'The brain is a very clever part of our body. It has to be because it is the most important part. From outside the brain is protected by the skull, here,' she touched the child's head, 'and inside it protects itself from all this bone,' she mock-knocked on the child's skull, he smiled weakly, 'by secreting a sticky fluid. The whole day it secretes the fluid and sends it travelling down your back and then absorbs it into itself. It is called the cerebro-spinal fluid, doctors don't have time so they call it CSF. I need some CSF to check ke bheja hain ke nahin.' The child laughed. 'Now, to check whether you have brains or not, I cannot hammer a big hole in your skull so I will just take it while it is travelling down your back. There.' The CSF withdrawn in the syringe was yellowish, the child obviously had an earlier injury in the brain area. Aruna proficiently filled vials, reorganized her white enamel tray and was gone.

Dr Sardesai watched her walk out of the ward filled with its sickness and fret, and the combined smell of sweat and urine. The realities of a hospital did not bother Aruna. The blood and the human waste and the pus, and the odours, she just worked right through them. Dr Sardesai thought, 'Like a gentle fair angel she . . .' Angel? Where were such strange words coming into his mind from! Dr Sardesai suddenly realizes that he had been staring at staff nurse Aruna Shanbaug right through as if entranced. Dr Sardesai is now angry that he is entranced.

Like Sister Durga Mehta, Dr Vidya Acharya was also an avowed KEMite. As the daughter of journalist G.N. Acharya who had been a part of the freedom struggle through his impassioned writing, Dr Vidya Acharya had as enormous a commitment to KEM as Sister Mehta. She worked with pride and pleasure, and considered herself fortunate to be in a hospital which had been the first in all of western India to institute a full-fledged department of nephrology. Much of the credit for this department went to Dr Acharya herself, kidneys fascinated her. Dr Acharya knew that even after retirement from KEM she would continue with her work in kidneys. Of course

119

retirement itself was a long, long way away. This was only 1971.

She had been asked if she would like to be on the governing committee of the Nurses Welfare Society, an election by the nurses themselves. Dr Acharya had agreed, she quite enjoyed the idea of organizing picnics, dances and dramas for the nurses. Poor things, they were so cooped up with all the pathos of the wards around them. Doctors on duty get to sit, nurses on eight-hour shifts are constantly on their toes. Or at least they should be, thought Dr Acharya with a slight frown as she passed Sisters Aruna Shanbaug and Prema Pai in the corridor. The two nurses were slowly walking towards the children's ward chatting away in Konkani. Dr Acharya stopped, turned around and called out to them.

'Good evening doctor,' they chorused like school girls.

Dr Acharya looked at them carefully. Cheery was fine but sometimes these young nurses could get really cheeky with the doctors. 'Are you reporting for night duty now?'

'Yes doctor,' again the chorus.

'What were the two of you talking about with so much interest?'

They hesitated. Sister Pai replied, 'Sister Shanbaug was just telling me about a Hindi film she saw yesterday with her cousins.'

'You like watching movies Sister Shanbaug?'

'Hindi movies.'

'Good, then perhaps you can think of some item to put up for the nurses social we are planning.'

Prema wanted to know why they could not go for a picnic.

Dr Acharya nodded, 'That too. You all are around 200 nurses. We will organize the picnics in groups since you all cannot go together because of your shifts. I was thinking of a small cultural programme before that. The nurses could perform skits or dramas and sing songs. I'm told some of your colleagues are very good dancers and singers. Can you sing Sister Pai?'

'Arrey no, not even to save my life. But I can act.'

'Okay I will send you a message once I have spoken to the other nurses and decided on the play. We're looking at doing this during the summer holidays when admissions and out-patient is slightly down. What about you Sister Shanbaug, can you do something?'

Aruna shook her head.

'Acting? Dancing? Singing?'

Aruna shook her head again. She is being shy, thought Dr Acharya.

'You like movies, do you not? Who are your favourite actors and actresses?'

'Vyjyanthimala, Raj Kapoor, Dev Anand. I cannot dance like Vyjyanthimala. I cannot speak Hindi like Raj Kapoor. But I can imitate the way Dev Anand shakes in his songs. Chalenga?'

It was a hot summer. KEM's wide corridors, high ceilings, long-stemmed fans and cool, stone architecture helped combat the heat considerably. But it was still sweltering. Dr Sardesai mopped his face with his huge white handkerchief, settled the square on the lines of its existing folds and put it back into the pocket of his white doctor's coat. He looked quickly into the neurosurgery ward. Where was she? He had been waiting for her to come back since what felt like forever.

Within two hours of the lumbar puncture incident

Dr Sardesai had given himself a sound mental shake. Look here Sundeep there will be enough time for such things later, he told himself and was very pleased that he was not fighting his self-remonstration. Discipline was the key. So whenever he had seen staff nurse Aruna Shanbaug in the last ten months he had maintained his standard cool demeanour and calm. He had chatted with her, professionally of course. It had occurred to him once, right in the middle of these professional chats, that he seemed to bump into her more often. Unexpectedly he would come face-to-face with her in the middle of KEM's corridors, their library timings seemed to coincide. But what an intelligent girl, not too many nurses were seen in the library.

And then suddenly she was gone, nowhere to be seen. He had looked in every single ward, at different times. He toyed with the idea of going to the matron's office and directly asking her. No, no, that just would not do; everyone would start talking and what would matron think? Could he check in the nurses quarters? But he was not even sure if she lived there. He thought she did, he had seen her jumping out of a taxi and rushing towards the building a little before dinner. She had looked beautiful. She was wearing a dress, like the Christian women in Goa, very bold for a GSB girl but it really suited her.

He cursed himself. All those small, oh-so-casual chats with her, not once had he asked where she came from, where she lived. It's not as if she hadn't replied in Konkani when he had subconsciously slipped into their language. Finally when Dr Sardesai could no longer recognize this feverish man which was supposed to be the organized, logical, coldly clinical himself, he exhaled and called everything to a halt. He sat down to seriously think about it in his room on the KEM campus. For the first time in his life he wished he smoked so that he could light a cigarette and drag on it, and drag on it. It seemed to help other men clear their thoughts.

Dr Sundeep Sardesai was a man in love. It was one of those truly enviable ones. Pure love at first sight. Dr Sardesai did not think of it like that and would never agree that Cupid had struck him pre-lumbar puncture. But there it was with Dr Sardesai taking an important decision. Yes, I want to marry her. He felt elated. Then he felt crushed. Suppose she does not return my feelings? Suppose . . . tchah-tchah, she's not like that. But just suppose she was responding to that Dr Samuel? He had heard bits of conversation among the doctors in their lunch-room. That Samuel was not even a competent doctor. He had seen him talking to her. Rascal. Maybe that's why she was wearing dresses these days?

Dr Sardesai exhaled again. He would start talking to her and see how she responded. He would take it from there. Suppose she did not show any interest? This time Dr Sardesai's exhalation held a philosophical breath. If she did not respond, he would just have to carry on as if nothing of importance had transpired in his thoughts. His heart would not break, medically it was not possible.

Dr Sardesai had reached the Udipi opposite KEM and asked the cashier for the use of the telephone. He carefully dialled the hospital's number and then asked for the matron. Matron answered in her office. Dr Sardesai asked for staff nurse Aruna Shanbaug.

'Who is this?' Matron sounded busy and irritated. 'This is not her private telephone. This is the matron's office.'

'Yes, yes.' Dr Sardesai tried to make his voice sound much older than it did. 'I am Aruna Shanbaug's uncle.'

The voice-over wasn't working. Matron now sounded suspicious. 'What uncle, from where?'

'Her uncle from Karwar. I am visiting Bombay so I

thought I would visit her also. Where can I speak to her?'

'Karwar? But she has gone there, to Haldipur, her village.'

So that's where she was from, some village called Haldipur near Karwar. He had never heard of it. 'Oh, I am from Karwar proper, Karwar city. I did not know she had gone to her village. I am her maternal uncle. No problem there I hope.'

'No, no. She is visiting her mother. As you must know she had not been there at all since she came to Bombay.'

'When is she expected back?' Each word dropped into the telephone heavily and took its own time to transmit. The pause between the reply was as if the answer had to come from a million miles away and not merely across the road.

'Next week. How long are you in Bombay?'

'I'm here, I'm here. Which ward will I find her in?'

'Ward? You can come to my office.'

'Yes, but supposing if I telephone her first they can give the line directly in the ward.'

'Personal telephone calls are not encouraged on the hospital line in the wards during duty, or any other, hours.'

Dr Sardesai had this enormously violent, utterly alien to him, urge to smack the heavy receiver onto the cuddapah-topped counter in the Udipi and then to methodically smash the entire instrument into very tiny, irretrievable pieces.

He changed tack. He knew the matron was also from somewhere on the Konkan coast; he spoke in Konkani.

'The thing is, I am staying at Borivli, at my brother's place, it is so far away. So I thought better to ring and come.'

Matron replied in Konkani. 'Of course. Just wait I will consult the nurses diary.' A rustle of paper. 'You can telephone next Wednesday. She is being posted to neurosurgery, afternoon shift. You can telephone around 4.00 p.m. and ask the telephone operator for neurosurgery. What did you say your name was?'

Staff nurse Aruna Shanbaug's maternal uncle from Karwar disconnected the line without even saying thank you.

It was a few minutes into the afternoon shift. Dr Sundeep Sardesai adjusted his stethoscope around his neck most professionally and walked over to the nurse's duty desk in neurosurgery most casually. 'Uh, Sister?'

The nurse on duty quickly stood up. 'Yes doctor?'

'Umm, I was told that staff nurse Shanbaug is on duty here?'

The nurse looked blankly at him.

Dr Sardesai decided to pull rank otherwise he would never be able to sort out this matter. One way or another, he thought with heightened determination. He raised his eyebrows and queried, 'Well, Sister?'

'She is not here, doctor.'

'I can see that.' He was amazed at his own capacity for such exaggerated patience. 'Would you know where she is?'

'No, doctor.'

'Would you care to find out for me?'

Can a blank look deepen? The nurse-on-duty's did.

'Sister, could you please pick up the phone and find out from whoever is handling the nurses' roster where staff nurse Aruna Shanbaug would be right now?' There, he had finally thrown caution to the winds. The nurse was bound to tell whoever she asked that he wanted to know. Then they would wonder why he wanted to know, after which they would probably equate him with that slimy Dr Samuel.

The nurse picked up the telephone receiver, began dialling, looked at him, hung up mid-dial and began organizing the desk in front of her. Dr Sardesai did not know what to make of this. He did not even know what to do if he made anything of it.

The nurse closed a register, tucked a ball-point pen into her uniform pocket, smiled sweetly and said, 'Any problem with bed nine call Dr Sunil Pandya immediately.'

'What! What?'

The nurse gestured apologetically, look beside you, and was gone.

He followed the nurse's gesture.

His lips were in line with her left ear. A tiny, perfectly formed, pink ear. Above which on her forehead was a small black lovely mole. Around which dangled a tendril of jet-black curly hair which had escaped from under her cap. She turned to face him and looked up, her eyes dark and shining. 'Good afternoon, Dr Sardesai.'

He cleared his throat, 'Ah yes, good afternoon.' What to say next, he had to take the lead in this matter, he had decided. 'I see you are late for the shift.' He cursed himself as soon as he had completed the sentence. This was definitely not the way to speak at such a time.

Her eyes still on him, she picked up her left arm, flicked her eyes to her wrist, looked up at him again, 'Nine minutes, fifty seconds, sorry', and continued to look at him with those bright eyes.

Dr Sardesai shifted his weight to the other foot. 'It's alright, it's alright. Um yes, thank you.' So saying he hurried out of the neurosurgical ward.

Staff nurse Aruna Shanbaug watched him going with a smile dancing in her eyes.


Nirmala waited till the coffee had arrived at their table before she could remonstrate.

'Really Aruna! What was the need to take a taxi from the theatre till here?'

'You wanted to walk and sweat?'

'Listen to this memsaab. Always taking taxis. Even when you come home on your off-days you run back in the evening in a taxi. Why can't you take a bus like everyone else? We would have taken a bus just now, it would have been minimum fare. So what if we had sweated a little? All of Bombay is sweating.'

'Everybody sweats so we must also? People sweat and then rub against you in the buses. It is horrible. The smell they leave behind on the rexine seats is also so horrible, I cannot bear to sit on them.'

'Maharani, thank your stars you do not have to travel by the local trains. Do you know from where all and how they come to work?'

'I hear enough of it from people in the hospital.' Aruna put on a sing-song voice. 'In a compartment which should accommodate fifty there are 300 every morning and evening. There are huts on either sides of the tracks and people from these huts grow spinach and other bhaajis upon which their children shit. These are then sold to us to eat.'

'Chhee chhee. Be serious.'

'I am. From the day I have come to know this I do not eat any green leafy vegetable in Bombay. I just thank God that I don't have to travel by those trains.'

'Aruna, I think this business of earning money and planning on further studies abroad has gone to your head. We are lower middle-class people. We will marry like this and die like this only.'

'Is this what happens to you when you watch Dilip Kumar in *Leader*, that too matinee?'

'Don't make fun of me. For the poor there is no hot or

cold. The rich sit in their air conditioning. It is only the middle-class who suffer in Bombay, in jampacked trains and crowded buses where the third-rate men rub against you and take their chance. Taking a taxi just because you are feeling hot does not make you equal to rich people. They speak differently, they react differently. They have some inborn authority with which they order people around. You try to imitate them and you will be like the dhobi ka kutta who finds rest nowhere.'

'You know who you sound like just now, Nimma? These religious pundits with big paunches who want to stay in business. They are always giving lessons in moral science. Like the politicians who keep people poor so that they can continue controlling them, priests use fear as the key. Don't do this, that will happen. If you do that, this will happen. You will be punished. God has meant you to remain meek and in whatever slot you are born in; don't worry, your reward will come in your next life. What about right now?'

'Right now I will order a cold drink, it is really too hot for philosophy. Will you share a Rim Zim with me?'

'No you go ahead. Have any more replies come for me from England?'

'Wouldn't I have told you if they had? The last lot which came, what did they say?'

'My matric marks were not good enough for one and the other expected me to pay for the studies.'

'See, I had told you.'

'I have sent some more applications.'

'You are well settled in your job. Why don't you settle down in life also? I'm sure Balakrishna will quickly find you a boy in Bombay itself.'

'Why can't I find one for myself?'

'Wai, wai.' Nirmala sounded amused as she agreed in Konkani. 'Find, please find one.'

'Actually, I already have.'

'Aruna, it is too hot for games.'

'No really. I am marrying a doctor.'

'Wha . . . Aruna, what are you saying?'

'Dr Sundeep Sardesai is interested in me.'

'You mean like in love with you? Really? Doctor and nurse. Like Raj Kumar and Meena Kumari in . . . in . . . that picture with the song Ajeeb dastaan hain yeh! Wah, just think, one nurse and now one doctor in the family.' Nirmala was beaming, she looked genuinely happy till her brow creased slightly. 'But then why are you asking me about further study forms from England?'

'Nimma, life is not an either-or. If I get a scholarship I will go. I can always come back and get married.'

'And he will be waiting for you at the airport with a garland in his hand, I suppose? Women do not leave their men and go away for long periods of time and that too, so far away. It is a stupid thing to do. You will come back and find him married to someone else. These days nurses have also become too bold. Or he might meet a clever lady doctor. Or his family will find him a nice gharelu girl, domesticated, who will bring double dowry because he is a doctor, not to forget that fridge and a Fiat. Plus she will bear him lots of children. Accha, never mind all that, what jaat is he?'

'Ours only. GSB from Goa, speaks Konkani.'

'When did he ask you to marry him? Shouldn't we go and tell amma, appa and Ramdas? Have you told Balakrishna the good news?'

'He has not as yet.'

'As yet, what?'

'Asked me to marry him.'

'Then, Aruna really! What are all these sand castles in the air?'

'He will.'

Aruna took a taxi back to KEM. Why constantly mortgage the present for the future?

In the best tradition of the Shanbaugs who had reached Bombay, Aruna was of assistance to all relatives who came from their towns and villages. They would reach KEM, locate Aruna and laboriously explain their relationship with her. There would be a father's fourth cousin; her grandmother's brother's son's somebody. Aruna never understood much of their explanation, frankly she did not even care. She paid attention because these people had sought her out, they were unwell and she was a nurse. Most times they just needed her assistance to jump the out-patient department queue; KEM being a free hospital, the lines at OPD were long.

But sometimes they were quite serious. Like her first cousin who came in complaining of a continuous nagging pain in her abdomen. She was sick and she was bewildered. Aruna took her to Dr G.H. Tilve who recommended an operation. 'Who is she?' asked Dr Tilve. Aruna replied without hesitation, 'My sister.' The 'sister' was admitted, operated upon and sent back home happy and cheerful; Aruna ensured this all.

One day her brother Sadanand showed up. It was like a meeting between strangers who had heard of each other; he had not really kept in touch with his youngest sister. Sadanand was a cashier in an Udipi in Kolhapur. He had been feeling odd for a while, somewhat bilious, and had been to several doctors in Kolhapur. None could effectively cure him. Then he had dropped Balakrishna a postcard about his health and he received one in return suggesting that he take some leave and come to Bombay since Aruna was at KEM. Aruna took him to Dr Sundeep Sardesai who was extraordinarily attentive. A few days later Sadanand had to return to Kolhapur and he went away saying, 'What a wonderful hospital. Doctors here treat you like you are of their family.' Staff nurse Aruna Shanbaug and Dr Sundeep Sardesai smiled at each other shyly. Bonding, seventies-style.

Balakrishna also left Bombay. The grapevine had told him of an imminent shutdown and sackings in Kamala Mills. He went back into the Udipi network and checked out the possibilities. Not in Bombay but back home, somewhere in the South where the people were a lot more decent, where human beings felt like persons living. Where you might earn less than in Bombay but you got in return value for your money through quality and quantity. You even got a good night's sleep on most nights. Balakrishna was informed of an Udipi being opened on the main road through Shimoga in Karnataka, the man was looking for a partner. Balakrishna resigned in a flash from the Kamala Mills dyeing department and was gone as fast as the first vehicle could take him away from a city he had always loathed.

If Aruna had the inclination she did not have the time on her Tressa to miss her guardian-brother. She had her hands full with Ramdas who had contracted typhoid. And who had turned overnight into an over-grown baby. Ramdas refused to come to KEM because he was petrified of hospitals. He had never stepped into one and was not likely to start now. He refused to take injections, he could not even bear their thought. He was hurting all over, feverish, fretting and impossible to manage. Their amma told Nirmala to phone Aruna who took leave and came with her syringes and sponges and a small bag of medication which she administered with precision. Injections were over before Ramdas could even yelp. Spongings were gentle but thorough. When her casual leave could no longer be extended, Aruna went back and sent Sister Usha Samant to tend to Ramdas for a day with a set of instructions that she be equally firm. Ramdas was right as rain in no time. He even got over his fear of injections and hospitals. He proved this by asking Aruna to find some time for him, he intended coming over to KEM to see an operation theatre.

They spat where they sat, they shat on their own doorstep. Aruna could never get over her revulsion for the filth Bombayites surrounded themselves with, and contributed to, in enormous measure. It was not just the slum people, the rich were just as bad. In fact it made them worse, since they were supposed to know better by virtue of their dubious wealth. Aruna carefully threaded her way through the maze of garbage-lined bylanes which led to the BDD chawls at Worli. This was another myth in Bombay, Aruna thought as she passed the first block of chawls. The Hindi movies always glorified these terrible places; the people who lived in here were shown as happy, healthy and good citizens. So wonderful was it in here that they did not mind laying down their life in front of the first demolition crane when the bad builders came. Basti ko bachaana was a big one in the Bombay movies. Save-the-slum pictures, produced by people who did not have any around their own bungalows.

The Bombay District Development Board barracks were built for their tommies by the British. Rows upon rows of single rooms, stacked one upon the other, in a sprawl of a hundred four-storeyed buildings. Near this small township of soldiers was stamped out a jamboree ground, this became the

Jamburi Maidan when the British left. The barracks turned
into the BDD chawls and, horrifyingly, into a model of sorts
for low-grade living all over the city. Single rooms measuring
ten by ten feet with at least six people crammed into each, ten
rooms to a floor with one toilet for all at the end of the
corridor. Several generations were hatched, matched and
despatched here, rabbits in time-warped warrens.

Aruna crinkled her nose as she adroitly side-stepped a
shower of sewerage. Bombay chawls invariably had broken
plumbing, BDD chawls did not see any reason to be different.
She quickened her pace, the sun had not set as yet but BDD
was a dangerous place. People broke glass bottles and stuck
them into each other first, they talked later. Full-fledged
fights broke out often and swords appeared as if from nowhere,
long, glinting, with evil edges. Confused children cried, battered
women wept, radios blared, bandicoots the size of puppies
foraged without fear for food between the barracks.

She did not really like the idea too much but there was
no question of refusal. Aruna had been invited by her sister
to spend the night in their kerchief-sized kholi in the Nehru
Nagar chawl behind BDD. When she was re-introduced to
her sister.by Nirmala's amma it was like meeting a stranger.
She was almost a stranger actually. Her sister had been
married off when she was all of fourteen. Aruna did not even
remember her face, never mind her wedding, she had been
that small. From Haldipur Shakuntala came straight to this
chawl behind BDD in Bombay. In keeping with the several
bits of nonsensical tradition associated with marriage
ceremonies, her in-laws renamed her Shantabai. New life, new
name; if it occurred to anyone that the husband was also
embarking on a new life they ignored it.

Her husband worked in an Udipi near Century Mills, he
subsequently switched to delivering milk bottles in and around

the sprawl of BDD chawls. Shantabai had some daughters, then a son; right through she assisted her husband in the delivery of milk bottles to augment their income. Mornings at daybreak, afternoons when the sun was at its highest and hottest, through the monsoon which further mucked instead of washing away the dirt, Shantabai would set out with a canvas bag clinking with the thick glass bottles. Exchange the empties, delivery, re-exchange the empties, back to delivery. Shantabai's legs often hurt, knees down; she tightly tied strips of cloth around them at different levels to ease the pain.

Aruna found the room without too much difficulty. Her sister was waiting for her with her family, and looked genuinely happy to see her. There was fresh hot food which tasted not unlike amma's, there was laughter and family gossip. Her nieces wanted to know everything about nursing. Aruna wondered where she would sleep. Nobody slept outside the kholi, not even the men, because the rats nibbled on their toes. Particularly heavy sleepers had been heard to get up with a shout when the rats hopped onto their chests to nip their chins.

A space was carved out for Aruna, near her nieces, on the floor, near the kitchen-side around which there was some haphazard green tiling. The room had divided itself unequally with a showcase that held up the wall. In this there were two matching china cups and saucers, a crude model of Gandhiji's three monkeys and the family transistor covered in plastic. In between the front door and the showcase was enough space to squeeze in a chair for visitors and the only other bit of elevated furniture in the house, a rusted metal single-bed. Under the bed was stuffed everything that would come in the way elsewhere in the room. Including several empties.

Aruna shut her eyes tight and tried to imagine herself coming from somewhere far away straight into a room like this one. She tried to visualize herself hauling heavy milk bottles all her life. Going nowhere else, milk-booth and back till the day she died. Then from here being carried out for the first time, feet-first, straight to the cremation ground. Before which they would lay her out on the floor between the bed and the chair for people to pay their last respects, covered with a few flowers and surrounded by her empties. Aruna sent up a one-liner of deep gratitude, there was so much to be thankful for. She also resolved to spend more time with her sister.

Dr Sundeep Sardesai entered the library with a new determination. Even his spectacles glinted resolutely. Today was the day, he was going to tell her that he needed to meet her outside the hospital. By now they had been talking quite a bit. He knew she would be there because he asked her about all her timings, he knew exactly when her shifts were and he knew what time and when she went to the library. He managed to know from her what herogiri dialogues that Dr Samuel was aiming at her. Why he even knew that she had seen *Sangam* and *Guide* twice.

He spotted her in the library near the newspaper rack. Her chin dipped down towards the paper on a swanlike neck. Her pink, baby-pink lips were pursed in concentration while she read. Dr Sardesai cleared his throat near her, she looked up as though expecting him. 'You enjoy reading the English newspapers everyday, is it not?'

Her eyes danced. 'I read the newspapers to improve my general knowledge and my English.'

'Commendable, commendable.'

'What does that word mean?' she asked in Konkani.

He explained, adding virtues to the word not as yet attributed in any dictionary.

'Thank you. I feel it will help me with my entrance exams.'

'Oh, you are sitting for some examinations?'

'Not as yet, but I think I am going to be accepted this year for pursuing higher studies in nursing in London. I am sure they will also have an entrance exam, like the one I gave here at KEM. Better to be prepared. Forewarned is forearmed. I learned that phrase from reading the middle-page of the newspapers.'

Dr Sardesai felt as though someone had boxed him hard in the solar plexus. What was she saying, she was going away! How could she do that, but if she wanted to study further who was he to stop her, how could he do it. He exhaled, now or never. Let her decide Sundeep, you just ask her the question.

He opened his mouth. Staff nurse Aruna Shanbaug looked at her watch and said she had to rush, she had a lot of work to do before she got ready for her night duty at neurosurgery.

She was gone before he could close his mouth.

1.47 a.m. and all was well at the neurosurgery ward. Patients rested, silence reigned. At the nurses duty desk Aruna sat embroidering the pallav of another sari for Nirmala. She had loved the first one, squealed excitedly, worn it and modelled it in front of Ramdas who immediately wanted the front of his kurta embroidered in some impossible pattern of entwined tigers and peacocks. A patient groaned, Aruna quickly set aside her embroidery and walked over. The patient sighed and settled in. Aruna walked back to her table and got a small, pleasurable shock. Dr Sardesai stood there, looking at her.

'Good evening Dr Sardesai,' she whispered.

'Marry me,' he said loudly.

Instinctively Aruna looked around the ward quickly. 'Shhh,' she whispered. 'Can't you ask me this outside the hospital?'

'What do you think I'm trying to do all these days? Every time I open my mouth to ask you to meet me outside the hospital you tell me about your chats with Dr Samuel.'

Aruna laughed softly, she had never been happier in her life. 'Tell me where you want to meet me.'

'Your shift gets over at 7.00 tomorrow morning. Meet me at the main gate at 7.02.'

Aruna shook her head in amusement. 'All these months and years you haven't said anything. Suddenly so much hurry.'

'Tomorrow evening near Hanging Gardens at Cafe Naaz, 6.00 p.m. I will be waiting for you on the uppermost deck.'

Aruna nodded happily.

He turned to leave and turned around again. 'Staff nurse Shanbaug?'

She looked at him.

'Say yes, right now.'

'Yes doctor.'

Love was quite heavily in the air at Cafe Naaz. Couples sat at tables absorbed in each other. They had just watched the sun set. Below and ahead of them, Bombay had begun twinkling in a sweeping curve. The Queen's Necklace shimmered. Sundeep slipped a small, thin gold band on Aruna's wedding finger. 'Do you know that a vein is supposed to go straight from this finger to the heart?'

Aruna shook her head, she was beside herself with happiness. Right now every vein in her body went straight to her heart.

'Aruna, now listen to me carefully. I've given you this ring right away because I never want you, or anyone in your family or among your friends, to think I am not serious about marrying you. But we cannot marry right away. We can't marry until I have a flat of my own to bring you to as a bride. For that I will first have to establish my practice, and for this I have to finish my MD which I will very soon, by the next year end. This does mean that we will have to wait to get married till 1975 or so. Do you understand?'

Her heart sank slightly. Almost immediately a thought struck her and her spirits rose again. She nodded.

'After we marry I do not want you to work.'

'No?'

'No.'

'But why?'

'No, that's all no.'

'Okay.'

'What will you do if you get accepted by any of those English colleges for nursing?'

'I'll tear up the letter from them and throw it away,' replied Aruna with a giggle.

'Why are you giggling?'

'Nothing. How much money does it cost to set up a private clinic?'

'I don't know, I have to see but I'd like it to be in an area where decent people live, where our flat would also be close by. I suppose that will cost a little more than going to the far-flung suburbs.'

'Still, some figure.'

'Deposit for a clinic space on rent, renovating it and

down-payment for a flat, hmmm, let's see. Around Rs 50,000 to start with.'

Aruna's eyes were like saucers. 'Ayyo, that much!' she gasped. 'You should let me work after marriage, so that I can help with such big expenses.'

Sundeep smiled. 'Aruna, I'm going to be a specialist doctor. I will make enough money without even needing to resort to dirty tricks the way some doctors do with patients these days. I do not want you to worry about money. When you come into my house it will be happily as Mrs Aruna Sardesai, future mother of my children.'

'Children!'

'Why, what's the matter, you don't like children?'

'No, no, nothing like that. After marriage all women are supposed to have children.'

'Why do I get the impression you don't like them?'

'You like them?'

'Me, yes of course. But I don't want to have more than two children.'

'Me too. And we can have them much later after we get married, no hurry.'

It suddenly occurred to Sundeep that he did not know her age. 'How old are you, Aruna? When were you born?'

'1 June 1948. I have just turned twenty-four.'

'Hmmm, we won't be able to wait too long after we get married to have children. If we marry in '75 you will be twenty-seven. Women should not have babies too late, it endangers the child and the mother.'

'Achcha, we will have both children, fatafat, one after the other. We will start when I am twenty-nine and a half.'

Sundeep laughed loudly. 'Come on let's go. Otherwise your hostel gates will close.'

While he paid the bill, Aruna looked at the lights twinkling below. Bombay had never looked more beautiful.

Her sister had not said very much when Aruna told her about her unofficial engagement. She did not even ask to meet Sundeep. 'Have you informed Balakrishna?' was the only question. Aruna said she had to speak to Balakrishna personally about something so she would tell him when she went to Shimoga. She had dropped him a postcard informing him of her visit in the near future. Her sister hesitantly began saying something but let her sentence trail, 'Long engagements . . .'

'What about long engagements?'

Her sister shook her head. 'Don't roam around with him, especially outside the hospital, too much till your wedding. Keep your dignity. A man loses interest in a woman when she loses her mystery.'

Aruna was so astonished that she did not know what to reply. Her sister shook her head again, this time a small, tired movement, picked up her canvas bag filled with its empties and wearily clinked her way out of the house.

The next time Aruna visited, her sister had a gold chain for her, in a twisted rope pattern. 'For your wedding, start getting your jewellery slowly together. I melted some of the gold amma had given me on my wedding day and made two chains out of it.'

'But these must be for Mangala and Savitri,' said Aruna referring to her teenaged nieces. 'It's not fair that I take one when you have started making jewellery for your daughters.'

Her sister was stoic. 'Take it. I'll melt some more gold when the time comes.'

Aruna wore the chain immediately. On it she hung a small pendant. It was Savitri's, she wasn't wearing it and she lent it to Aruna. The pendant was hexagonal, with a flowery design within the hexagon and a border of tiny, suspended gold beads. It was pretty.

Usha Samant returned from her one-month-long leave to her village near Poona. Her sharp eyes noticed the new gold immediately. 'The bride is getting her ornaments ready, I see.'

Aruna blushed. 'What ornaments. My sister gave me the chain, the pendant has to be returned.'

'Is it? Then who is marrying Dr Sardesai, matron?'

They both giggled at the thought. Matron was a much older woman; a comfortable, maternal woman whom the nurses liked.

'So when is the wedding?'

'Still time.'

'All the nurses are talking about it. They envy you. You better marry him fast, otherwise one of these nurses will slyly slide into the picture.'

'And I will just sit and watch? Let them try, just let them try.'

'Oh ho, listen to this one! Still it's better to have the mangalsutra faster around the neck. Have you started collecting money for it?'

Aruna turned off the light in their room and smiled in the dark. The mangalsutra was already in the making. The money being collected for the ticket to London had come in handy.

'Turn off the damn radio. I want to sleep. This is certainly one of the many reasons why I wish you would get married first thing tomorrow morning.'

'You mean there are lots more reasons why you wouldn't want to be my room-mate?'

'Go to sleep Aruna, dream about your doctor-boyfriend.'

They really are a good match,' remarked Sister Premila Kushe as she watched staff nurse Aruna Shanbaug and Sundeep Sardesai walk ahead of them in the corridor.

It was a lazy, relaxed Sunday. It appeared that Dr Sardesai was on his rounds and Aruna was accompanying him. Sister Kushe was also on her pre-lunch rounds, walking till ward four with her was senior assistant matron Durga Mehta. Sister Mehta had returned enriched from the Royal College of Nursing in London and was in the process of trying to institute small, but relevant, changes for the betterment of nurses at KEM.

'In fact they are a right fit,' continued Sister Kushe. 'Physically also.' Sister Mehta was thoughtful, 'In our time did we have the guts to even question a doctor?' Sister Kushe replied, laughter mingling with genuine joy in her voice for the couple she could see ahead, 'Doctors don't marry nurses even today. I doubt if there will be another doctor-nurse marriage in KEM itself for a long time after this one. This is what makes this couple so special. It is a real-life romance.' They turned into ward four.

Aruna trotted alongside Sundeep, content, happy. And as always when she was with him, full of questions and conversation and observations. It was as if she had finally found a mental mate. The Chinese might have described their meeting as the perfect combination of yin and yang. He was dark, she was fair. He was ruminative, she was exuberant. He was the slow-fuse, she the fire-cracker. Today she was off but Sundeep was working so she had worn her uniform and appeared by his side when he started on his rounds. He was not expecting her, he had looked surprised but welcoming. 'I don't know what matron is going to say to this but the patients of KEM I am sure will be very grateful that off-duty nurses turn up for work.'

They walked into the children's ward and the two nurses

on duty nudged each other. 'Look at that docile little lamb walking obediently beside him, does he know he is the sacrificial goat? Nice bakra she has caught. Now she will follow him everywhere like a bakri or one of us will catch him, no?' The other nurse pursed her lips. 'Naseeb-naseeb ki baat hain. Fate.'

Aruna could have told them that destiny is according to thought. Or is it?

Aruna's big bubble of happiness was pricked just a bit when she was informed of her transfer to the dog lab. The board outside the huge room with its doctor's cabin, research and operation area on the terrace of KEM read: Surgical & Medical & Gastroenterological Experimental Laboratory. On the other side of the terrace were the kennels. Stray dogs, and those without collars, were caught by the BMC from Bombay's streets and kept for eight days in quarantine. The BMC's dog pound would also wait for any claimants. Often tearful owners would rush in, identify their dogs and walk away with them without even a word of gratitude for the corporation. Unclaimed, quarantined dogs were supplied to KEM for their experimental laboratory, simply called the dog lab. Even the wheelchair for humans—supplied as an oversight to the department and never sent back—had dog lab neatly stencilled in red on its back.

'I am a nurse,' she told Sundeep, almost tearfully. 'I have to look after people. Why should I go to the dog lab?'

Ever practical and the long-term thinker, Sundeep said, 'There are several bright sides. You won't have shifts in duty, it will be only the day shift. You will have no work-stress at all. It's a no-pressure posting so matron will easily grant you leave since you want to go to Shimoga. And the best part of all is that the dog lab in the CVTC basement is not operational as yet. So you will only have to sign in there. The entire day will be spent in this building in fresh air and good light.'

A new building had come up on one of the two extra sites that KEM had purchased at nominal cost from the BMC during its inception. It was across the road from the original stone structure and compared poorly in architecture. Tall, ungainly, painted a hideous pink, it was the CVTC, the Cardiovascular Thoracic Centre. But what it lost out in looks it made up in service. The number of people flocking to the free CVTC out-patient department grew every year. The OPD was at road level, on the ground floor. Below it, in the basement, was supposed to be the CVTC dog lab. However, it had not been made operational at the time the building was inaugurated and even till now. There were steps leading down to the basement, a door opening out into a long corridor on the right of which were dumped old files, medical records which by law could not be destroyed for a set period in time and a few mangled skeletons of rusted hospital beds. Straight down the corridor were two rooms, one opening into the second. The first the nurses duty room, the other the intended dog surgery and experimentation laboratory.

Doctors involved in experimental heart surgery on dogs preferred to work in the existing dog lab on top of the old building's terrace by habit. Besides, it was a much brighter place to work in than the dank, dark and dismal CVTC basement. Nurses were routinely assigned on duty at the CVTC dog lab. They checked into that duty room and quickly crossed the road to the other dog lab. They felt spooked in the basement.

Aruna didn't even like talking about it to Nirmala. 'Miserable,' she said.

'Which one are you referring to, the dog lab or your trip to Shimoga?'

Aruna had convinced matron to give her leave before she took on the dog lab duty. 'Both,' she replied. 'Just thinking that I have to report to the dog lab from tomorrow onwards is making me sick.'

'Why should it bother you so much? Just think of it as another job, 9.00 to 5.00.'

'Nimma, would you like to see dogs being killed in front of you every morning and afternoon?'

'Arrey, I didn't know you were an animal lover.'

'What does this have to do with loving animals? You mean if I don't love animals I should not mind if some are torn open every day?'

'Achcha baba jaane do. Tell me about your trip to Shimoga. Did you tell Balakrishna about Sundeep? What was his reaction?'

Aruna looked at Nirmala and wondered whether to tell her everything. She then decided against it. Some day Nimma might tell Sundeep, he would be furious and all that was unnecessary. She could have written to Balakrishna about Sundeep a long time back but she decided to visit him in Shimoga specifically so that she could ask him for a loan of Rs 50,000. She had told him it was for Sundeep's dispensary and that she needed it at the end of this year. He was a doctor, going to earn a lot of money, and he would start repaying the loan immediately. Balakrishna had asked her to look around his Udipi. 'Remember as you look that I am a partner in this place, and then tell me if I have the Rs 50,000 to give to you.' The conversation which followed had been equally dispiriting.

'Well?'

'Yes, I told Balakrishna about Sundeep. But somehow he did not appear too happy.'

'Maybe he has a boy in mind for you.'

'Not much point in that now, is it? Besides, how can there be anybody better than Sundeep?'

'Maybe Balakrishna worries that Sundeep will expect a very large dowry since he is a doctor, with a very grand wedding. Maybe he does not know Sundeep is GSB and also speaks Konkani. Maybe he is just upset that he is from Goa, how to check on the families of these out-of-the-state people. By the way, has Sundeep spoken to his family about you?'

'No.'

'Why not?'

'He says there is no need. He will tell them after his clinic is settled. When he is completely financially independent, his family might not have too many objections.'

'Why should his family object to you?'

'Why do families object? Caste, sub-caste, class, colour, character. Even if all these are okay, there is dowry.'

'Sundeep will stand by you, no?'

'You have met him when you came to the hospital, what do you think?'

Nirmala was succint, 'I like.' A thought struck her, 'He does not ask about your immediate family?'

'He has sort-of asked earlier, I have not said too much. It is best this way, this is how it must stay.'

'While you have been talking about Balakrishna, I've been thinking that . . .'

'Oh imagine, she thinks also!'

'Shut up. It's always nice when a girl's husband-to-be first meets some males from her family. Your brothers are all . . . well, they are not here for you at this time. Let us keep my appa out of this, he is also very old-fashioned. Why don't you introduce him to Ramdas?'

'I have been thinking that myself.'

Dr G.B. Parulkar, cardio-vascular and thoracic surgeon, sensed staff nurse Aruna Shanbaug's hesitation on her first day at work at the dog lab. He had heard of her engagement to that young Dr Sardesai, he noted she was pretty.

'Young lady,' he said, 'suppose your husband had to undergo sudden and immediate heart surgery. Would you like it if the surgeon cut him open and then couldn't decide between using one technique and another to try and save his life? Would you understand it if the surgeon told you that he could not make out which was a safer procedure because he had never done it before? Therefore do not underestimate laboratory work. Labs are always ahead of clinical work. We establish the safety of any procedure in the lab first, we need to do this. As an animal lover you will think of me as a beast for doing this to the poor, defenceless, innocent things. Would you rather I did it to your relatives?'

Inspite of herself Aruna was interested. 'Why dogs? Why not monkeys which are closer to humans?'

'Monkeys are both expensive and difficult to procure. Their maintenance and feeding would also be a problem for us. Monkeys would be unmanageable for our work. As we all know monkeys are not unlike humans, they would be difficult to handle.'

Everyone in the lab laughed. There were technicians Sambhaji Jethegaonkar and Pandurang Nemane who handled the heart-lung machine, the perfussion, everything that would have been used in the technical aspects of an operation on a human being. There was staff nurse Mary Joseph who also reported to the CVTC basement. The animal attendant Laxman Salunke and the sweepers Udayvir and Sohanlal joined in the general laughter too, although it was very apparent that they had not understood a word.

Aruna had more questions. 'Abroad also they use dogs?'

Dr Parulkar was pleased that she was being so attentive. She is good-looking and bright, she will be an asset as a doctor's wife to young Sundeep. 'They use several animals, they also use dogs. Their dogs are so big there, especially in America, almost like calves. When we Indian surgeons go there they are amazed at the precision of our fingers and our skill. They don't know it is because we have worked with such puny animals.'

Everyone laughed again, including the attendant and the sweepers. Aruna wanted to know what was the first operation Dr Parulkar had performed on the dogs.

'Let me think, that would have been in 1959, a long time back when I was a lecturer. We started the dog lab then. At that time we did very simple heart-lung exercises, simple to us now but very exciting then. There were several in-built problems, like the blood of dogs is very vulnerable to plastic tubes. More deaths as a result. But then their blood groups are not strong like humans so a little bit of mismatching was alright. We did heart transplants which included myocardial preservation. At any normal time have you felt your heart beat? Think of a surgeon taming that heart for surgery, keeping it tamed through surgery and then bringing it back to full beat. Taming the heart is no easy task. You could say it is a muscle with a mind of its own. But there will come a time, soon, when we will subdue the heart down to twenty per cent of its pumping capacity and still make it come back completely after surgery. There will be such machines and there will be surgeons so skilled in the technique that they will match their precision with that of the machine to produce medical miracles. Do you know how all this will happen?'

Everyone shook their heads in the negative.

'Exactly the way it has happened till now. With us performing our operations first in our dog labs. Right?'

'Right!' everyone chorused.

'Right, let us scrub down and prepare for the operation. Please bring a dog from the kennels, a small one will do.'

Aruna felt slightly nauseous, more so when Sohanlal brought in the canine from the kennels on a dog chain. It was a white, fluffy pomeranian and it was happily wagging its tail. Aruna swallowed, this just wouldn't do. She would have to resolutely bite down her bile. She managed with some very deep breaths and scrubbed down for the operation. One more operation in the dog lab and Dr Parulkar was impressed. Staff nurse Aruna Shanbaug was not only good-looking and bright but also very sensitized during the operations. She understood exactly what the doctor wanted. That Sundeep Sardesai was one lucky dog.

Ramdas thought Aruna was the very lucky one. He was impressed with Dr Sundeep Sardesai. He was, in fact, in awe of him. Ramdas with his traditional horror for hospitals, doctors and allopathic medicines had never met a doctor before on a personal level. Now Ramdas' awe was mixed with delight. Aruna coming into his life like an elder sister had introduced him to the pleasures of being professionally nursed when he had typhoid. Next time onwards when he was sick—and may that take its own time, he was in no hurry to test it himself—he would happily go to Dr Sardesai, uh, Sundeep.

Aruna had organized their meeting, she had chosen the place with care. An Udipi would not do, they were vegetarian places. To save on excess taxi fare, it should not be too far from the hospital. It should be comfortable for Ramdas to come from Agripada as well. It should not be too expensive, after all they were saving for his dispensary, but it should be somewhat posh. It should serve sensible non-vegetarian but tasty food. It should not serve alcohol, Sundeep did not smoke or drink, thank God. Aruna settled on Hotel Persian Darbar, opposite Palace cinema in Byculla.

The fake-glass chandeliers overhead glittered satisfactorily. Families clustered at tables laughed, chatted, ordered far too much food. Fathers sat children on their knees and fed them bite-sized bits of roti, momentarily relaxed mothers looked on indulgently. Soon all this would be hers too, the closeness and the cohesiveness of a family. It should be. Very soon.

Aruna looked at Sundeep and Ramdas tucking away into a fragrant biryani, chatting away in Konkani like long-lost friends. She tuned in, they were talking about Udipis in the city. Ramdas, keen to impress upon Sundeep his knowledge of the subject, pointed out that GSB sons in Bombay were not as keen in taking over the running of the Udipis from their fathers. They wanted to become engineers and doctors, no offence meant to Dr Sardesai of course, he added hastily. The Shettys and their sons would take over the running of the Udipis, by which time everybody would be selling idli-vada-dosa and this would make for so much competition that the Udipis would be forced to sell Chinese food.

Sundeep laughed but said Ramdas was probably right. Another factor would be the rising rentals on commercial space, this would force all restaurants to broad-base their menu. Ramdas asked if rentals on doctor's dispensaries were also very high. 'He is going to be a specialist in a clinic. He's not going to run a dispensary,' interjected Aruna loftily. 'What do you think, he is some small doctor with a dawakhana and a silly compounder?' Sundeep shushed down Aruna, an emboldened Ramdas informed her that she must have chewed on blades as a child. The conversation on rentals resumed with Sundeep elaborating on his professional and personal plans, they were very closely interlinked, he pointed out. 'With men it is always like that,' nodded Ramdas in complete approval and agreement.

'Why?' asked Aruna very suddenly.

'Why what?' questioned Ramdas.

'Why should men put all their personal plans always on hold for work first? Isn't personal happiness and peace equally important? Why should a woman come second to work? Women don't do that to men. Men even get angry when women try to put their work first.'

Sundeep was listening to Aruna very attentively while looking at a glass of water on the table. He did not take his eyes off the glass as he said, 'I am not putting you after my work. I have no home to take you to, I have to work first to achieve this.'

Ramdas made warning eyes at Aruna, do not let that tongue of yours run away with you again.

Aruna ignored Ramdas. 'Why can't we work on buying our home together? We can stay in a rented flat in the meanwhile. Hundreds and thousands of couples do.'

Sundeep was quiet, still looking at the glass. Ramdas realized that he had to do, or say, something as the male of Aruna's family otherwise she would really upset Sundeep and then God knows what would happen. 'Look here Aruna, I know you are the last person to listen to anybody. But this is not a good time to suddenly start doing chik-chik. No need to nag. Let him at least finish his MD, it is only a few months away, at the end of this year. Let him get his clinic space, then you two can always have a fresh round of discussion. Is that okay Sundeep?'

Sundeep looked up from the glass at Ramdas who was peering at him anxiously and nodded his assent.

Nirmala had much to say after Ramdas narrated the conversation at Hotel Persian Darbar to her. Aruna and she were having their customary coffee at the Udipi closest to the Mahalakshmi mandir. 'I don't know what has got into you Aruna. All this time you are okay, suddenly you start rushing him. Must be all those modern women's magazines you keep reading. The women who write in those women's magazines, do they themselves follow what they want ordinary middle-class women to do? I really wonder.'

'I just want to have a normal life, like normal women with normal families. What is wrong with that?'

'Nothing is wrong with it. But in the beginning itself Sundeep explained things to you, and you agreed. Did you not? Then what is the hurry?'

'Why delay?'

'Are you worried something will happen in the middle? Has Sundeep said anything?'

Aruna was silent. Nirmala ordered another round of South Indian filter coffee. From a height she expertly poured the scalding hot contents of one tumbler into the dabra, the small steel bowl sitting on the table, forming cream-coloured froth, and passed it on to Aruna, 'Do you know why they do that in the South?'

'To cool the coffee.'

'Tchah-tchah, what kind of Kannadiga are you? Filter coffee is served with pure milk. When the milk is heated milk-cream forms on top. But when poured into the tumbler and mixed with the filter coffee that disgusting brown skin appears on top as it cools. The froth on top prevents this from happening while allowing the coffee to cool in its own sweet time.'

Aruna had not been paying attention.

'Aruna, you have been out-of-mood ever since you came back from Shimoga. You are that upset about Balakrishna's reaction? Forget it yaar. We are there for you.'

'You are not there, you are getting married in May. Where will Mrs Nirmala Telang be staying after her wedding?'

'He has booked a flat in Borivli.'

'So far!'

'Yah, it's very far. I really don't know how I will manage those crowded train rides to and fro from Borivli. By road it's impossible, someone was telling me from Borivli to Agripada will take me at least two hours by bus.'

'Anyway you are not working, so it will be only the occasional local train ride into the city. You can carry your peas along, I am told the women in the women's compartment peel their dinner vegetables on their way back home in the train itself.'

'And if I run short of spinach I'll just lean out of the running train and grab it from the side of the tracks,' added Nirmala chuckling.

Aruna gave a wan smile, then sighed. 'Back to the dog lab tomorrow. I'm hating the thought.'

'You still feel bad for those dogs?'

'More so, ever since I've discovered that their food is being stolen by one of the sweepers.'

'I don't understand. Why should a sweeper be concerned with a dog's food? And how can anyone steal dog food, chhee, chhee.'

'Nimma, good mutton and milk is being served to the dogs, not some sidey-rubbish left over from the butcher's. The food comes from the patients' diet department, it is wholesome, clean and fresh. We have ten dogs at any given time in the dog lab. Can you now see how much of milk and meat that horrible sweeper can sideline day after day when he gets it from the diet department?'

'But how can you be so sure that it is he only who is doing it? There may be other sweepers also involved.'

'The other sweepers are not authorized to go to the diet department, only Sohanlal is. Before Sohanlal the animal attendant Laxman Salunke got the food from the diet department and fed it to the dogs. Since Laxman is on leave from Diwali the job of getting and feeding has been given to this Sohanlal.'

'But how do you know he is not giving the food to the dogs? Do they tell you?'

'Don't joke. I know because I have observed what is happening. The dogs have started looking hungry. They howl. The day I catch him red-handed I'll have him sacked. As it is he is very bad at his work. He's arrogant. I've already complained once about his arrogance to the custodian, Jaisinh Jadhav. Technician Jethegaonkar asked him to do some other urgent lab work which Laxman used to do. He flatly refused. Then I asked him to run an errand for me, to go to the laundry to pick up my clothes, Laxman used to do these small things for us. The way he answered back, as though I was kachraa. I had to complain to Jadhav who came to the dog lab and reprimanded him in front of all of us.'

'Okay, enough of all this now. Don't you get involved with all the internal rubbish of the dog lab. This sweeper's name suggests he is from up north somewhere. People from the north are very rough, no point crossing them. Do you hear me?'

'Tomorrow if I am in the maternity ward and I find some nurse is not giving the babies their milk, will I not do something about it?'

'It is not the same thing.'

'It is, to watch a sin taking place and do nothing about it is a bigger sin. Besides, it's my department. I am posted there and it is my responsibility.'

'How long are you going to be there in this damn dog lab?'

'I don't know, but I have been thinking that since the dog lab posting my timings are more regular, I should shift out of the nurses hostel.'

'Oh really, and go where?'

'To my sister's at BDD chawls.'

Nirmala called for another round of coffee. There were times when Aruna's brain raced far too fast. 'First of all, you don't like BDD chawls. Secondly, what will you achieve by shifting there?'

'They cut hostel and food expenses directly from my salary. If I'm not staying in the hostel, all that money will be saved. I can set that money aside for the deposit on our rented flat. When we get our own flat the deposit can be used to buy things for our house.'

'So you have decided that you will not wait till the end of 1975. Means you will be married within the next one year. Nice. But does the bridegroom know any of this?'

Aruna shook her head. 'He will not agree, so what's the point in asking? Might as well just do it and present it as something that cannot be changed. Wait I'll tell you the word, I read it in the papers that day. Inevitable.'

'Are you going to save so much money that you have spent so much thought on it?'

'I hear an LIC advertisement on the radio quite often. They sing a Hindi poem. Boond boond se nadi bane, nadi nadi se saagar. In other words, with boonds, that is drops, a river is formed, and with rivers, made the ocean.'

'Very nice. But what makes you think you will save any

boond by shifting to your sister's house? Her situation is not good, you only told me. So money will have to be spent on food anyway. An additional expenditure, which you do not incur living in the hostel, will be the bus fare to and from the hospital. One good thing since you have met Sundeep and started worrying about this dispensary and flat business, you've completely stopped taking taxis.'

'Nimma, I've worked it all out. The money which I will need to give my sister for my food will also feed one more person in the house, so she will be happy to have me. This is how it is with poor families, I have seen amma stretching money and food in Haldipur to unimaginable limits. As for the bus fare, there's a slightly shorter cut from behind BDD and Worli to Parel which I have been using. I will keep walking it.'

Nirmala rolled her eyes heavenwards. 'Even God will not understand how you think. I absolutely forbid you to shift out of the hostel, I do not even want to discuss this with you anymore. You are overdoing this. Imagine thinking you can walk through all that wet garbage and slush during the monsoon.'

'I won't have to. I will be married by then.'

Sister Shashikala Vaaran realized she had not been the only one. Two other nurses had told her of a similar experience in the not-too-distant past. It had been established by all that Dr Sundeep Sardesai was a kind, patient and good doctor. He had also established that he thought of nurses as human beings instead of treating them like glorified medical ayahs the way some doctors did. Not unexpectedly then, nurses had been approaching him first when they felt ill or when their relatives came to KEM for treatment. Lately, though, nurses were having second thoughts. Dr Sardesai's fiance, staff nurse Aruna Shanbaug, had been using that sharp tongue of hers like a saw on them; the last recepient had been Sister Shashikala Vaaran.

Sister Vaaran had taken an aged uncle to Dr Sardesai and had been both, pleased and thankful for the diagnosis which prescribed very little strong medication. The next thing she knew she had Sister Shanbaug standing in front of her in the staff room.

'Is there only one doctor in KEM?'

'Obviously not,' said Sister Vaaran who could be quite crisp herself.

'Just keep that in mind in the future.'

'What will happen if I don't?' wondered aloud Sister Vaaran.

'We'll have to see when the time comes.' With that Sister Shanbaug left the staff room.

Sister Vaaran watched her trim figure go with interest. Sister Shanbaug was her senior by a few years, for as long as Sister Vaaran could remember she had always been dressed like this, neat and tidy. She's good-looking, thought Sister Vaaran, she need not worry about losing him. Maybe it's just her military-type nature, she feels she has to be kadak all the time. Sister Vaaran had seen Sister Shanbaug on duty in the wards. She would behave like a red-belt, not the blue-belt she was, the way she would check the toilets attached to the ward, the patients themselves and the beds they slept on for whether their bedsheets were turned correctly into hospital corners. Sister Vaaran thought Sister Shanbaug was a very disciplined nurse, very committed. Everybody had some fault, maybe Sister Shanbaug's was the muscle in her mouth.

People in the dog lab also thought that Sister Aruna

Shanbaug behaved like a red-belt, they just did not have the guts to say this to her. She might have even been pleased to hear it, this alleviation of rank. She checked the heart-lung machine, the cardiac defillibrator, the respirator, all the other tiny instruments that were so important in cardiac and vascular surgery, the sutures, the drugs, the gloves and the linen. Linen. This blood-soaked lot had not been washed from the morning's operation. Setting the instruments to be sterilized for the afternoon's surgery, Aruna looked for Udayvir or Sohanlal. Udayvir had not come to work that day, Sohanlal stood on the terrace behind the kennels smoking a bidi.

Aruna sniffed, smoking was clearly not allowed on the premises. She looked at the smouldering bidi and said shortly, 'Smoking is not allowed in the dog lab.'

Sohanlal looked straight at her, 'This is the terrace.' He was squat, dark, heavily built, with flat, glittering eyes.

'Please come in immediately,' she said, crossed the terrace and entered the dog lab to check on the sterilization. Sohanlal took his own time in getting there. 'Why is the linen from the morning's operation not washed as yet?' Sohanlal stood there and stared at her, his eyes glittering. Aruna repeated her question.

'I will do it with the afternoon operation's sheets.'

Aruna raised her eyebrows. 'This is also how you feed the dogs, only once a day, isn't it?'

Sohanlal said nothing, his face was impassive, he crossed his arms over his chest, kept staring at her.

Aruna felt uncomfortable. 'People who steal food meant for dogs will die like dogs themselves.'

Sohanlal uncrossed his arms, leaned forward as though about to walk up to Aruna's table, changed his mind, mocked her with his glittering eyes and walked out of the dog lab without taking the blood-soiled linen with him.

Aruna found herself shaking. Stop it, she told herself, you can't allow some sweeper to frighten you like this. She picked up the internal line and asked the operator to connect her to custodian Jaisinh Jadhav. When he came on the line she told him clearly of what had transpired and asked him to treat it as her second complaint. She did not tell him about her conviction that Sohanlal was stealing the dogs' food, for that she would get the proof and have him sacked once and for all. Right now it would be her word against his, she didn't see any reason why what she said should even appear to be suspect.

The silence in the vicinity was suddenly shattered by the sound of several people rushing up to the dog lab, talking loudly among themselves. They were strangers, visitors, what were they doing here? They were from a group of dog-lovers which claimed to be attached to the Society for Prevention of Cruelty to Animals. They had heard that surgeries were being performed on dogs here, that the animals were being kept in inhuman conditions, that they were not being fed at all and to stop them from howling with hunger their vocal chords had been chopped off.

The agitators stood in front of the nurses duty desk and very loudly began demanding to see the dogs. The dogs in their kennels had by then sensed a strange presence and set up a volley of barking. There they were, all around her, humans and dogs barking away. Aruna sat at the duty desk, feeling her strength draining rapidly out of her. The voices and barks receded suddenly in a swathe of sound, Aruna closed her eyes for a fraction of a second to enjoy what appeared like weightlessness. There was a hand on her shoulder, 'Sister?' Aruna swallowed, told them they were welcome to check the kennels but could she please see the dean's written permission allowing them to be on the premises since these were not visiting hours. They said they didn't have it. Aruna picked up

the phone and called security who came and whisked the
agitators away to the dean's office.

When Sister Prema Pai came looking for Sister Aruna
Shanbaug for some 'time-pass on the terrace' till lunch-time
got over, she found her holding her head in her hands, her
elbows on the table, eyes downcast, looking completely lost
and tired. Like a child who has been out to the circus, all
alone, for far too long.

Turning-points in a life do
not necessarily have to announce themselves with fanfare or
come underlined. Sometimes they do not even have to appear
as turning-points; it is enough that they happen so that subconsciously stock can be taken, and apparently solid decisions
be reviewed.

When she woke the next morning, Aruna felt emotionally
younger, lighter, almost free. Nirmala would have described
it as Aruna's pre-Shimoga self. She hummed as she dressed,
the radio on and waking Usha who liked to sleep late when
she had to report for afternoon shifts. Usha chucked her
pillow at the radio, narrowly missing it. Aruna turned up the
volume on the radio, picked up the pillow from the floor,
walked over to Usha's bed, yanked her up by the neck of her
nightgown, dropped the pillow under her head, let go of her
nightgown to allow her head and neck to flop onto the
pillow, smiled and left for duty.

Usha was slightly amazed. 'She has actually left the radio
out and gone instead of locking it up the way she has been
doing all these years. Somebody is in a really good mood,
doctorsaab must be setting the wedding date today.'

Aruna clocked in at the basement in the CVTC and

quickly crossed the road to the old stone building, ran up the stairs and rapidly wrapped up her morning duties in the dog lab. When the clock struck 10.00 a.m., she told Sister Mary Joseph to cover for her and made her way to the ground floor of the main wing. Crossing the dean's office she walked three doors down and turned into what they called nursing establishment. Every nurse who had been through KEM—including Mrs Marion McCarthy who was the head of the nursing department founded officially in 1926—first became a file. Each nurse was also numerically stored in the several steel cupboards lining the walls of nursing establishment, according to the year of joining.

It took some time for it to be calculated that staff nurse Aruna Shanbaug had a total of 113 days paid leave to her credit. Could she take it all at once? That would have to be checked, said the lady clerk, depending upon the casual leave Aruna had taken, and whether medical leave could be bunched with privilege leave. Unpaid leave? Until three months should not be any problem, replied the clerk. Could paid and unpaid be taken one after the other? Paid would have to be taken first, anyway what was all this about? If staff nurse Shanbaug told her the reason, accordingly, she could advise her on how best to juggle the leave.

Aruna smiled, 'I'm getting married.'

The clerk was enthusiastic, she had heard of this doctor-nurse romance and the staff nurse's name but had never seen her. Pretty girl, she looked so happy too. 'That's very nice, congratulations. When is the wedding date?'

'That's what I'm trying to decide through the leave-position.'

'You can apply for your medical leave separately, but you will have to submit a doctor's certificate.'

'That should be no problem at all.'

The clerk returned Aruna's smile with a second thought. 'I am not sure if doctor-husbands can sign medical certificates for their nurse-wives if both of them are attached to the same hospital. I will have to check.'

All the checking and cross-checking took its own while. No one appeared to know the answer to the clerk's second thought, every one agreed it was an unusual case indeed. The dean's personal assistant was also at a loss when posed the question. Finally it was decided that the query would be addressed to the BMC. A phone call was put through, this was an answer only the relevant section-head could give, he was on leave. No they did not know for how long, try next week. 'Arrey but the nurse has to apply for leave accordingly, to get married.' 'Oho asa kaay, then better to consult the deputy commissioner's personal assistant.' He was not at his desk, call back after fifteen minutes.

When Aruna left nursing establishment around lunchtime she had filled two forms. One informed nursing establishment that she would not be staying in the hostel, she would be a non-residential nurse from 1 November 1973. The second form was her leave application, beginning 1 December 1973.

There wasn't all that much to do in preparation for the wedding. It would be a simple one, in the temple in front of God. Whoever wanted to attend from the family could, they needed the money for their flat, so they could not afford to make a big fuss. Book a big hall because you have to call so many people, then feed them, smile at them while they give you rubbish gifts you do not want and watch them waste the food your hard-earned money has paid for. The next morning everybody goes to the toilet, there goes the money too. An indirect way of flushing cash. No their wedding would not be like that, Sundeep would see her logic.

She would have to get a gold ring made for Sundeep, she knew his size and would order it when she went to pick up her mangalsutra which was lying at the jewellers. Nurses were not allowed to keep ornaments in the hostel, she would take the mangalsutra directly to BDD. She would need a small cupboard for her clothes at BDD, she would pick it from the pavement cupboard stalls at Dongri. Sister Placida D'Silva had done that when she got married last month. The Dongri pavement cupboard stallwallahs purchased second-hand cupboards from people, repaired them, painted and polished them really nicely, and sold them as good as new. They even delivered the cupboard to your house for a small extra cost on a handcart. She would have the cupboard delivered to BDD.

Instead of a small one, should she buy a big cupboard for both of them? When she had gone there with Sister Placida, they had chosen a big wooden one for her and her husband. It was solid wood with nice carving on the top. The cupboard seller quoted a fancy price saying it was an 'antick', the family had to sell it because they had fallen on bad times. Sister Placida had immediately said if that was the case she definitely did not want the cupboard, why bring bad luck into your home, that too at such a high cost. The man had eventually sold the cupboard for much less.

She would take Sister Prema Pai with her to choose the cupboard, before that she would need to go to the bank. The Canara Bank branch was right here near the hospital, she would keep this account open until they moved into their own flat. New flat, new bank account with new surname, new life; of such pleasant thoughts are plans of new beginnings.

Sundeep's plan of which speciality to choose had also begun crystallizing most satisfactorily. He had, in his methodical manner, made a list of his areas of medical interest. By a fine-toothed process of elimination, which included the weighing of pros and cons, like long-term growth of the disease, he had arrived at diabetes. Just in case he had erred in judgement, he had sat Aruna in front of him and debated diabetes with her. At the end Aruna said she thought it was a great idea because people would never stop being greedy for sweets. Sundeep doubled with laughter and then quickly sobered up when he heard what Aruna had to say. As always he was amazed how much Aruna had her ear to the ground.

She had heard that a particular doctor in KEM was planning on opening a special diabetes centre in Chembur, why didn't Sundeep go and speak frankly to him. Sundeep hesitated. Go, she said.

'He might take it amiss. He is a very senior doctor,' pointed out Sundeep.

'His seniority is all the more reason why you should go to him right away. If his knowledge is true and for the benefit of mankind, he will have no ego about sharing it with you. Senior doctors taking junior doctors under their wing is part of our Indian tradition, the guru-shishya parampara.'

'What?'

'Pandit Ravi Shankar said in the papers the other day that it was his duty to teach young Indians how to play the sitar, it was part of our guru-shishya parampara. Teacher-student relationship, you know.'

'It amazes me, how carefully you read the newspapers. The doctor might not have read Ravi Shankar's noble words in the papers, he might not even care and might simply throw me out.'

'You do not know that until it happens, which it might

not. If he does throw you out he is stupid and it his loss. I'm saying try, what do we stand to lose? Go.'

Sundeep went. The doctor knew of Sundeep, had heard of his excellent academic and practical performance and was so impressed by Sundeep's sincerity that he spoke with him at length about his plans for starting the diabetes hospital in Chembur. It would take time but till then he saw Sundeep working in this diabetes department and some day, depending upon his performance of course, he saw Sundeep taking over as head of the department.

Aruna was ecstatic. These were all very good signs. She used the opportunity to tell Sundeep about her plans to shift to her sister's and her application for the long leave which had been granted. Sundeep smiled his agreement.

Ramdas finally made his quantum leap. He stepped into the hospital all by himself, quite pleased that he had conquered what now appeared like an utterly silly phobia. Aruna took him around KEM, introduced him to several doctors as 'my brother' which made Ramdas feel very grand. She showed him an operation theatre, how it functioned, explained all the machines, turned on the overhead saucer lights for his benefit. She took him to another operation theatre where, from an ante-room, she let him watch an operation in progress for a few minutes. Ramdas remarked that it was all very cold and clinical, not at all like in the movies.

'That's because there's no background music in real life. Haven't you ever noticed how in the Hindi movies they always have heartbeats in the background of an operation scene, dhak-dhak, dhak-dhak, even when it is not a heart operation?'

Ramdas wanted to see where Aruna worked. She pulled a face, 'I don't like working there at all.' He wheedled her into it, she took him up to the dog lab. It was a very light day, no operations scheduled. Everyone was sitting around in the dog lab reading papers and magazines including the sweeper Inder. Aruna pulled out some money from her pocket and asked Inder to get a Mangola for Ramdas from the KEM staff canteen. 'Can you send them for personal work like that?' asked Ramdas.

'I should not, but we all do when there isn't any other department work.'

'They never refuse? Supposing they do, it will look so bad.'

'These are not permanent workers, they are badli. The ones who are part of unions can be difficult. Of course, there are some of these temporary fellows who don't even do what they are paid to. Come on, let me show you around the lab and kennels till your Mangola comes.'

Ramdas was pleasantly surprised at the cleanliness of the kennels. 'In fact everything in this department is so clean and neat.'

'Of course, it is my department, I make sure it's always like this.'

'The dogs also look tidy and well-fed.'

'That is now in the last few days because Inder has been taking care of them. That other horrible sweeper Sohanlal has not been turning up to work which is very good for the dogs. Sohanlal steals their mutton, like a vulture. I am just waiting for some proof. The next time he does it, I will report him immediately.'

Ramdas looked perturbed. 'Maybe you should just warn him.'

'I have, twice.'

'You mean you have called him a thief to his face?'

'Yes, seedha bol diya.'

'Aruna, these people are bhangees, scavengers, you must see aagey-peechey with them. Be careful.'

'Of what?'

'I don't know, just be careful.'

'He also drinks up their milk outside the diet department itself. I don't see how he can take that much milk home without being caught.'

'Maybe he is very poor and therefore hungry all the time.'

'Inder is also a sweeper, he is also poor. So is Udayvir, the other sweeper. They do not steal. Being poor does not give you the right to be wrong. There is also a big difference between genuine hunger and greed for anything including food. This is applicable to everyone irrespective of whether you are rich, poor or middle-class like you and me.'

'Where is the inclination for such philosophy in a place like Bombay?'

'This is not philosophy, it is religion. All religions teach the same good morals. In Bombay the temples, mosques and churches are so crowded, I wonder how many people in them are actually learning from their religion.'

They leaned against the parapet of the terrace and looked at the backview of Bombay in wide-angle. Smoke-stacks rising from mills freely spewing black poison, low urban sprawls under them. Huddled, resentful structures harbouring inner-city hate.

Sister Prema Pai and Aruna emerged from the movie hall giggling. They had been in splits for the better part of the film, sending out little explosions of uncontrolled laughter in the otherwise quiet, darkened theatre. Bar two or three half-hearted shushes from the balcony area, nobody objected. There weren't too many to object, Plaza cinema at Dadar was almost empty. The film was a re-run of an old one, undoubtedly a disaster when it had first been released.

Aruna and Prema had entered on a whim. They had come to Dadar to do a reconnaisance on a wedding sari for Aruna. Neither had liked anything, their next search for a wedding sari was going to re-commence, on their next leave, at Matunga. 'Something in silk but simple and South Indian will be just right,' felt the bride-to-be. Both were specific about their choice of colour, red. Auspicious, what was more it would sit very well on Aruna's fair skin.

All sojourns outside their immediate environment have to be rounded off with a good bout of snacking before returning to yucky dinners, it's an unwritten rule followed implicitly by all hostelites. Aruna dragged Prema to Dadar TT to the snack shop famous for its super-soft dhoklas and crunchy kaanda bhajiyas. They stood on the pavement outside the shop and ate, traffic roared and dispersed in all directions around Dadar circle. 'Why do they call it Dadar TT?'

'Gote illa.'

'What?'

'That means I don't know in Kannada,' said Aruna. 'You should know anyway, you are born and brought up here.'

They asked the man dispensing the bhajiyas and bhel puris. He said maybe the TT stood for tram terminus as this used to be the last stop for them. He asked if they wanted a round of paani puris. 'No, no I have to go home and eat,' said Prema. 'Yes, yes,' said Aruna.

Prema watched Aruna opening her mouth wide to

accommodate the entire puffed puri with its spicy filling and liquid. Some of it spilled over her lower lip, dribbling down the side of her chin. Prema felt a twinge of irritation. 'How do you manage to eat that much and still remain so slim?'

'Gote illa.'

'Nothing happens to your skin either. I eat one deep-fried snack and pimples erupt all over my face.' The irritation increased.

Aruna shrugged, tipped up her chain to pop another puri into her mouth without getting its paani all over her face.

'You are lucky,' said Prema, 'very lucky.'

'You are casting the evil eye on my looks,' laughed Aruna.

Prema laughed as well, but her eyes did not. 'Not just your looks. I wish I had what you did.'

'I read this in a magazine just yesterday, if wishes were horses beggars would ride.'

Prema flushed with anger. 'Come on, it is getting late, let us go.'

'Late? But it's only six o' clock. What's your hurry? Come on let's go see what the movie is at Plaza. I've never seen a Marathi movie before. If it's interesting we'll watch it.'

'Then it will get really late, your hostel gate will close and my mother will throw me out.'

'We'll leave the movie half-way if it's boring. Come on!'

The film was meant to be a weepie, at least two hankies. Aruna and Prema could not stop laughing at this retrograde rubbish. There was a joint family and everyone sang songs together. But then the wicked, wicked daughter-in-law, the soonbai, came and ruined everyone's happiness. The father-in-law just fell down and died mid-dialogue, the mother-in-law started coughing, one brother left the house in disgust, the other got kicked out by the evil soonbai, the daughter of the house was made to do the dishes, this went on and on until the director ran out of ideas on how to be horrible to humans without physically hurting them.

After the interval the director focussed on the wicked woman's continuous attempts to become pregnant and failing each time. Finally, she met a sadhu who said this was because she had been a witch to her in-laws, only after her paschataap—deep, heartfelt, enormous repentence which could possibly include grovelling—would she conceive. The woman ran home and clutched her coughing mother-in-law's feet, a giggling Aruna and Prema made their exit to the bus stop.

'Supposing her mother-in-law were to give her one kick and say she did not care if her husband's family name didn't carry on, she would not forgive the witch, that would be funny.'

'Suppose the witch had to turn around and tell the sadhu to get lost,' laughed Prema, 'that would have been really funny. She should have told him she would adopt a child instead of changing her personality.'

Aruna burst into a fresh set of giggles. 'Then she would have offended her husband also. Males are so particular about their own seed. I realized it the other day when I was assisting Dr Pardanani on one of his operations in the dog lab.'

Their bus arrived, it was jampacked, they pushed their way in and stood on the steps between the upper and lower decks to continue their conversation. Prema said she did not know what Dr Pardanani specialized in.

'Arrey, all this only. Andrology. Mardon ki mardaangi, their internal-external plumbing.'

'Oh, like that! Yah that makes sense then, working with dogs.'

Both laughed. Aruna explained that the doctor had been trying to get a silicone shunt in place. 'If the vas deferens is cut and the male wants to have a child, this would act like a rubber-band of sorts.'

'The government should ban all doctors from doing anything scientifically that would increase the population. Stop all research on reproduction until the population stabilizes.'

'Pass a law in Parliament, every second child has to be an adopted one. That will help both adoption and population contol.'

'Would you, adopt I mean?'

'I don't know Prema, it would also depend on Sundeep. I would not mind having one and adopting one. It would be a good thing to do provided we treated them both equally.'

'Hmm, one's own blood could get all the attention making the adopted one feel neglected.'

'Actually, I was worried about it happening the other way around. Because the child is adopted you lavish extra attention on it and wind up neglecting the natural one. If you adopt you really have to maintain a balance, not to spoil or neglect the child even if you have only one child and it is adopted. Would you adopt, Prema?'

They moved around on the staircase to allow passengers from above to disembark at their stop. The bus screeched to a halt, passengers would have been thrown against each other if they had space to move. Prema noted drily that the bus was the best example of how childbirth should simply be banned for the next five years in the country. 'My sister was married to this haraami who has a reproductive problem, he was really scum, and they just shoved all the blame on my sister. My father took up the matter with her in-laws to set things right but haraamipana runs in that family's blood. He even suggested that no matter where the fault lay, they could think of adopting an heir to their family name and wealth. You know what that old bat, my sister's mother-in-law said? "No, who knows what kind of blood will come into the house".'

Aruna was quiet, this was the first time Prema was talking about her family. 'Maybe by blood she meant madness or something. Suppose there had been insanity in that child's parents' or grandparents' line? Imagine thinking you are doing such a noble thing and you wind up adopting a nut. Is madness hereditary?'

'Like that the child could have diabetes or be prone to cancer. Or some new disease which we don't know about as yet but which becomes very important fifteen years later and the child would have those germs all along. Maybe the child is being adopted for furthering the lineage and turns out to be impotent, how can you ever tell.'

Prema nodded, 'If bad luck has to come, it will no matter what.'

'If you are saying that, does it mean you would adopt?'

'The way things look, my sister is back at home as a divorcee, there are other problems, I do not think any decent proposals will come for me from the community. There will only be the kind who call themselves innocent divorcees, or there might be widowers with ten children who will want me as their unpaid ayah. So I don't think marriage is in my naseeb. Maybe I should adopt a child.'

'That would be very, very bold. But do they give single women permission to adopt?'

'I don't know. I will ask my father who did all that research on adoption to try and save my sister's marriage.'

'Supposing they do, is it correct to bring a child into your house and not give it the love of both a father and a mother?'

'I could try, I need not lie to it that I am its natural mother. In fact I would not, just in case the poor child grows up thinking it is a bastard because of my bad behaviour.'

'Then why adopt, why not sponsor a child in an orphanage, his food and education? I see a lot of articles on that in the papers and magazines.'

'So that there will be someone to look after me in my old age.'

'But that is selfish!'

'You think natural parents have children for any other reasons than sex and selfishness? If they were unselfish wouldn't they raise better citizens instead of the junglee children we see these days? Okay here's my stop, I've got to get down. See you tomorrow, ta-ta.'

Aruna reached her stop, disembarked and walked to the hostel. There was a note waiting for her with the watchman from Sundeep. It was cryptic, its contents struck a crippling blow.

'Diabetes department head died suddenly at 6.30 p.m., age forty-three.'

Neither had slept much in the night. Sundeep looked completely shattered. Aruna was distraught. The heat and noise were adding to it. Everyone in the hospital appeared irritated. Septembers were not supposed to be so warm, out-patients were sweating as they pushed around trying to get the maximum in medical treatment at KEM. Battered ambulances rolled up at Casualty and there weren't enough gurneys. There weren't enough helpers either, relatives were carrying their own patients on stretchers. People were everywhere, it was the morning visiting hours, the wards were full, the OPD was jampacked, each patient had come with two relatives. There was just no place to sit down together and feel the full impact of what had happened yesterday evening.

Aruna took Sundeep up to the terrace at the dog lab. They leaned against the lab's wall near the kennels, trying to avoid the hot sun. They did not talk. Sundeep crossed his arms over his chest, closed his eyes and rested the back of his head against the wall. Aruna reached out hesitantly, touched his upper arm and stroked a small section of it as though comforting an infant. Sundeep, with eyes still closed, caught her tiny hand in his and settled it on his arm. Aruna inched closer and set her head on it, she closed her eyes. It occurred to neither that this was the first time in their close-to-four-year-old relationship they had physically, intentionally touched each other. Together they leaned against the wall in the half-shade, in grief at what had happened, in relief that they had each other no matter what.

Aruna felt uncomfortable, a prickling sensation; she raised her head from Sundeep's arm and opened her eyes to look right into a dark, flat, glittering pair staring at her from across the kennels. She gasped in fright. Instinctively Sundeep clasped his arms around her, 'What happened?'

Aruna gestured with her head for Sundeep to look towards that side of the kennels. Sohanlal did not move an inch, he continued looking at them. Sundeep dropped his arms from around Aruna, 'Come, we'll go downstairs.' They went towards the stairwell, Sohanlal followed them, Aruna dug her nails into Sundeep's arm. They stopped, Sohanlal stopped, 'Salaam doctorsaab.' Sundeep acknowledged his greeting with a curt nod, sheperding Aruna out of the area. Sohanlal stood at the door of the terrace watching them go down the stairs.

'Does that that fellow always stare so insolently?' Sundeep asked when they settled in with their fruit juices in the small restaurant across KEM's main gate.

Aruna nodded, 'That's Sohanlal the sweeper who steals the dogs' food.'

Sundeep was quiet. Aruna sipped her sweet lime juice and looked at him, 'What will we do now?'

'Carry on as if nothing happened.'

'Means?'

'I have to give my MD exams in three months, there is so much to complete in terms of preparation for it.'

'Then?'

'I will set up the clinic as originally planned and look for attachments with other hospitals. I don't know if it will be far more difficult now but it will certainly appear so.'

'Yes,' said Aruna very quietly. 'Everything will become far more difficult now.'

A low note of panic came into Sundeep's voice. 'Don't become non-residential just yet. Cancel your leave, let me get my practice on its feet.'

'Sundeep somebody else has died, please do not kill me because of it.'

'Don't be dramatic Aruna.'

'I'm not. You don't understand, maybe you don't want to.'

'That's not fair. Alright, if you think I don't understand you explain it to me.'

Aruna took a deep breath. 'What has happened cannot be altered. Maybe this is for the best even though I don't understand how it can be possible. Anyway we have to look ahead. After your MD in December you will leave KEM to start private practice along with your hospital attachments. You will have to stay somewhere from January, where?'

'With my brother and his wife in Sion.'

'For how long?'

'Till we get our own flat.'

'No matter how long it takes? Supposing some other unexpected shock comes up, the way it did yesterday? Why should your sister-in-law tolerate your presence for so long in her small house?'

'I had not thought of it like that,' admitted Sundeep. 'But we won't have any more setbacks after this. I was depending on external factors, this happened. Henceforward I will be self-dependent.'

'Then let us be self-dependent together. We will find a small rented flat near wherever you decide to have the clinic.'

Sundeep's brow creased. 'I still wish you would not become non-residential from November itself.'

'I have informed them ages back. You know what a long waiting-list there is for hostel space, by now they must have allotted it to some other nurse.'

'They can always re-adjust for two-three months. You come straight to the rented place from the hostel.'

Aruna laughed. 'We will need the money saved to buy ceiling-fans for our home.'

Sundeep joined in the laughter, instantaneously wiping off his face the years which had accumulated overnight.

Things looked much better already.

Usha sounded unexpectedly unlike herself, 'In my own way I will miss you.'

Aruna folded another sari and put it into her small bag. 'You are saying this only because you know your next room-mate will not tolerate any of your bad moods. Often you can be so sour that if I were to keep a litre of milk in front of you it would split and become paneer by itself in no time!'

'Very funny. Tell me, I have been watching you these past few weeks with your packing, why are you doing this bit-by-bit? I know you don't have a big suitcase, I don't have one either, we could have always borrowed one if you wanted to take it all in one shot in a taxi.'

Aruna shook her head. 'Thanks, but it has been quite easy for me to carry my things in small bags when I walked it to my sister's.'

'You could have at least taken a bus.'

'I would have needed about six bus rides to and fro, and it's not like the bus goes to my sister's door. I have to walk quite a bit anyway from the bus stop. But thanks for your belated concern.'

'Does your mother know you are getting married shortly?'

'No.'

'Don't you want her to be there for your wedding?'

Aruna set the bag on the floor, sat on the bed stripped down to its mattress and folded her legs under her. 'When I was in Haldipur my mother found fault with everything I did. When I was leaving Haldipur to become a nurse, I had to get passport pictures for my forms. I got it done in Kumta, we didn't have a photo studio in my village, and I got one photo enlarged and framed which I gave to my mother. When I went the last time to visit I noticed that she had put it up right next to the photos of gods and goddesses and my dead relatives. My mother's mental attitude is different, you could say my full family is like that. Therefore, I doubt it very much if anyone will mind about not being told in advance.'

'You will not mind not having a normal wedding?'

'What will come afterwards will be so normal and wonderful that it's worth everything. God is being so kind. Imagine, He is getting me married to someone who was just four hours down the highway. He sent us both to Bombay so that we could meet here.'

'Highway? What are you talking about? Or have you suddenly become as mentally different as your family?'

'Never mind, you won't understand. Chalo I'm going. See you in the hospital from tomorrow.'

'Aruna, you've forgotten your bucket under the bed.'

'Look what's in it.'

Usha pulled out the bucket from under the bed. Its contents slopped on the floor. 'Kanji!'

Aruna smiled sweetly. 'That's for you, my good-bye gift. I've also left instructions with the staff kitchen that fresh kanji be delivered on your off-days.'

'Swine!'

'It takes one to recognize another. Ta-ta.'

Sensible routines are best established swiftly, they become easier to slip into and follow. Aruna would wake up before much of the chawl so that she could use its common toilet while it was relatively dry. She would be bathed, dressed, sipping her cup of tea when her sister would hand over a small dabba with her lunch. Each morning when leaving she would remind her sister that the bucket in which she had soaked her clothes was not to be touched, she would be washing her clothes herself in the evening when she returned.

She would sling her brown handbag on her left arm and then secure it under her armpit for safety; Bombay's roads were filled with bag-snatchers. She knew that Bombay's local trains were filled with chain-snatchers who grabbed at the dangling gold, she didn't take a chance on that either, her chain was safely tucked into her blouse. With her dabba in a small separate plastic bag from that of her uniform so that the smell of the food would not seep into the fabric, Aruna would walk briskly to KEM through the back-lanes brimming with garbage, and reach the CVTC basement by 7.30 a.m. Sister Mary Joseph would arrive a little after Aruna.

There were several nurses, specially the older ones, who preferred to come to work and go back home in their saris. There were two reasons for this, the most obvious that they felt uncomfortable in their uniforms, which in effect were 'dresses' anywhere outside the hospital. The younger nurses who might not have minded coming to work dressed for it, found that they couldn't because of the enormous distance they had to travel between work and home. Crisp uniforms didn't stand a chance in the people-crush of changing buses and trains. As for the colour white, within the hour of wearing it reflected the grey of Bombay's sea. For all these nurses and their uniforms, a changing room with lockers had been provided on the fifth floor of the CVTC.

Sister Mary Joseph, and every single nurse before her who had been assigned to CVTC dog lab duty, never took the trouble of going up to the fifth floor. They changed in the defunct dog operation room in the basement, a 413 square foot space with windows in the northern wall, shut to the sun and breeze and secured with iron grills. It was the easiest thing to do, report for duty in the duty room, use the cupboards there as lockers, and change in the attached dog surgery. Why go till upstairs twice a day when one could just get on with one's work? True the dog surgery room was dark and airless, but all of the CVTC dog lab in the basement was miserable. It was even a little frightening, that's why the nurses assigned to it never changed alone but always in the company of each other. Nurses never even entered the basement alone if they could help it.

The senior nurses were aware that these Sisters were changing in the CVTC dog lab. Every now and then they would remind the Sisters that it was against the rules, some of them had even visited the basement and wondered aloud why the girls would want to change in a place which felt 'like a mortuary'. The girls would apologize, take the elevator to the fifth floor for a few days, then forget about the rules once again. This had been going on ever since the CVTC building had been built and nurses routinely assigned to CVTC dog lab duty. Routine can also be numbing, it occurred to no one that nurses could directly report to the dog lab on the terrace even if the official records had to suggest a bustling lab by assigning nurses to it on paper.

Aruna, like all others before her and Sister Mary Joseph with her, changed in the dog surgery. She would reach by 7.30 a.m., set down her personal and plastic bags on the duty desk, open her brown handbag and pull out a tiny purse made of cane. The purse opened out into two to reveal red lining, she carried her change in it, in the mornings she would put her gold ring and earrings in it since jewellery was not allowed on duty.

By which time Sister Joseph would arrive. They would take turns in changing in the dark dog surgery, saris would be neatly folded along with blouses and petticoats, put into the plastic bags and all of these would be locked in the duty room cupboards with the keys in their uniform pockets. Lunch bags would be carried with them to the dog lab on the terrace before which Sister Joseph would lock the CVTC dog lab, walk down the corridor, lock the main door to the basement and put the keys in her pocket. A duplicate set of these keys were kept in ward 31 upstairs, in custody of the night-nurse on duty. Sweepers assigned to clean the basement had to collect the keys from her at 7.00 every morning.

Duty ended at 4.30 every evening, Sisters Shanbaug and Joseph would unlock the basement, walk down the dank corridor, quickly unlock the duty room door, let themselves in, unlock the duty room cupboards, unlock the dog surgery, change there, lights out, lock up and leave within twenty minutes. Aruna would walk back to BDD chawls, wash her soaked clothes, assist with the evening cooking and then curl up with the magazines she would pick up from the lending library near KEM. Sundeep was very busy with his studies, she met him at lunch-time every day on the hospital campus. The first twenty-two days of November 1973 passed in such a routine.

Also being seen as routine by both, Aruna and Mary Joseph were the stern reprimands they received from assistant matron Durga Mehta when she heard they were continuing to change in the dog surgery. 'Give me one reason,' she asked of them, 'why you should not want to change in the rooms assigned for nurses to do so.' Both of them looked at the floor, assistant matron Mehta realized she would have to get stern to enforce discipline. She discussed the matter with matron Belimal and it was decided that the next time nurses were found to be changing in the dog surgery they would be issued memos following which there would be punitive action.

Sister Mehta received a phone call from her home, Amreli in Gujarat, that her mother had suffered yet another stroke which had left her paralyzed once again. Sister Mehta left for Amreli by the night train but not before handing over temporary charge to senior assistant matron Kusum Upadhyay. Who kept an eye out for Aruna and Mary and summoned them. 'Assistant matron Mehta has spoken to you both. Now I am speaking to you as your senior assistant matron. I know you will not listen, all you young girls never do because you do not have the patience to benefit from our experience. However, it is in your interest to listen this time. When assistant matron Mehta comes back she and matron Belimal are going to get very strict on this issue. Now go, I have warned you, be careful.'

That night the dogs in their kennels on the terrace of King Edward VII Memorial Hospital howled.

They howled again soon after, on the night of 25 November 1973. They howled together, they howled for long.

The dean heard them, late into the night, and spoke to the security chief who went up to the terrace to check. 'Perhaps it's because it is a full moon, sir. Dogs are known to go mad on full moon nights.' The dean told the security officer to inform the dog lab in charge in the morning about the howling. 'We don't want the Society for the Prevention of Cruelty to Animals to turn up again.'

The dog lab in charge was informed in the morning of what the dean had said, and she knew exactly why the dogs had been howling. They were hungry. They were being deprived of their meat and milk by Sohanlal. It was a hectic day, three operations, Dr Parulkar's was the first. Staff nurse Shanbaug watched sweeper Sohanlal carry away the dead dog for disposal, she instructed sweeper Udayvir to take away the blood-soaked linen for washing and called for sweeper Inder to get the food for the dogs from the diet department. Sohanlal returned, went into the kennels, came back and said he was going to fetch the food for the dogs.

There was ice in Aruna's voice. 'That will not be necessary. Someone else will be going to the diet department from today. Henceforward you will bring the dogs from their kennels for the operations, do the dead dog disposal, the soiled linen washing and kennel cleaning only. Another point, I have observed you dragging the dogs with unnecessary force from the kennels. Please stop strangling the dogs like that, with their own chains.'

Sohanlal's eyes glittered. 'Sisterji, you worry so much

about dog hunger and dogs being strangled. What difference does it make if you or I take extra care when doctors kill them every day over here?'

Aruna's voice was so soft that others present in the dog lab could barely hear her. 'How dare you question what the doctors do here. How dare you compare yourself with any of us. Keep to your limits, remember that you are a sweeper, a bhangee. The next time you open your mouth I will be forced to give a written complaint against you to the dean. You will be sacked on the spot. Now get out from here and stand near the kennels till you are summoned.'

Sohanlal looked around the dog lab at the others watching him and addressed technician Sambhaji Jethegaonkar, 'You all, including her, ask me to do your personal work and I do it. I am not paid to do your work.' Jethegaonkar, taken aback, said, 'If you have a problem tell the dean.' Sohanlal looked again at Aruna and walked out.

The second operation went on till lunch. The third took place soon after lunch, a long operation which went on till 3.45 p.m. Everyone was relieved when the doctor left and the sweepers began the cleaning. Aruna sent Inder to get tea for everyone from the canteen. Udayvir and Sohanlal were cleaning up the operating area, separated from the nurses duty desk area with a half-partition.

'Quite tiring,' said Sister Joseph. She dug into her uniform pocket, pulled out the bunch of CVTC dog lab keys and slid them across to Aruna on the table. 'Before I forget let me give them to you. I am on leave for two days, tomorrow and the day after. I will be back at work on the 29th.'

'You better remember to take the keys back as soon as

you get back,' said Aruna, 'I am on long leave from the first of December.'

Inder came back with the tea, Aruna asked him to serve himself, Udayvir and Sohanlal too. 'Everyone has worked very hard today,' she smiled. There was chatter, mild banter. The technicians wanted to know why Sister Shanbaug was starting long leave in December, 'might be some good news she does not want to share with us'.

Aruna blushed, 'Not that I do not want to share it, the actual date has not been decided as yet.' There were general congratulations, a clamour for a treat before she started her leave. Inder said he wanted sweetmeats, shaadi key pede, for all three sweepers. Aruna consulted the doctors' dog operation register and said alright, a big treat for everyone at 3.30 p.m. on November 30 after the scheduled surgery.

Sohanlal collected the empty cups from everyone to take them for washing, he hung the long dog chain scarf-like, around his neck like a dupatta, while he did so.

The next morning there was more than just a nip in the air, a Bombay-style winter was announcing itself earlier than expected. Aruna pulled out a cardigan from her cupboard and put it on. She was a quick dresser, a very organized one too. Clothes to be worn to work the next day would be decided upon and sorted out on a hanger the night before, the hanger would be kept to the left of all the clothes on the hanging rod in the cupboard.

Her sister gave her the lunch box, 'Yes, yes I know, you have soaked your clothes, no one is to touch that bucket, you will wash them yourself in the evening.'

The morning was misty with the smoke of small fires lit

all over Bombay, by the poor on its pavements, to ward off the chill. Aruna reached the CVTC basement, it was darker and colder than usual. Inder was sweeping the corridor, 'Namaste nurseji, aaj thoda late ho gaya, bahut cold hai na.' 'Namaste, andar wala rooms ho gaya?' Inder said yes, he had finished sweeping the dog surgery and duty room, she could go in.

Aruna hurried in, locked the duty room door behind her and quickly changed in the dog surgery. She pulled out her cane change purse, put in her earrings and Sundeep's engagement ring. She remembered to take out the laundry slip for her handbag with money for it, she would send one of the sweepers to collect her silk sari from dry-cleaning later in the day. It was a rani-coloured silk, a cross between deep purple and pink which looked really nice on her, Usha had helped her choose it in a Matunga sari shop. Aruna folded the money into the laundry receipt, slipped it into her uniform pocket along with the cupboard keys, put on her cardigan, picked up her small tiffin box, locked up behind her and asked Inder to lock the main basement door when he finished with his sweeping.

The first operation was scheduled for 10.15 a.m. Sohanlal brought the dog in from the kennel on its chain, dragging it with brute force. He hung the chain around his neck and sat in the wintry sun on the terrace while the doctor completed the operation within fifteen minutes. The dog was medicated and bandaged and Sohanlal carried it to the post-op side of the kennels. He returned to the duty desk with the chain still hanging around his neck, 'I am going to the diet department for the dogs' food.'

'No,' said Aruna sharply, 'I have already told you yesterday that your duty does not include feeding the dogs.'

Sohanlal said nothing, he sat down in the dog lab with the chain still around his neck. Inder came up and Aruna sent him for the food for the dogs. Udayvir arrived, Aruna asked Sohanlal to take the linen used in the operation for washing. 'I am paid to be a sweeper here, not a washerman,' he replied looking all the time at Udayvir.

Aruna instructed Udayvir to wash the linen. Then she drew a sheet of paper towards her and started writing the complaint to the dean. Prema arrived for her customary 'terrace pey time-pass', Aruna told her to wait till she finished writing this letter to the dean about Sohanlal stealing the dogs' food. Do it later, said Prema. They chatted, Aruna told Prema that Sister Mary Joseph was on leave for that day and the next, so would she come with her when she went to change in the dog surgery. Prema shivered, 'The vaatavaran there is so bhayaanak, that place is so spooky I don't know how you can even bear to step in there. Why did you not directly go upstairs to the fifth floor for changing when you knew Sister Joseph would not be there?' Out of habit, admitted Aruna, she would remember to go upstairs tomorrow. Would Prema come with her today? Prema agreed to meet her at the CVTC OPD on the ground floor at 4.30 p.m. sharp. 'Don't get late, I have to reach home in a hurry today,' she said and sped down the stairs.

There was a telephone call from Sundeep. What was she doing just now, the weather was so wonderful he didn't feel like studying, could he buy her a quick coffee in the canteen? Yes, oh yes, and she was gone in a flash. A coffee, a small stroll on the campus, some shared smiles, a few important questions like 'What did you have for breakfast today?' and it was time for Sundeep to study and Aruna to return to the dog lab.

She barely had time to finish her lunch before the doctor arrived for the afternoon's operation. It began at 2.05 p.m. and went on till 3.30 p.m. Sohanlal had dragged another dog in again, the dog chain was then back around his neck. Inder took the dog's dead body for disposal, Udayvir took the linen for washing, Sohanlal sat by the phone on a small stool after cleaning the operating area.

'Tomorrow morning,' said Aruna to Sohanlal, in a cold and clinical voice, 'I am going to complain about you personally to the dean. This is your last day in KEM.'

He looked at her, unblinking, his black eyes glittering, not moving an inch, his thick-set body on a stool with a chain around his neck.

Technician Pandurang Nemane suggested they play cards, he pulled out two well-worn packs from his cloth satchel. Sambhaji Jethegaonkar thought it was a good idea and suggested they play cards in the doctor's cabin. Aruna looked around for Udayvir and Inder to send them to the laundry, Jethegaonkar said Sohanlal would go. He asked Sohanlal to get him a packet of Milan supari, Aruna handed over the receipt of the Whiteway Laundry with five rupees. The phone rang, Sohanlal picked it up, handed it over to Aruna who listened and hung up. 'That was Prema,' she said, 'from the Casualty. There has been food-poisoning in Mahim from mithai served at a school prize-distribution function. Lots of children are being brought in a very serious condition. Adults also. Prema wants me to call her neighbours to inform her father that she will be late today.'

Sohanlal took the chain off his neck, and trailing it in his hands he let the chain rattle right down the stairs, as he left to run the errands. Aruna made the call for Prema. They sat in the doctor's cabin and started their card game. Sohanlal came back with the sari and supari when the last hand had been dealt, he made to return the change to Aruna who gestured that he could keep it. At 4.30 p.m. they stopped the game. Aruna took out her watch from her uniform pocket and tied it around her wrist, she always took off her watch during operations.

They collected all their belongings, Aruna debated aloud whether she should call Prema in the Casualty or go there and tell her that she had spoken to her father. Prema's father had said that if she was going to get very late she must stay the night in the nurses quarters, not attempt to come home in the dark. Aruna decided to tell Prema this personally in the Casualty, it would not be professional to call her on that telephone line in the middle of such a big emergency. They left the dog lab, Sohanlal locked the department and ran down the stairs ahead of them.

The Casualty smelt of rotten eggs and faeces. Adults moaned, children sobbed, their little bodies jerked violently as they retched. IV tubes snaked all over the ward, doctors and nurses tended to patients swiftly. The adulterated mithai cases were still coming in. Prema had her hands full, Aruna assisted a bit with some of the patients, helped Prema locate a few veins for fresh IVs, she did not have to do any of this since she had not been asked to assist by the doctors or the senior nurses present. But she just couldn't walk into a ward filled with fresh patients, deliver a message and walk out. 'Okay,' said Prema with a sudden grin in the middle of administering a tranquilizer, 'you have done your duty, now go home.' She nodded when Aruna gave her the message that she stay back at the nurses quarters if she got too late.

Aruna dodged the ambulances, gurneys and people outside the Casualty and made her way quickly across the street. She ran down the basement stairs, the CVTC main door was unlocked but not ajar. Inder must have forgotten to lock the door in the morning. She let herself in and locked the main door behind her, walked swiftly down the corridor, stopped and walked back. She rechecked the basement door, pulled the additional latch into place. Walking quickly towards the nurses duty room, she unlocked it, entered, pushed open the door which swung back half-way behind her and unlocked the cupboard in which she set the silk sari packet from dry-cleaning and her dabba. She pulled out the plastic packet with her clothes and unlocked the dog surgery door to change.

In the darkness of the basement, on the other side of the half-open door, a man silently shifted his position slightly to monitor her movements. He waited, his eyes glittering, a dog chain tied around his waist under his shirt. Watching the virgin bride within. Any moment now, this dulhan would be ready to be disrobed.

# Towards an Elusive Mukti

A nagging ache in the temples, occasionally accompanied by a mild cold. A general puffiness of the body with a slight swelling of the fingers and the ankles, painfully tender breasts. A mood swing, nerves on edge. Pain; in the knees, the lower back, the lower abdomen. Cramps in the uterus, when that tiny, expandable bag tucked into every woman's body sheds its inner lining month after month—among several unfortunate women every twenty-three days—for three to six days in a row.

In middling to severe cases—some gynaecologists opine that both menstrual haemorraghing and intense pain are direct results of the woman's state of mind—the uterus turns into a throbbing wound. The inner lining tears itself off the wall with ferocity, bit-by-bit, sometimes in little chunks, sometimes in tiny strips. This can happen at any moment, the woman could be shopping or asleep, she gasps with the unexpected viciousness, some women double over. The brain takes charge, there is an irritant, a foreign object within the body which needs to be expelled; the uterus reacts to the message. The woman's opening expands, a rush of bright-red blood, an agonizing contraction and again expansion, the ejection of liver-coloured, differently shaped blood clots. Not unlike giving birth to a baby every four weeks. The uterus now aches dully.

Before all this there is a week of PMT, or pre-menstrual

tension; after the period there is PMD, or post-menstrual depression. Women who don't have any of these may consider themselves blessed.

Aruna Shanbaug is not blessed. She is partially brain dead. She is blind. She cannot speak. She has atrophying bones, wasting muscles. The joints at her fingers, her wrists, the knees, her ankles are bending inwards. To try and straighten them is to cause her pain. She feels pain, this part of her brain is a sly survivor, it continues to be healthily alive. She gets her periods, these are excruciatingly painful periods.

She is in this 'convalescent home', in a far-flung Bombay suburb, from 10 February of this year, 1977. She is drugged, moaning and a bloody mess. Her periods have arrived. She also has the beginnings of several bed sores, lice in her hair and filth on her body including carelessly cleaned flecks of drying faeces. She is wasting away, but her spirit is not allowing this process to be rapid enough to invite an early death.

Her nurse colleagues from KEM have come to visit, they take one look at her and mobilize assistance. A social worker is contacted to speak to some politicians, letters are written to newspapers, telephone calls organized from ostensible strangers to voice their objection to the dean of KEM Hospital and the municipal commissioner of the Bombay Municipal Corporation. The BMC buckles, not in the face of such organized public opinion but with the thought that now if Aruna Shanbaug dies it will be known that it was the city corporation which ordered what has started amounting to an excruciatingly slow—and pain-wracked—murder.

On 10 March 1977, exactly a month later, Aruna comes back home to her hospital bed attached to ward 4.

She is cleaned up thoroughly, medicated, bandaged. Her hair is completely shaved off because of the lice. Her position is changed every two hours, she keeps going back to her favoured foetal postion. Soon she is put on FDHP plus two eggs, Full Diet High Protein. She screams. She laughs. She shouts. She weeps.

Things are back to normal in the life of twenty-nine-year-old staff nurse Aruna Shanbaug.

Dr Sundeep Sardesai stands at Aruna's bedside looking down at her, he hesitates, then he pulls up the stool which has come with her from ward 33 and sits on it. He does not take her hand in his, she is knocked out with the anti-convulsants that have had to be administered over the last twenty-four hours.

He speaks to her, in a very low voice, just a few sentences compared with his earlier long, detailed chats with her. 'Tomorrow is the first of May, my wedding day. My family and friends have fixed this marriage for me. She is a genuinely nice woman, I should not do anything to hurt her. I cannot see you after this. I will be coming to KEM but I will not visit you. There will be talk about this and my marriage around your bed, you will have to listen to it, I'm sorry. If you can, please forgive me.'

Dr Sardesai gets up from the stool and goes to the little locker on the other side of her bed. He looks for the new packet of bindis he had purchased and put into her locker as soon as he had come to know of her return to KEM. The packet isn't there, he rummages around the locker, he cannot find it, he looks helplessly around the room. He goes to the door, turns around and looks at Aruna, walks swiftly back to her bed and folds her limp body into his arms, her arms fall by her sides. He cradles her head in his palm, kisses her cold, unresponsive lips. This is the first time in their four-year-old relationship that he has kissed her. The salt of someone's tears sting his lips. And then he is gone. This time, forever.

Dr Sunil K. Pandya pulls out a sheet of paper from a stack, printed on the other side, kept for recycling. He pauses, pen in hand, gathers his thoughts, and begins writing a letter to Dr Charles Randall in the United States of America at the Seymour Hospital in Seymour, Texas.

Dr Pandya has secured Dr Randall's address with some difficulty. He had been flipping through an old issue of the *Reader's Digest* when he came across an article headlined 'The Eight Year Sleep of Gene Tipps'. The eight year sleep referred to a coma, patient Gene Tipps was able to come out of it with some radical, hitherto untested, medical intervention by one Dr Charles Randall. It could be said, generically speaking, that this Dr Randall had revitalized the patient's brain.

Dr Pandya had first written to the *Reader's Digest* in Bombay, addressing his letter to the editor explaining why he needed the addresses of Gene Tipps and Dr Randall. After a while the editor's secretary had replied saying they had written to their American edition which had specified that the patient's address could not be given. Dr Pandya wrote back saying he would be content with the address of Dr Charles Randall, could they please let him have it. A reminder followed in the mail, along with a telephone call. The address of Dr Randall finally arrives.

With a five paragraph medical summary of Aruna

Shanbaug's condition, Dr Pandya writes, 'Could you please advise about whether you feel that general anaesthesia or intubation with hyperventilation etc are likely to help our patient? Could we please have a detailed medical account of the pre-operative status, exact anaesthetic procedure used during the operation and the sequence of post-operative care in Gene Tipps? Any other help which you can also render will be greatly appreciated.'

The secretary types up the letter and has it posted immediately. She puts a copy under a file marked 1973 and the letter A. Dr Homi Dastur has devised a simple, but fool-proof, method of filing all the neurological cases which come to his department. Either under diagnosis. Or the year of the patient's entry under their care and alphabet of the first name of the patient.

'Why first name?' the secretary had once asked, 'why not last name as is the common practise?'

'Surnames change when women get married,' Dr Dastur had replied patiently. 'Of course in India a few men also change their wife's first name on marriage. Mercifully for our filing system, as also for those women, this doesn't happen too often anymore.'

The secretary does not need to file Dr Randall's reply under 1973, A, because it never arrives.


Nephrology specialist and nurses in charge, Dr Vidya Acharya is trying to explain one simple point to the staff nurses—that they have become far too possessive of Aruna Shanbaug. 'I understand that she is your colleague and your feelings run strong because of all that she has gone through. But you must also understand that she is a patient.'

'You want us to be indifferent to her?'

'You are using the wrong word, you are not indifferent to patients in KEM, at least not as yet. You need to be detached with Aruna's treatment just like you are with that of other patients.'

'If we had been detached she would have suffered very badly before dying in some rubbish bin for human refuse.'

'All credit—and I do not say this because we are having this conversation now—goes to the nurses of KEM for Aruna Shanbaug's maximum rate of recovery. But why must you surcharge the atmosphere with so much possessiveness and anger when we even think of trying a new line of treatment on her?'

'She is not a medical guinea pig that every time some new treatment for the brain is heard of, you all should run and try out some experiments on her.'

'We tried a new method of physiotherapy. You all stopped it because it hurt her, obviously it will hurt, she has not used her limbs in a while. We tried taking her out of the room on a wheelchair, she screamed, you all stopped it. Concern is all very well but does it ever occur to you that you might be a stumbling block in her treatment?'

'Like we were a stumbling block when you all looked the other way when the BMC tried to kill her?'

'The point right now is this. We are doctors, each time academic friends and colleagues of ours from all over the world come to Bombay we invite them to KEM to specifically examine Aruna Shanbaug. Some of them make suggestions, you all take kindly to only a very few of these. Presently there is this Swedish team in the city, visiting at Bombay Hospital, and we are requesting them to come over and see Aruna. Please do not question their motives or look at them with suspicion, they are professionals, treat them with the respect they deserve. Please assist them in her examination.'

The Swedish team suggests the stimulation of Aruna's brain through mild shocks with sensors and probes.

'She is not your laboratory monkey. Nor is she your medical basket-case where everyone can toss in their untried ideas.' So saying, the nurses veto the suggestion.

Dr Acharya sighs, people can be difficult to reach. When Dr Jeevaraj Mehta, the spirit behind KEM, died earlier this year the hospital waited for his body. He had suffered from tuberculosis, his one lung had been removed. He had wanted this to be handed over to research along with all the other organs the hospital could put to practical, or best, use. When he was sick he had told the KEM doctors, 'I belong here, my body should come back to KEM.' Dr Jeevaraj Mehta acccordingly mentioned this when he drew up his will.

So when The King Edward VII Memorial Hospital was informed that one of their founders and first dean was dead, they made all the preparations at the hospital, and they waited to receive his body. But it did not arrive because his distraught wife refused to send it.

May 1978. It is hot, so hot that the air itself seems to sweat. Senior assistant matron Kusum Upadhyay wipes her brow and tries concentrating on the otherwise simple task at hand, the rescheduling of nurse shifts. It is not helping that she can hear Aruna shouting from down the corridor. She has been shouting since the morning. Sister Upadhyay pushes back her chair and leaves her office to walk down the corridor. She is met half-way by trainee nurse Christine Gomes. 'Sister, I was coming to see you.'

'What is it?'

'That nurse, uh Aruna Shanbaug, she has been shouting from the morning.'

'I am aware of it.'

'The patients in ward 4 are getting very agitated.'

'I was on my way to her room, you can come with me if you like.'

The young Christine Gomes falls in step with her senior assistant matron, she has seen Aruna Shanbaug once before, she had peeped into the room when she was asleep. However nothing has prepared her for the sight of a bony, wild-eyed woman with hypertonic limbs screaming hoarsely and continuously. Without realizing it Christine clutches Sister Upadhyay's arm.

'Aruna? Aruna! Stop this, you are disturbing other patients.'

There is an immediate cessation of sound in the darkened room. Sister Upadhyay briskly pulls back the curtains, opens the window and turns up the fan. 'I thought as much, you were shouting away because you wanted some attention, well what is it?'

Aruna cringes away from the afternoon light pouring into her room, she wails aloud. The trainee nurse stands in a corner rubbing her forearms, she has goose pimples. Sister Upadhyay bustles about, straightening the bedsheet, changing Aruna's sanitary napkin made out of a folded piece of padded cloth.

'I know you are in pain because you have your periods. But such pain is to be borne.'

She gestures to the young girl, let us leave the room. Outside in the corridor, Christine meekly asks of her senior assistant matron, 'Can I please ask you a question?'

Sister Upadhyay hesitates, then decides she will answer this child's questions on Aruna Shanbaug, God knows there are lessons in this for all of us. 'I'm going to ward 4 on a round. You can walk with me and we can talk. Come.'

'Does she always shout like this when she wants attention?'

'When it gets very bad she does. Earlier there were so many of her batchmates, even her immediate juniors, who would make it a point to collect around her bed and chat with each other so that she could feel like a part of them. Life is so strange, when she was a working staff nurse she hardly socialized at this level with her colleagues, she kept mostly to herself. Anyway, now most of her colleagues have gone, they are married, they have moved to private hospitals. The new ones, like you, don't know her at all.'

'You were among them, Sister Upadhyay, when they shifted her to that other place?'

'You are asking whether I was in agreement about her being shifted?'

Christine is frank. 'Yes.'

'I felt that it was better if our person was under our care. But I saw it from the administration's point of view too, they were not wrong in wanting a bed to be vacant for patients more deserving of treatment.'

'You mean because she is brain dead she is not deserving of treatment?'

'She is not entirely brain dead. I cannot answer the rest of your question because it is an extremely subjective matter. A decision on this subject is an outcome of a very individual thought process . . . I think it is very ironic, the more medical sciences advance the more heated will be the debate on mercy killing in the future.'

'Is that what it was supposed to be for her when she was sent away, mercy killing?'

'It could be looked at like that as well.'

'Do you think she would have been better off dead?'

'I told you, answers to such questions can only be very subjective. But I do not think there can be too many people in this world who want to suffer, be a burden on others including their own children, be dependent on a breathing-machine and then die physically several years later.'

Aruna starts shouting again, a patient in ward 4 complains loudly about it.

'I am told that some senior nurses feel this would never have happened to her if she had had to obey orders?'

A question rephrased, an answer in contemporarily structured sentences; but the dilemma continues to echo for Indian women over generations.

Sister Upadhyay smiles sadly, 'How often this question gets asked in so many different ways. The answer is the same but somehow this reply keeps refusing to fall into place for you young girls. Let me put it this way. In English the words are man and woman, this does not symbolically signify the difference as much as our Hindi words do, nar aur nari. The woman has that extra letter because she has to take that extra precaution. I know it will sound old-fashioned to you. It sounded very out-of-date to Aruna when I told her she should not change in the CVTC basement. You young girls don't want to take advice from elder, more experienced women because you think you are part of a more modern, better world. Some things do not change, in fact men becomes more bestial as women become more like them.'

Christine crinkles her eyebrows trying to absorb it all. 'Sorry Sister I did not understand. Are you saying there should be no progress for women?'

'What is the meaning of progress? How do you define it? And at what price do you want this progress? At the cost of your virtue? The way things are going today's generation might think of virtue as merely that easily discardable small piece of skin. But because I, an old woman, am saying this you will laugh at me when I tell you that for a woman virtue is connected with self-respect. Virtue goes beyond a hymen hidden in one part of a woman's body, it is also her mind, and the resultant way she looks at the world.'

Aruna's shouts pierce the ward, more patients fret and grumble. Sister Upadhyay sighs, 'Come with me, you can give her the pain-killer injection she has been asking for from the morning.'

Trainee nurse Christine Gomes proficiently administers the injection. Sister Upadhyay smiles her approval. Outside the door Christine once again asks a question. 'Last one Sister. Why is God making her suffer like this?'

'Do you believe in rebirth?'

'Christ rose from the dead. But I don't know for myself, I've never thought about it.'

'According to us Hindus there are rebirths. Perhaps she is paying for what she did in her last life. Perhaps, like your Jesus Christ, she is paying for all our sins. And if none of these thoughts can give us any comfort, perhaps we must just finally believe that there is no God, Aruna Shanbaug's plight is proof of it.'

On 20 March 1980, at 1.30 p.m. Sister Prema Pai goes into Aruna Shanbaug's room and finds her on the floor. She is unconscious. Sister Pai involuntarily clasps her hand to her mouth to cut off her own scream and runs to matron Durga Mehta's office.

Aruna is quickly, and thoroughly, examined. She is found to have a bite on her tongue.

There is an immediate enquiry. It is about to be concluded

203

that when the student nurses came in for the sponging and the feeding they forgot to raise the specially added baby railing on Aruna's bed. All these years it has been this railing barrier which has prevented her from falling off the bed during her several bouts of restlessness. But then both the student nurses insist that they did remember to raise the railing; when they are told that no action will be taken against them if they tell the truth they swear it was not their negligence.

And then Sister Prema Pai looks at the calendar, seventy-three plus seven equals eighty. There is horror in her voice as she asks, 'Is that sweeper free, has he come back from prison? Last time he had almost bitten off her lower lip, how can we be so sure that it is not he who has bitten her tongue?'

There is a shocked silence. 'But the rape happened at the end of November, so seven years means that he would come out only in the beginning of December.'

Somebody speaks very, very softly, 'Suppose he has been let off earlier for good behaviour?'

The Bhoiwada police station is informed at 5.10 p.m. Is this a complaint, who is the complainant, do you suspect anybody, KEM is asked. No, we are just informing you. What are we supposed to do with this information, the Bhoiwada police wants to know. We do not know, let it be on record that we informed you. How can it be on record when you are just telling us on the phone, please tell us exactly what role you want the police to play just now without your lodging a complaint or anyone coming forward in person from your side to give us something in writing. The way it stands right now is that someone from the hospital is phoning to say that a patient has fallen off a bed.

Rumours start floating in KEM. Someone saw him on the road, someone saw him entering the hospital, someone is certain they saw him go towards ward four on the day of the incident. But on questioning they change their minds, they can't say for sure it was sweeper Sohanlal, it has been so long, they do not properly remember what he looked like.

Which is when every one realizes that there are very few in the entire hospital who would know what Sohanlal Bhartha Walmiki looks like. There is no photograph of him on file because he was a badli, a worker hired on a rotational, temporary basis. Sweeper Sohanlal's father, Bhartha Dhekolia, has long since left the hospital. This means he could be standing right there, in front of any nurse and no one will know. This also means that he could be going in and out of the hospital during visiting hours, and could well have slipped into staff nurse Aruna Shanbaug's room that day any time till 1.00 p.m.

The window is found wide open in Aruna's room when it should not have been. Another badli worker says he was sweeping the grounds in the area near the window when he saw a man prising it completely open and looking into the room. He shouted, the man ran away.

Bars are welded onto the window in Aruna's room. Matron Durga Mehta is still uncomfortable, she discusses this with her colleagues and they have a big lock purchased. The huge lock is fastened into place on the door to Aruna's room. Very strict instructions are issued, the door is to be unlocked only for routine activities like feeds, changes, sponges, baths and medical checks. The door is to be unlocked by a staff nurse and locked again by that nurse, the key is not to be handed over to anyone other than a staff nurse. Should there be any slippage in this very serious action will be taken.

And so Aruna exists. Locked in such a private hell mentally that it pins her down physically to one bed in a world shrunk to one room. Now geographically delineated with a lock. The man had come back to complete her incarceration.

27 November 1980. A mere seven years have passed, but enough has happened in them to last several people many lifetimes.

In another world, working in its own time-frame, Haldipur in Karnataka, Aruna's cousin Bhaskar Shanbaug now lives in the big house as caretaker. The house which the yejaman built in teak and sturdy pillars takes some looking after, Bhaskar says it would be easier if there was not so much dirt being thrown up by the enormously heavy traffic on the highway near their gate. He asks how Aruna is, 'When she came to see her mother the last time from Bombay she also visited us, she looked so smart and happy.' Aruna's mother has passed away without knowing of what has happened to her daughter, no one bothered to tell her. Three of Aruna's six brothers have also died.

Sadanand, who had visited her at KEM and whom she had taken to Sundeep for treatment, died of prostrate cancer. It was a bitter battle against cancer, their eldest brother Balakrishna took him to the Tata Memorial Hospital in Bombay, and the Manipal Hospital at Manipal in Karnataka. Sadanand worked as a cashier at a restaurant in Kolhapur, once his savings were exhausted Balakrishna paid for the rest. Sadanand died in pain.

The end was equally indecent for the other two brothers, whom the villagers of Haldipur politely describe as 'mentally slow'. One was standing by the side of the road after lunch, gazing into the sky. It had been a colourful morning, it was Haldipur's annual jatra day and he had enjoyed the rathotsav, the chariot ceremony. A tempo hurtled down the wrong side of the highway and fatally knocked him down.

And then there was the other one, on his own in the house who fell ill, stayed ill for some time and eventually went away.

Death discriminates.

$A$nd continues to do so a decade after a life became so completely worthless.

Meanwhile more people move on, move away.

Like matron Durga Mehta who is in tears. This is her last day at KEM, she had joined the institution in 1951. Thirty-two years of living in, and caring for, a hospital along with its patients. Sister Premila Kushe enters the room and stops in embarrassment. 'Sorry matron, I did not realize this would not be the right time to wish you good luck.'

Matron Mehta quickly dries her eyes. 'No, no it is okay, I was just a bit overwhelmed.'

'I think I understand how you must feel, I know how deeply you care for KEM. But Sister, this is the first time I have seen anybody feeling bad about a promotion!'

Durga Mehta shakily joins in the laughter. 'I know, I now am the superintendent of nursing services at the Bombay Municipal Corporation. I hope to help push decisions in a direction which would help nurses in all BMC run hospitals. Here's hoping it is not the other way around!'

Both laugh, Sister Kushe helps Sister Mehta carry her luggage to the waiting vehicle.

Another Mehta enters Aruna's life when Durga Mehta leaves, albeit indirectly. Harkishen Mehta, no relation to Durga but he knows her well and has had her interviewed for his magazine *Chitralekha* which stands for the goddess of luck. *Chitralekha* and its editor Harkishen Mehta have certainly been lucky for each other, the magazine and the man have attained unparalled success in Gujarati journalism. A general interest, family-oriented Gujarati weekly with timely cover stories, *Chitralekha* bears Harkishen Mehta's stamp through and through with his attention to detail. Not for nothing is Harkishen Mehta called the 'Manmohan Desai of Gujarati journalism'.

For the uninitiated, Manmohan Deai is a Gujarati director who made mish-mash Hindi movies, utterly bereft of strong storylines, chock-a-block with impossible coincidences and crammed with every conceivable emotion for every section of the audience. Animal lovers are treated to the sight of a man-eating, hungry tiger bowing to a defenceless, emotionally distraught mother; or perhaps the scene was meant for what in a section of Gujarat is referred to as a 'maavadyaa', a fully-grown, mother-doting male human.

Not surprisingly, not every Manmohan Desai film is a hit but those which are box-office block-busters are enjoyable to the very end, what the audience refers to as paisa vasool or value for money. Hindi film critics kindly referred to his style of movie-making as 'chaar aane ki murgi, baaraah aane ka masala', or the meat of the matter is but a quarter, the rest is mere masala. Doubtful then, if Harkishen Mehta should take the comparison to Manmohan Desai at its face value.

Harkishen Mehta is certainly a spin doctor, though, when it comes to his serialized story-writing. Every week, after the rest is read and absorbed in *Chitralekha*, subscribers eagerly turn to the last few pages for the story. He writes the chapters weekly, sometimes a few hours before the pages go to press, weaving in and out and around characters with their own complicated lives enmeshed in complex situations which invariably involve cliff-hangers and these enthrall the readers so, it unfailingly makes them buy the next issue.

On 5 December 1983, Harkishen Mehta puts out the first chapter of 'Jad Chetan' and has as his central character a nurse who is in a coma after a rape. He had visited KEM and met Durga Mehta to ask her a few questions on the Aruna Shanbaug case, the rest of the questions were on how nurses function, how doctors interact, how a hospital is run. Jad in Gujarati means inanimate or inactive, Chetan is that which is lively, spirited. He specifies that none of what he writes purports to be the true story of Aruna Shanbaug, however he acknowledges that her rape and consequent coma is his take-off point. He names the nurse in his story Tulsi, after the sacred Indian plant which gives forth beneficial properties when it is watered well and tended to with respect.

'Jad Chetan' appeals to the male reader, it is a kind of localized 'General Hospital' in print. And it touches a chord among the women. Harkishen Mehta is only a quarter of the way through his serialized novel when he begins receiving letters, and phone calls, that he bring Tulsi back to consciousness. The demand grows, it becomes insistent from Gujarati subscribers all over the world, *Chitralekha* has an international edition. Bowing to popular demand, he works it into the story and Tulsi comes out of her coma medically unscathed. She also recognizes her doctor fiancé and happily waltzes off with him into the closest sunset.

The fortnight after which Tulsi opens her eyes in print is utter mayhem for associate editor Bharat Ghelani. He has to deal with the congratulatory calls, there are also the bouquets of flowers and mithai delivered in person by delighted readers. There are telegrams too, and letters, one envelope from Baroda has cash carefully stuffed into the folds of the paper which reads, 'Amoe Tulsi maate maanta maani hati, amaara taraf thi aa agyaar rupya na penda khaay lejo.' ('We had pledged to God that we would distribute sweets when Tulsi came out of her coma, here are Rs 11, on our behalf kindly buy yourself sweets and eat them.')

'Jad Chetan' continues without Tulsi till 14 January 1985.

'Why won't she die?'
There is a whole new set of staff nurses freshly graduated from the in-house training programme, Sister Christine Gomes

is listening to them talk in the staff room. They already sound patient-weary, she thinks. Sister Gomes is getting married soon, she will then join her husband to continue working in one of the Middle Eastern countries as a nurse.

'Because we look after her.'

'You mean if we did not feed her or neglected her she would die immediately?'

'Not necessarily. The human body can stay quite some time without food. And all the time you see poor people lying on the road for weeks on end, they stink but they do not die. I think medically it is called chronic wastage.'

'And imagine, you hear of young, healthy people going like that, in just a snap of the fingers, while playing tennis or something.'

'They are lucky.'

'You are calling somebody young and healthy dying suddenly, lucky?'

'Not just them, I am also calling their family lucky.'

'Tchah, how can you talk like that, in such a heartless fashion?'

'I am being practical. Lots of people keep wanting to live at any cost, even if they have to take hundreds of tablets for it. Then there are lots of other people who keep moaning the fact that their family members died young or suddenly or both. I wish I could say to all of them, release your fear of death. Take a good look at Aruna Shanbaug in our hospital and thank your stars that your child did not suffer even one per cent of this.'

'You think she is suffering because of the sins of her parents? My grandmother used to tell my mother good parents make for a bright future for their children. And even unthinkingly wicked parents—who have caused another's child hurt—will be punished by having to watch their own children suffer.'

'Yah, I agree. I've also been told that the sins of the parents visit the children.'

'In this life itself. No past and future bunkum.'

'Maybe that is what they mean when they say that actually there is no heaven above and hell below. It is right here on this earth and you visit both places several times in your present life according to your day-to-day thoughts and deeds.'

'Aruna has been in hell every single day for the last fourteen years. What is the explanation for this?'

'You mean the non-medical, religious one?'

'Obviously!'

'There is no answer. Just as there is no answer to why she is not dying when people tougher than her have died from far lesser causes.'

Sister Christine Gomes speaks. 'You may laugh at what I feel. I think she will not die for quite some time. Her spirit will not let her die till it is sure that the rapist gets proper punishment from God. This is her spirit's way of shaming God into getting her real justice, where his suffering will be far more severe than what she is going through. It might be impossible to believe that anyone can suffer any more than her, but then Jesus, Aruna's Bhagwan, your Allah, all represent the same creator, He has his ways. For example if you take his voice away from a singer, her feet away from a dancer, his sight away from a painter, then what is left in that person's world?'

There is a small silence, some nurses have been nodding while listening. One of them asks, 'But what possibly can he stand to lose? He was a sweeper, he cannot rise too much beyond that so what would he have to lose when his time comes?'

Another answers. 'Who knows, maybe God will give him

plenty first to snatch it all away in one shot. They say the mills of God grind slowly but they grind very fine. But Sister Gomes, whenever his time comes how will he know that he is being punished for what he did to Aruna Shanbaug?'

Sister Gomes thinks a bit, she now realizes why Sister Kusum Upadhyay had thought it important to give her measured answers. She also understands, now and unexpectedly in a flash, how much those answers have helped her qualitatively mould her life. 'Does it really matter if a person does not know what he, or she, is being punished for? But I think every person does know, people might like to pretend they do not. Deep in every conscience is a check-list, genuine prayer helps us keep track of it. By genuine prayer I do not mean standing around and singing God's praises the way these fanatics and communal-minded people do. Sincere prayer is continuous soul-searching, constantly updating that check-list.'

'If God is so great and just, why did He let off that sweeper so lightly?'

'Because God can only help those who help themselves.'

'If God is so good why did He let this happen to her?'

Sister Christine Gomes smiles. Once upon a time, not too long ago, she had asked this question herself. 'I don't know. Maybe because there's no God up there, all our Gods—like our demons—reside within. Or maybe because He wants all of us, batches of nurses, Indian women, to understand something —which would be beneficial for us—through her plight. To learn some lessons which would help us and we in turn would pass on to our daughters.'

'Understand what, learn what kind of lessons?'

'I don't know as yet. But this may be because we all think lessons have to be big and they have to come announced— something like how the Ten Commandments came—or with

212

a lot of noise and breast-beating. Perhaps Aruna's story has already taught me several small lessons which are significantly altering my life and I have not realized it as yet. What I can tell you right now is that my lessons will probably be different from the ones you learn from it.'

The strange case of Aruna Shanbaug continues to confound people, her spirit travels all over the country and then crosses its borders, compelling people to reach out to her in whatever form they can. Like Praneswar Bokade of Raipur in Madhya Pradesh who simply addresses his letter to Dr S.K. Pandya, Neurosurgery, King Edward Hospital, Bombay. The inland reaches Dr Pandya's desk without any delay. Writing in Hindi Praneswar says he has heard on Radio Ceylon about 'behen' Aruna Shanbaug who is lying 'behosh' for the last twelve years. He is praying for her to regain consciousness, he would like them to know that.

Well-meaning cranks also have their say. Some offer sure-fire faith-healing, some insist on the hospital contacting the evangelist Dhinakaran, someone sends a little bottle of oil for 'massaging her hands and legs so that she can open her eyes', and yet someone else requests that the thread she is sending may please be tied around Aruna's wrist immediately so that she can be better in no time.

One man's evil against the good intentions of several. The balance refuses to right itself.


Would evil also be the word to describe the winds blowing since a while over Bombay; puffing up in great gusts from the pipe of a man who is determined to throw out several people from the city? The South Indians, the Gujaratis, the Muslims, anybody who does not have his kind of chip on their shoulder. All these are the 'outsiders', frighten them into submission, fear is the key to local rule, later that of the state, who knows about tomorrow.

Actually this is one man who can make the difference, truly the city needs someone authoritarian like him to save Bombay. It is showing signs of beginning to sink under the continuous onslaught of being taken for granted. But this must remain Bombay's biggest tragedy. Just when there is someone who can positively influence the city's contemporary history, it must still suffer. More so under this man and his henchmen , for they are in a hurry, no time to carry an entire city along, no inclination for niceties. First divide, and then rule, who says the British did this best?

This fetid wind has to blow right into the BMC, already reeking from the stink left behind by another differently perverse political party. In any institution where human endeavour makes for much of its moral fibre, such ill winds can only affect honest administration. When the wind picks up speed it can almost blow away 'honest'; which leaves 'administration', another blast generally takes care of much of that.

When in Rome, etc, etc, several officers succumb, they have been waiting for this excuse. And then the whole thing begins to smell like Rome in the midst of one of its debased orgies. It occurs to a journalist covering the BMC beat that if the Romans were to put this one particular deputy municipal commissioner into a toga, he would probably be delighted. As it is, his shirt buttons are open to the waist displaying a huge, nauseatingly hairy chest on which sits an enormously elliptical gold coin suspended by a finger-thick gold chain. His habits run to wine, women and song, he shares these interests with politicians of every hue thus ensuring that he can keep the drawer in his desk filled, how else will the coins and chains and chicks keep rubbing against his well-fed, pampered body?

This man likes his women well-endowed, in return he endows them with expensive gifts which cost him financially nothing: an out-of-turn promotion, a not-applicable housing allotment, a job for them, their husbands, offspring. It is a good life, no one to answer to because he never leaves behind his traces, he ensures the connivance of at least one corporator from whichever party rules the BMC during that time. Now his personal assistant, a pleasant enough woman, has asked him for a favour. She wants her doctor-daughter to get that job in KEM. Another doctor is being called in, he is coming from America specially for it, but finally it is her daughter who should get that posting. The BMC officer will obviously oblige, his PA knows far too much of his dealings. Go, he says grandly, rest easy, this will take time but tell your daughter it shall undoubtedly be done.

On 6 December 1988, Dr Rajesh Parikh comes to his first day of work at KEM. His flight came in early this morning from America. KEM could not give him much time to leave the Johns Hopkins hospital in Baltimore, Maryland, so he has packed what he could, leaving his wife with their infant to do the rest and follow. Dr Parikh thinks of KEM as his extended family, he has been brought up on its campus since his father was a long-serving, respected doctor here. He, too, has graduated from the medical college attached to KEM Hospital.

In 1984 he was offered a fascinating research and teaching fellowship at Johns Hopkins, he had asked KEM for study leave without salary for two years. KEM had sent its file to the BMC, the ultimate boss, which had turned down

Dr Rajesh Parikh's request. They were well within their rights to do this, but it helped Dr Parikh after he quit KEM since Johns Hopkins gave him an extension on his fellowship. His learning curve was going upwards swiftly, his contribution to the medical profession could not be discounted, he got a letter from India saying KEM was looking for a department head. Johns Hopkins agreed to release him although he had another nine months of his fellowship left. What is more, he could carry over the research funding from the United States for collaborative work at KEM.

So here is Dr Rajesh Parikh, India's only neuropsychiatrist, utterly jet-lagged but delighted to be back at his alma mater first thing in the morning. He's looking forward to a lot including the sharing of all that he has learnt with the medical students at KEM. His is a new branch of work in the country. Examining the neurological basis for psychiatric disorders and also the psychological manifestations of neurological disorders. Simply put, to connect brain to behaviour to thought to feeling and consequent action; an attempt to understand thoughts and emotions in terms of the complex functions of the brain.

Dr Rajesh Parikh reports to his department at 8.45 a.m. At 9.00 a.m. he is served with a legal notice from a woman saying she had been promised this job. The case goes to court, it is thrown out. The woman appeals, again her case is thrown out by the courts. Relieved, Dr Parikh gets on with the job of setting up his department, what keeps coming up is that he can't ask for too many work facilities since he is not officially a department head. That's a mere formality, he thinks, since he has already been promised the job as department head. He was told on the telephone, when he had called from America, that as soon as he came in he would be officially made department head.

He is not. So Dr Parikh takes up the issue with the dean who directs him to the BMC. He makes several trips from Parel to Dr Dadabhoy Naoroji Road to meet the deputy municipal commissioner in charge of such matters. Each time the secretary smiles and assures him that he will receive the official notification of his promotion soon. During one of his visits, where his distress is apparent on his face, he is told that there will be a meeting to decide whether Johns Hopkins can be considered on the list of BMC's 'approved' hospitals since this is where he has come from. Rajesh Parikh cannot believe his ears, but then again since all these things are only formalities, as the BMC's official has told him last month, it should be alright.

The meeting—between one BMC official and some corporators to find out if Johns Hopkins can be considered a good enough hospital to hire a specialized doctor from—takes its own time to get scheduled. Dr Rajesh Parikh begins spending almost all his time either physically at the BMC or on the phone to it. Yes, says the personal assistant of the deputy municipal commissioner, I am trying to schedule it but everyone's timings just won't match. Eventually the meeting is scheduled, but it is not held. This happens once again, and then yet again. Three meetings scheduled but not held to find out if a proven specialist can be hired from one of the world's premier medical institutions.

On 4 June 1989, Dr Rajesh Parikh puts in his resignation papers at the King Edward VII Memorial Hospital, they are forwarded to the BMC and his resignation is accepted. Word gets around quickly, Jaslok Hospital gets in touch with Dr Parikh. He tells them very honestly that he had never thought of working in a private hospital, so geared had he been towards concentrating on the government-funded KEM. Jaslok gives him time to think, they treat him like a

217

professional. Dr Rajesh Parikh joins The Jaslok Hospital & Research Centre on Pedder Road as their consulting neuropsychiatrist. He receives several things—apart from a cheque which KEM could not even think of matching—including genuine interest in his work and facilitation from this hospital. The happy by-product of this is what every doctor, advocate, engineer, journalist, any thinking working person, longs for but does not too often achieve: professional satisfaction.

Yes, he feels a small twinge of regret when he enters KEM and sees the medical students. He won't be able to teach them, he will not be able to share his knowledge. Well, he pacifies himself, perhaps when he is old and very grey, that is if he doesn't go bald first, and not into a full-time job. Dr Rajesh Parikh is visiting KEM to wrap up the last of his paperwork. As he is leaving the dean's office, something takes him towards ward four instead of his waiting car. He sees the lock on the door of the room attached to ward four and speaks to the nurses on duty who shrug. They do not know very much about that woman inside, she is not really a patient but they feed and sponge her on their duty times. She is far too awkward too handle and she keeps screaming and laughing like a madwoman.

Dr Rajesh Parikh visits the matron and has a detailed chat with her about Aruna Shanbaug, her actions, reactions, body language, quiet moments. He then walks to his car in deep thought. Brain stem damage results in peals of laughter and crying. Sometimes it can even be seen in ostensibly normal people, they cannot stop laughing or crying. Some of them even articulate this to him as their problem, 'That day, doctor, I just could not stop laughing.' Dr Parikh is the only neuropsychiatrist in the world to measure pathological laughter and crying. His work merits mention in the medical dictionary.

He drives out of KEM, possibly for the last time in his life, his thoughts on Aruna Shanbaug. The possibility that the rape continues to influence her behaviour cannot be discounted.

But now, of course, even if KEM lets him do it, it is far too late to expect anything out of such an examination of those aspects; sixteen years is too long a time.

The post denied to Dr Rajesh Parikh goes to the daughter of the secretary scheduling those three meetings which never took place. She is 'highly recommended' by two corporators from the pipe smoker's party. The lady uses her position, and its resultant perks like free but specialized hospital care, paid maternity leave et al, to have two babies. Soon after, she moves to Australia with her husband; the migration had been applied for around the same time she had started jockeying for the job at KEM.

A nurse is horrified as she watches a very senior doctor stuff his trouser pockets with fistfuls of tablets and slip other medicines indented for KEM patients into his bag. She tells her colleagues about what she saw, they shrug. Oh, he has been doing this ever since his wife started running that nursing home near their residence.

A doctor who has been working on an honorarium at KEM, continues teaching students even after all honorary doctors are stopped at KEM and full-time doctors appointed in their stead. The honorary doctors used to teach the students as well, some classes were held till 3.00 a.m. When the full-timers took over as heads of department they also took over the teaching. The doctor who continues to teach now practises elsewhere but comes in the night to KEM and teaches the students free of cost.

He is asked to stop by the administration which views him with suspicion, 'Why should you be teaching our students without expecting anything from it? Also, you are using our class room and electricity without paying for it. Your teaching is also creating confusion in our students' minds because it is different from that of our full-timers. Stop your class on our campus immediately or we will be forced to take action.'

The doctor rents a small place and puts up a blackboard on one wall. He apologizes to the students for having to charge them but he is helpless since he now has overheads; the students do not mind. They come to him in droves, from another medical college as well. The doctor now runs one of the busiest coaching classes for medical students in the city.

Those bad winds, where all they blow in Bombay.

Late 1990. A middle-aged woman of medium height, medium build, medium colour, steps out of her bungalow behind KEM in the dark. Clad in a simple cotton sari and shod in sensible chappals, she softly begins her nocturnal walk around the hospital campus. She has been doing this very often in the last one year since she has been appointed dean of KEM. She is the first woman dean of KEM. Earlier, in 1986, she became Maharashtra's first woman dean when she was promoted at Nair Hospital, in central Bombay. Dr Pragnya Pai, a paediatrician by specialization, is married to a fellow doctor. Theirs has been a love marriage, she is a Gujarati, he a Konkani.

Dean Pragnya Pai's eyes and ears miss nothing as she walks silently, and alone, across the campus. This nightly criss-crossing has given her the kind of graphic insight into the deterioration of KEM which no written report can ever present. She has seen things, heard conversations, and acted on them in a manner which has made people wonder how many informants she has in the hospital. The truth is that dean Pai has made far more enemies than friends.

Drugs in the dank and dark mortuary among the dead bodies. Slum and pavement dwellers from the vicinity washing their clothes on the premises, using the hospital's toilets and bathrooms on a daily basis. A full-fledged bar selling country liquor on the orthopaedic terrace. Sex in a disused shed. This is but a tip of the iceberg uncovered by dean Pai, so much cunningly concealed is being carried out still among several levels of staffers at KEM. This includes not just the menial staff and very obviously the hospital security section, but clerks, administrators, doctors and nurses as well, some of whom are sharing the spoils with their colleagues at the Bombay Municipal Corporation.

Mrs Pragnya Pai reaches ward four and stands in the unlit alcove to listen to a conversation between two young nurses. One is urging the other not to do something with the threat, 'Dean madam la saangu ka? (Should I tell dean madam?)' Far from feeling pleased that her name is being invoked to set things right, dean Pai feels sad. Will they not do things the way they should be, for themselves, for a better quality of life? Why should fear always be their key? A sound emerges from the room attached to ward four, a low-pitched moaning but loud enough to carry till her. The moaning slowly picks up into a wail, one of the nurses nudges the other, 'Go, give her a sleeping shot otherwise she will be a major headache all night.' Dean Pai silently moves away.

The next one week finds dean Pai feeling utterly perplexed, enormously frustrated, frighteningly helpless. A very large batch of final interviews are coming up for several vacancies which need to be filled in the hospital. She has just been informed that all the employees have already been chosen, she also knows how much money each one has paid to whom to secure which job. The final interview is but a sham, this has been happening all too often in the past and the system is too well entrenched to even make a dent in it so late in the day. If she raises it as an issue now, the entire matter can rebound on her; it can be seen as her private witch-hunt which will bear no result, who leaves traces after all?

On the morning of the final interviews dean Pragnya Pai studies the rule book and sails into the conference room. She announces that she, personally, will be sitting in on each and every final interview. There is a stunned silence, there is shock, there is fidgety protest, 'Madam all these are far too small matters for you to bother about.' Dr Pai smiles, 'Please, let me, it has been a while since I have been part of a hiring process.' The interviews take place, people are hired according to their merit. She has read that there is honour among thieves but she is not too sure of this lot, so Dr Pai also ensures that the bribe amounts are returned to those who had paid them.

And so it goes on, each week a new face of human venality. But Dr Pai does manage to make the time for staff nurse Aruna Shanbaug in the ante-room of ward four. She holds her hand, Aruna does not react with fright which is what she normally does with strangers. She speaks with her in Konkani, Aruna cocks her head, her eyes rotate, Dr Pai talks, Aruna listens like an unsteady, but not unhappy, child. Trainee nurses are brought in regularly, on dean madam's orders, to read to Aruna.

Dr Pai also tries to bring Aruna back to the land of the living through the food she enjoyed. She brings fish curry-rice from a Konkani restaurant in Dadar and has it fed to her. Aruna loves it. Idli-vada-sambar follows, with mango during the season. Fish curry-rice is the reigning favourite, dean Pai keeps up a steady supply from the restaurant. Then the KEM canteen cook hears of this and insists that he will send the fish curry-rice, please not to order it from outside the campus. Dr Pai offers him payment, he refuses. Goodness begets goodness. Aruna's taste buds redevelop quickly, she begins spitting out the occasionally uncooked omlette being mashed into a mush and fed to her at breakfast time. Now that she has been fed her spicy sambars, she also displays a contempt for watery dal and rice.

Dean Pai does not know that Aruna is cortically blind, most nurses around her also do not know this, so she tries to bring back colour into Aruna's life. The white curtains surrounding her are pulled down and replaced by those with gay patterns. Printed pictures of film stars and of nature cut out from magazines are plastered all over the bare walls. Aruna's bony wrists are adorned with glass bangles, they tinkle, she tinkles them some more with jerky movements but then these have to be removed when she breaks one of them while thrashing about in her agitation.

So that she does not hurt herself when disturbed, dean Pai has a special bed made for Aruna, padded and adjustable. Softer bedsheets are put on it. Softer pyjama sets are ordered for her to wear to avoid rashes. Softer diapers are stitched so that there is less chafing. Dr Pai also restarts physiotherapy.

She also has a wheelchair specially designed to support Aruna while she is wheeled out of her room and around the gardens. This is a disaster, Aruna cringes when she senses strangers and then howls in despair under the beneficial morning sun in the garden. Several attempts at these 'walks' come to nought, in fact a minus, as Aruna goes into severe distress when exposed to a non-contained world; the wheelchair is abandoned.

'I feel so bad for her. How long will she be able to bear it, madam?' asks her personal assistant Rama Malik.

Doctor Pragnya Pai looks resigned. 'We have this saying in Gujarati, Rama. Maandi shareer no kaam chhe, mrutya samay no dharma chhe. Illness is the function of the body, death is the tradition of time. As long as I am here, and Aruna is here, I have to keep her comfortable.'

As a believer in passive euthanasia, Dr Pai also discounted some friends among her family when she said their grandfather should not be put into the intensive care unit. Her grandmother, all of eighty-nine, leaned over to put some ghee from the katori in her hand in to the khichdi on her husband's thali. She lost her balance, fell over, fractured herself. The operation was successful but the grandmother died in ten days. This was the beginning of the end for the grandfather. He fell very sick, the family said we must shift him to the intensive care unit right away, Dr Pragnya Pai said no. The younger lot, including her grandfather's son, saw what she was trying to say, the elder relatives have yet to forgive her.

Her grandfather died with a very sweet smile on his face; Dr Pai is always grateful to God that she had the guidance not to prolong her ninety-five-year-old grandfather's agony and death.

$\mathrm{D}$r Shashiprabha Satoskar stops at the circular patch of green inside KEM's main gate and watches the gardener at work. Dr Satoskar is the medical officer, she came from Kolhapur as a student to KEM in 1951, and stayed at the hostel, since then KEM has been her home. With a small garden attached, Dr Satoskar has been working to green the KEM campus as best as she can.

'There, maali take out that weed,' she instructs the gardener. 'Have you checked on the stems of the Christmas tree?' Dr Satoskar has had this sapling planted a while back, it is growing to be her, and the garden's, pride and joy visible to all who enter the hospital from the main gate. The maali mumbles that he has checked the branches of several trees on the campus, a small dose of pesticide will not hurt. Dr Satoskar nods, makes a mental note about the requirement and enters the hospital building.

She meets matron Premila Kushe at the entrance. 'Matron, I was just coming to your office.'

'Anything specific, doctor?'

'I wanted to give you this transistor for Aruna. Dean Pai has suggested we keep playing her some music.'

'This is very kind of you, I will start playing it from tomorrow for her.'

The next morning, after Aruna is bathed, changed, fed and patted into place, matron Premila Kushe turns on the transistor and stands by to watch her reactions.

The sounds of an abhang, a Marathi religious song, fill the air; the song floats towards Aruna and surrounds her with its serenity. A look of peace filters across her face, and then, ever so slowly, Aruna Shanbaug smiles.

Matron Kushe finds herself smiling too, what a pleasure to see this unfortunate child happy. To the best of her knowledge Aruna has never smiled before, any of the nurses noticing it would have made it a point to mention it if she had. It occurs to matron Kushe that this is the first time in approximately nineteen years that staff nurse Aruna Shanbaug is smiling. She straightens the curtain in the room and goes to the door, she has decided to leave the transistor on for a while.

The abhang ends, the announcer starts the details of the next song, Aruna screams.

Matron rushes to her bedside, Aruna's face is contorted in

terror, she is screaming and screaming. Matron Kushe quickly turns off the transistor, comforts Aruna until she calms down a bit and then, puzzled, leaves the room to get some medication. What might it have been, just when she was smiling? The answer strikes her as she is locking the door, the announcer's voice was that of a male.

Aruna is more disturbed than she generally is, over the next few days. She alternates between hysterical bouts of laughter and hyenaish howls of agony. Her screams bounce off the walls, her laughter echoes right down the corridor till matron Kushe's office.

Premila Anant Kushe covers her ears with her palms, trying to block out the sounds. She closes her eyes, but she cannot block out the image of Aruna screaming and laughing, laughing and screaming. Continuously. Without any expression at all on her face.

In the dog lab on the terrace of the old, stone building, there is a severe shortage of dogs. Earlier the Bombay Municipal Corporation followed a set procedure, unclaimed dogs were dealt with or quarantined and sent according to their specifications to KEM's dog lab for experimental surgeries. The Society for the Prevention of Cruelty to Animals, as also several other dog loving activists in the city, bore down upon the BMC. Because of their combined pressure, unclaimed dogs are sterilized by the BMC and sent back into the streets. Net result: among other things, they can run around biting bystanders but the dogs are not as freely available to those surgeons at KEM needing to test a procedure before trying it on a human being.

Across the road from the old, stone edifice, it is the

regular, crowded out-patient department morning in the Cardiovascular Thoracic Centre building. Some patients mill about awaiting their turn, not everyone can be accomodated on the moulded bucket chairs fixed onto the floor. A teenaged girl walks up to the nurse on duty to find out when the doctor will arrive, she is carrying her cardiograms in a plastic bag with blood-red, cupid type hearts and on which is emblazoned Love-ly Menswear, Lalbaug.

Assistant matron Vaishali Gawde enters the CVTC with a visitor, they both go towards the back of the ground floor and then descend by the stairs into the basement. The place is brightly lit with tube-lights, cooled with fans, spanking clean, lined with lockers and beds and cheerfully painted walls, some people relax in a small sitting-room type of arrangement watching a Manmohan Desai movie on a tiny television set. It is not one of his best, *Naseeb*, though a telling title as a depressed Manmohan Desai slipped—or was it jumped?—to his death from on top of the water tank of his office building in crowded Khetwadi.

A loudspeaker suddenly crackles to life, will the relative of patient on bed number so and so please come up and see the patient? 'Dean Pai installed this so that the relatives do not have to sit around near the patient's bed all the time,' explains assistant matron Gawde cheerfully. She is a fair, cherubic woman, pleased to be part of something pleasurable. She gestures around the basement and tells the guest, 'This used to be the CVTC dog lab; that room there with the beds, where that man is reading on his bed, that was the dog surgery. This entire area was closed down in 1973-end after which it became even worse than it used to be. It was filthy, water seeped in from outside the building through these walls and stagnated in sticky pools on these floors, big rats ran all over the place. It would be completely flooded during the monsoon months. When dean madam came she changed everything.'

Dean Pragnya Pai almost had the basement reconstructed to stop the seepage and leakages. She had it completely cleared out of its moulding files and furniture, and then replastered, repainted, rewired and converted into a small shelter for the relatives of those patients who come from out of Bombay for their treatment to the CVTC. She set up sixty-one beds, seven separately for women, and added a bathroom facility, locker, fresh bedsheets, a dining room, TV area and living room. All this took a lot of patience and time, and some money for which dean Pai had no hesitation in sending around a hat—donations big and small were cheerfully accepted. She set up Sanyog, a specially formed trust to take over the responsibility and management of the day-to-day running of this place.

Twenty years after the use of that dog chain here, the basement was reopened in 1993 to people who came from Madhya Pradesh, Gujarat, Maharashtra, Karnataka, and the Andaman Islands, accompanying their relatives with hope in their hearts that this broken part would somehow mend at KEM. In the twelve months of 1996-97, 1,517 relatives took shelter under Sanyog's umbrella. In return they paid five rupees per bed, per day.

'Five bucks a day only! It's wonderful what your dean madam and KEM are doing here,' remarks the visitor. 'Why didn't anybody think of doing this as soon as they closed down the basement two decades back?'

Assistant matron Vaishali Gawde looks around the place, 'It had to wait for another woman to try and set things right, and it had to be at the right time because too much had happened just then.' Then she adds what she had said in 1973, as she thinks of that day and that time when she was unmarried and the young Sister Shashikala Vaaran, 'Every thing changed after that.'

Especially a change of attitude towards work for most of the nurses, slowly it was time for retirement from KEM for the rest.

Sister Sulochana Beechi, the first nurse to tend to Aruna in the dog surgery after the rape, is now the matron at a hospital in Mount Abu. Sister Premila Kushe is matron at a hospital on Bombay's Eastern Express Highway; she earlier commuted to work everyday and shifted to living on the hospital's premises after a speeding car knocked her down at 7.00 one morning on the highway. It was a hit and run, the driver did not stop, no one else did either. Sister Kusum Upadhyay runs an orphanage in the central suburbs.

Sister Durga Mehta, completing her posting at the Bombay Municipal Corporation's main building at the Victoria Terminus in the early nineties, lives in her ancestral home at Amreli in Gujarat. Close by she runs the Bhaagini Chaatralaya. The Bhaagini Chaatralaya is a kind of home-away-from-home hostel for girls from the neighbouring villages whose parents would not send them for any kind of higher education if there was not 'a trusted place' for them to stay in. That the Bhaagini Chaatralaya has been welcomed by both the parents and the girls is evident in the fact that Durga Mehta had to have an extension constructed to accommodate the growing list.

Dr Shashiprabha Satoskar moved on as medical superintendent at the nearby Bai Jerbai Wadia Children's Hospital where she is as involved as she was at KEM in the greening of the premises. The Christmas tree at KEM is now tall, strong and healthy.

Dr Vidya Acharya retired after forty-one years at KEM and is now a travelling professor, apart from a practising consultant, on the several aspects of nephrology including kidney donation. She ensures that she also visits smaller hospitals in semi-urban and far-flung places, 'Life should not be a series of mindless seminars in five-star hotels.' Dr Acharya is unstinting in her praise for the nurses who looked after Aruna. 'They took care of everything, her bowels, her bladder, her uterus.' Including her life no matter its quality, ensuring that their colleague did not die. A relay of nurses, in hindsight have they done the right thing?

'I do not know, at least not in Aruna Shanbaug's case,' replies Dr Acharya frankly. 'What I do know is that it is a life completely wasted. Unless, of course, her family turns up from somewhere to give it in writing to the hospital that they do not mind her eyes being donated after her death. Think about it, she came to this tragic state of affairs because she tried to do good for her department, she has suffered her entire life for it. She has perfectly healthy eyes but is blind, and then when she dies her eyes could give sight to two others who are alive. Apart from the irony of it, think of the blessings for her next life, also applicable for those in the family who facilitate such a good deed. Incidentally, there is a section of the inner ear which can also be donated immediately after death. I am told Aruna Shanbaug's brother does not come to the hospital because he is still worried he will have to take her home. Well, he can always absolve all responsibility for her on a twenty-rupee stamp paper stating that the hospital is in charge ever after. That should be enough, whenever the time comes the dean and other doctors at KEM can take care of the rest. I am sure they will be happy to do so, specially since eye donations are on an increase in our country.'

Today is 1 June 1997, staff nurse Aruna Shanbaug's forty-ninth birthday, nobody remembers this because there is nobody left to keep track. Ironically enough it is a different kind of special day for Aruna anyway, it's bath day.

Sister Bhakti Kubal enters the room and prepares to lift her onto a gurney with another nurse's help. 'If I take male assistance to lift her onto a stretcher for her bath, she screams.' Nurses now speak in low voices in Aruna's room. 'If she hears any voice in this room which is unfamiliar she moans.' Bath is a cumbersome procedure, Aruna is a featherweight but her body is constantly at variance with her. Her brittle bones can break if her hand or leg is awkwardly caught even accidently under her lighter body. 'She has stopped menstruating recently,' says Sister Kubal. 'After their periods stop, women tend to easily fracture their bones, so I am extra careful.'

Her skin is now like papier maché stretched over a skeleton, Aruna is also more prone to bed sores. Every now and then she is turned around in bed so that she does not get these sores. Her wrists are now twisted inwards, her fingers too, which are bent at the joints and then fisted into her palms. 'I put oil on her hands to try and prevent this as much as possible, specially since her nails grow into her palms as a result and tear into her own flesh. It really hurts her when I unfold her fingers and cut her nails, but what am I to do? I feel so terrible even when I am brushing her teeth, they are decaying quite badly and causing her immense pain.'

Food is completely mashed and given to her in semi-liquid form. Bread and omelette soaked in tea, her favourite fish curry and rice blended together by hand, ditto idli and vada in the sambar, mango which she loves is fed in part pulverised form. But she cannot eat a full meal any more, her digestive system shuts down after one idli or a few spoons of curry and rice. And Aruna cannot be given any liquids, she chokes. A journalist visiting dean Pai for permission to do a piece on Aruna brings her a fresh sweet lime juice from the Udipi opposite KEM. She feels foolish, and guilty, when she is told Aruna cannot drink anything. She then feels nausea when she is told they will try and mix it into the rice during the afternoon feed.

The journalist gets her permission and does the piece, the response is unexpected, concern pours in from all over the country. But it does create a security problem for KEM. People turn up wanting to see her. A woman barges straight into the dean's office with a child on her hip and a man by her side to ask, 'Woh rape kareli nurse kidhar hai?' ('Where is that raped nurse?') Dean Pai gestures towards the statue of Ganapati in her office, points at the idol's heart and replies, 'Look in there, you will see her.'

Another middle-aged lady says she is in between trains, her train from Dadar to back home in Poona has been delayed by a few hours. So she thought she could drop in and see that nurse she read about. Permission is denied since Aruna's room is not a tourist spot.

A male singer comes with his harmonium, there is some hesitation, then two of the nurses stand by when the man sings soothing bhajans for three-fourths of an hour. Here is a male voice, a strange one, there is only a look of peace on Aruna's face.

Another man walks into the matron's office and says he is a wealthy textile merchant but he cannot read English. The assistant in his shop had remarked to him about this article in an English paper and then, upon his request, told him the story in Hindi. It was written in the article that this nurse liked music, is it true?

Matron replies that she has come to this hospital only recently, the journalist who wrote the piece knows that nurse since much longer. If she has written that she liked music, then it must be true.

'I will give,' says the man, 'a radio cum tape-recorder for her with some cassettes.'

Thank you, says Matron.

'But I have a condition.'

'Sorry sir, no conditions here.'

'But you listen to me Sister.'

'I said I am sorry, no conditions.'

'No you listen to me, I just want to see her.'

'Out of the question, we are not permitting anyone to see her.'

'I must see her, I will see her. Otherwise I will not give the two-in-one.'

'It is alright if you do not. Good day.'

The man turns up twice again, saying he has already purchased the electronic appliance for that nurse, now he just wants to see her before he hands it over. Matron consults dean Pai who asks whether it appears the man will keep visiting the hospital and making a nuisance of himself. Yes, says matron, he has already been here thrice and the last time he refused to budge from my office till I said I would have to ask you. Dean Pai feels that there is no point not getting rid of the man, show him Aruna from the door and make it quite clear before doing so that we do not expect to see him again. If he comes again, we will have to call our security to deal with him firmly.

The man peeps into Aruna's room and is gone.

A faith-healer woman comes from the western suburbs, Versova. She is given permission to pray by Aruna's bed but not touch her, a student nurse is stationed on one side to keep an eye on the proceedings. She telephones matron next day to tell her that she has been in communion with Jesus last night.

233

She asked Jesus about a tentative date of Aruna's departure from this world. He replied that 'he was thinking about it'.

The lady who gives Reiki is much simpler to deal with. She sits at Aruna's bedside serenely with her palm outsretched and her lips moving silently. After she is done she thanks the staff and says she will henceforward be giving the Reiki from her home, it will reach Aruna, please do not worry.

There are offers for clothes, books, food, money; these are all politely declined, Aruna has no active need for any of these things, the hospital provides all that she does need. Bar one need, which no one seems to be in a position to give her gracefully, not even God—her release.

# 27 November 1997.

Twenty-four years after it all.

Balakrishna Ramchandra Shanbaug, Aruna's brother and guardian for a while, is seventy-one years of age now. The shift from Bombay to Shimoga has been beneficial for him and his family. Business has also been good, his restaurant on one of Shimoga's arterial roads has done well for itself. He and his wife live in a pleasant home in a decent colony, his daughters are married.

'They kept saying leke jaao, leke jaao, take her with you. Where would I have kept her?' he asks, 'What would I have done? That dean Deshpande kept insisting that I take her away, every time he saw me he would say so, so I had to stop going. He just would not understand that it had nothing to do with compensation. Anyway how could anything compensate for what she lost? I did the best I could under the circumstances for everyone in my family. I looked after my mother and brothers in Haldipur and sent them money, I had my other brother treated for cancer till his last breath. Now it is too late for even me, I have very high diabetes and cataract.'

Balakrishna's voice is very resigned when he questions the point of having feelings on any subject. 'What is to be done with feelings when that is all they are—feelings? If you cannot do anything about those feelings, if you are not in a position to do anything about them, what is point of having them? Like I sometimes feel that all of this is a purv janam ka problem. My family suffers the sins from the past life. Well, if this is how it really is then all our next lives are assured of much better times. In the meantime when she dies, and if I am still around, I will go to Bombay and take her to the samshaan ghat for her last rites.'

Such can also be the kinetics of karma.

$D$r Homi M. Dastur, who revived the moribund department of neurosurgery at KEM and set it on its professionally committed course—thus unconsciously playing guru to a number of dedicated doctors— has retired long since from the hospital, though not from professional practice.

He carefully goes through the xeroxes of Aruna Shanbaug's case papers. 'She had a distinct improvement during the first month, then it plateaued. Her improvement was with those brain cells where the activity had gotten suppressed, these slowly came back to complete being. The damage does tend to be irreversible if you stop the supply of oxygen to the brain beyond three minutes, I do not mean an exact 180 seconds here. She has suffered all-round damage to her brain as also to the brain stem. In those days there was no C.T. Scan to show the structural damage, today you could get a pictorial representation of the damage although not at the cellular level.'

Dr Dastur shakes his head in the negative at the unasked question, 'We have the C.T. Scans and the MRIs but there is no treatment, really, today which would be any different from the one administered then. Except perhaps that somebody might try the hyper baric method where there can be the delivery of oxygen at high pressure to the brain. But even this would have to be within six hours or so of the mishap. It is whatever is left of her brain which is keeping her alive; the parts which Aruna Shanbaug needs the most are dead a long time ago.'

Dr Rajesh Parikh agrees, but says he would not subscribe to therapeutic nihilism, that they cannot do anything any more for Aruna Shanbaug. 'Science is the sum total of our existing knowledge. Alexander Fleming found penicillin when examining fungus in a dish, once upon a time tuberculosis was a death disease. Today heart transplants are being done, brain transplants are being tried out in the United States of America and Mexico. Agreed that it is not a routine thing but brain cells from the human foetus are being tried on patients with Parkinson's disease.'

Dr Parikh says Aruna's injuries also correlate with her behaviour so an MRI would not go amiss. 'Today a Magnetic Resonance Imaging is so simple, and all it takes is twenty minutes. The MRI will show us the extent of the damage to her brain and we may, accordingly, be able to reduce some areas of her suffering. The chances of her walking again are non-existent, I doubt very much if she will ever see again or regain her speech. But she might just live like this for a very, very long time so we can ensure that she is made more comfortable.'

KEM does not have an MRI facility. But it can be done

at Jaslok Hospital where a top-of-the-line machine is shortly to be installed.

This means KEM giving its permission, and if it is granted Aruna Shanbaug being taken out from the hospital after twenty-one years. How will she react when she feels the sun on her face and then the movement of an ambulance; when she hears the strange voices of male attendants and the incessant roar of traffic as the vehicle takes her from Parel to Pedder Road and back; when she feels the touch of male doctors and an alien environment; when her sense of smell tells her . . . can she smell?

But with the shock of suddenly having to take her out of her protective cocoon and re-introduce her to the land of the living, albeit for a brief while, what can happen to Aruna till she reaches that MRI machine?

Dr Sunil Pandya explains that the human brain has evolved in stages, it has taken more than millions of years of evolution. The most primitive brain had as one of its primary functions the protection of its organism, the other was to find food. 'For the protection of its organism the brain developed the mechanics for recognition, after that it developed a memory pattern. Recognition without memory is of no use. So when it perceived a danger, the brain went into recognition, memory; fight or flight. The human brain still has this primitive brain, fight or flight, as its basis.'

There is no flight for Aruna, no fight in her frail body anyway. The undamaged part of her brain can still react though, and she can scream, and yell, and weep, and laugh since it is all the same to one part of her brain now. She could get convulsions in the ambulance. She could even die of fright right there under the MRI machine, her broken heart could just stop beating.

Would that be such a bad thing, or a good thing to happen?

# 16 January 1998.

Newsline, a gutsy city broad-sheet sold as part of the *Indian Express* everyday carries a story headlined 'Death no release at KEM morgue'.

In summary, the story says that the morgue of The King Edward VII Memorial Hospital has been closed for repairs since September 1997, when its ceiling caved in. Different officials of the Bombay Municipal Corporation give the reporter different dates when she questions them about how long the repair work will take and, indeed, when it will start.

The deputy city engineer says that the work will begin by the end of February. 'The mortuary building is a heritage structure. Though all formalities concerning tenders are over, we need clearance from the heritage committee. It will then be put before the standing committee.'

V.P. Mehendale, assistant engineer of the municipal head office and heritage conservation, informs the reporter that KEM and the main building of its attached GS Medical College are among the tweny-three listed heritage sites under the BMC. He adds, 'According to our phase-wise restoration plan, these salient buildings will be repaired in the next budgetary year. We will check on the condition of the mortuary then.' A budgetary year runs from April to March of the next year.

But post-mortems have to be conducted so that the dead can be despatched their way without undue delay, and dead bodies have to be kept somewhere. The bodies are being kept in the cold room of the anatomy department which happens to be on another part of the campus. Post-mortems are being conducted in a room adjoining the morgue with its non-existent roof. The bodies are carried by workers from the cold room of the anatomy department to the morgue, this would normally take around twenty minutes of walking. But then these are a different breed of employees, the bringing of a body can take up to forty-five minutes, that's if there is no staff shortage. If there is, workers wait for another body to arrive so that they can bring both bodies together to the morgue. This can take for as long as it needs for someone to die, be declared dead and then earmarked for a post-mortem. There is a short cut if a relative wants to speed up the process, pay the employees a reasonable enough amount of money to galvanize them into movement.

Not that this would enable them to use the shorter route, they have been instructed to use the longer one through the hospital building for a reason. The anatomy cold room is located in the college building right opposite the canteen. Students, doctors, nurses, relatives of patients and visitors could be having a cup of tea at the canteen and be confronted with the unpleasant sight of bodies, not necessarily in good shape—or one piece—being carted to the make-shift morgue.

The fifteen by twenty foot cold room is meant to be a storeroom for unclaimed and donated bodies which would be used by medical students for their dissection. But only three of the fifteen trays which house the bodies function smoothly, twelve trays are jammed shut. The morgue waiting to be repaired has twenty-seven boxes to store bodies; around fifty bodies lie stacked on the floor of the morgue. A doctor recalls the time when a rat nibbled off a ear from a corpse before it could reach the post-mortem table. An attendant is morose, 'Bodies with gangrene start smelling. Summer will set in within the next 60 days, bodies will rot even more quickly and will stink like anything.'

The *Express* Newsline story also carries a box in the main story about thirty-eight-year-old Dilip Patil who met with an accident at Vikhroli on December 31. He was operated at KEM, he died on 13 January at 9.45 p.m. His relatives were told that night by the hospital that there was no staff, the post-mortem could only be conducted the next morning. Patil's colleagues came at 6.30 a.m. and were informed that the doctors would be present at 9.30 a.m. Meanwhile the mortuary attendant telephoned the Coroner's Court at J.J. Hospital to seek permission to conduct a post-mortem. The constable on duty at the Coroner's Court granted the permission, the mortuary attendant informed the concerned doctor at KEM. The doctor did not turn up, they waited for a while and then Patil's relatives went to the college building to call the doctor. The post-mortem was conducted at 1.30 p.m.

Patil's people then had to rush to Vikhroli Police Station to obtain an NOC, or No Objection Certificate, they were in luck and did not have to wait for hours on end because the police official on duty was present at the station itself. Clutching this piece of paper the relatives rushed to the Coroner's Court at J.J. Hospital for the other set of relevant papers which could get them the dead man's body for its last rites. Only a Bombayite would understand what it means—physically, financially and emotionally—to rush from Parel to Vikhroli to Mohammed Ali Road and back to Parel within five hours in the thick auto pollution, the noise, the humidity, the traffic, the crowds. The phrase 'running from pillar to post' sounds like a joyride in comparison.

To get his mortal remains back it took Dilip Patil's friends and relatives a full twenty-two hours after he died.

It takes for ever, and then an age, for some people to realize that they do not need to physically be at Nariman Point to prove to themselves that they are in business.

Nariman Point is Bombay's Manhattan without the every-two-seconds-one-wailing-siren of the latter during the nights. In fact it is very probable that the Bombay police heaves a sigh of relief when Nariman Point empties itself out every evening; in doing so it disgorges some of the real rogues. By night Nariman Point is somnolent, stacked with silent skyscrapers watched over by their own security. The only hectic signs of life are apparent at the five-star hotel, The Oberoi; and diagonally opposite, at split mezzanine levels, where there is coursing news adrenalin at the Indian Express Towers.

To find parking during the day at Nariman Point, to wait in the interminably long queues for elevators at each of these towering fire-traps, to actually get cooped into one of these thousands of matchbox-like offices for the better part of a working life, this is a cakewalk when compared with trying to reach the place everyday. Nariman Point is South Bombay's tip, connected with the rest of the city through roads, and traffic conditions, which can treble the time of any twenty-minute journey. Local trains, which bring in the bulk of the white-collar workers here, terminate at Churchgate and the distant Victoria Terminus railway stations; they bus or cab the rest of the way, adding to the stress, noise and auto pollution.

Not that these are any of the city-concern factors which finally gets several people to start shifting. It is the cost of real estate which does it, business magazines often calculate that the per square foot cost of Nariman Point is the highest in the world. Those who rent realize they can rent at lower cost elsewhere; those who own and occupy decide to rent out to a fresh set of suckers and buy more, cheaper, somewhere else and move in there. But where?

The answer pops up in Parel and its surrounding areas where the textile mills have pretty much closed shop, where excess mill land is slowly being converted into residential buildings. Here the existing administrative structures of these once busy material factories can be turned into brightly-lit business cells. At much lower cost when compared with Nariman Point. The advertising agencies are the first to move to Lower Parel, symbolic that another set of yarns will now be spun here.

Lower Parel is rechristened Upper Worli; this automatically gives Worli, once the social back-of-the-beyond bar its sea-facing bungalows, some status. And this brings in more people, it really is alright now to say that one's chauffeur took the parallel Tulsi Pipe Road to save time. Nothing is down-market any more, how can it when it is today retro-chic? The other side of Worli does even better, entire corporate office buildings come up like Mahindra Towers with its contemporary Indian architecture including an interesting choice of exterior paint and exquisitely manicured penthouse gardens. To cater to this corporate world at their lunch time come in trendy Maharashtrian-Konkani cuisine restaurants like Viva Paschim and young couples, chefs trained at the Taj and at Singapore's Raffles, like Namrata and Dhiren Kanwar who set up their gourmet kitchens close by.

Somewhere in the middle of Upper Worli, actual Worli and Mahindra Worli with their lunches of curried clams and quiches with salads tossed in a 'lite' dressing is still the BDD chawls. Here in this sprawl, surrounded by all sides with real estate and social reconstruction, things remain pretty much the same the more they change elsewhere.

Money plants grow out of a kind-hearted cooking medium's used five-kilo jerry cans where earlier there were rusting dalda ka dabbas. Cable wires snake in and out of the hundred-odd buildings, connecting the chawls to each other, collectively they accept satellite-beamed images of another

India vastly different from the one they also watch on their main channel, Doordarshan. Either way, it is all only non-expensive time-pass, the advertising on the satellite channels even more enjoyably non-believable than the programmes.

Behind the BDD chawls are still the several shanty slums, illegal structures regularized by successively regressive politicians developing and pampering their vote banks. And among them is still Nehru Nagar where Shantabai Vasudeo Nayak continues to distribute milk, her burden ironically increased by progress; the switch from heavy milk bottles to the lighter plastic bags has made it possible for her delivery to accommodate much more. It tells even more on her legs, they hurt badly, she ties a few more strips of cloth at different levels around each of them to ease the continuous ache.

Shantabai's daughters are married, her son is a peon in a bank at Andheri, her daughter-in-law is from Belgaum and her first grandchild is a pretty little thing called Vaishali. 'Aruna was even more khubsoorat than her as a child,' she says suddenly, flatly, her eyes on Vaishali frolicking on the floor. 'I went, you know, to see her but I wasn't able to have a look. My daughter had her delivery at the nearby children's hospital, it is quite close to KEM so I walked across to it. They had locked Aruna's room, I told them I was her sister, they said they did not know who had the key, I said okay forget it, and left.'

Anger suddenly explodes in Shantabai's voice, 'They kept saying that I must take her home so I stopped going there. Then they tried to shift her to another place for ever, pack bandh kholi mein rakha tha. Room khali kar dene ka tha, bahut khatpat kar ke waapas laaya. (They moved her to an airless room elsewhere because they wanted to vacate their room, we managed to move her back into KEM after a lot of trouble.)'

The anger subsides as suddenly, she sounds tired as she recalls the time she went to the court, 'They gave us back the things stolen from her except the pendant, they did not return that. I saw that fellow there in the court, people wished him dead at that time. He cannot die, how can he until she is alive? Someone told me that he had shifted to Delhi after his release from jail, he has changed his name and is working in another hospital there as a ward boy.'

When is she planning on trying to see her ailing sister again? Shantabai's eyes go blank as they swivel to the clock on the wall, it is mid-day, time for another batch of deliveries. She picks herself up and leaves her kholi, a large canvas bag in hand. Without saying a word, and wearily.

The nurses are up in arms, they have collected at assistant dean Nirmala Dixit's office to jointly voice their long-standing complaint about the ward boys, attendants, sweepers and other servants.

'They are just never there when you need them,' points out an elderly nurse. 'Each ward is packed to capacity with patients, how are we supposed to manage on our own? And it is sheer hell every summer, when almost all of them take leave at the same time to go to their native places. Relatives of patients have to empty their pots in the dirty toilets, they have to push the gurneys and carry the stretchers themselves. Relatives of patients bring food from home, there are fruits and other eatables, all the leftovers are put into bins at the end of the ward. Used dressings, cotton wool with blood and pus on it and other materials are also put in the bins. Everything piles up because there is no one to maintain cleanliness and hygiene in a proper way, and then everything stinks. It is just terrible, it has become unbearable, can nothing be done?'

'KEM's budget for the financial year of April 1997 to March 1998 is Rs 40 crore,' says dean Pragnya Pai. 'Of this sixty-five per cent is going towards paying salaries. Yes, sixty-five per cent where there is hardly any productivity because there is far too much of job security. There is poor accountability in all spheres of government today in our country. This is to be expected, I suppose, in a system which encourages the hiring of people for several other reasons other than their abilities. Politicians do not want what they see as their vote banks to develop the courage to compete openly. The net result is that mediocrity keeps scoring because there is no such thing as meritocracy.'

And the wage bill keeps rising as mediocrity holds everything to ransom with the threat of strikes. In the year 1990, KEM has an OPD attendance of 14,28,064 patients, there were 63,695 admissions and 57,386 operations. The budget for that year was Rs 18,99,41,740. In 1994 there were 16,01,041 patients with 61,186 admissions and 62,370 operations. The budget for this year was Rs 31,15,61,000. During the year 1995 to 1996 there were less admissions and operations but a higher budget of Rs 35,57,02,000. In this year there were 59,516 admissions and 60,430 operations. The out-patient department did register a higher number of 16,27,342 but the new cases among these were 4,43,287. The new cases in OPD in 1994 were not very much lower, 4,37,114.

Some more number crunching in the year of the Rs 40 crore budget with sixty-five per cent of it going towards just salaries. In the 1,800 bed hospital, 1,750 beds are completely free. There are 630 staff nurses with another 366 trainee nurses. KEM has 500 resident doctors and 370 senior doctors.

Ministers and their relatives down to their drivers, other

state government satraps, BMC bosses and their minions—they are all known to throw their not inconsiderable weight in regard to all the above all over the city. Much of this works with intentionally vaguely worded letters followed up by tough-sounding phone conversations, during such calls threats about transfers are common. Since much of this can rarely be proved, it is politely termed as political interference. All of which gives rise to several enemies inside the walls, a fort divided is doomed to fall.

Dr Pai recalls the time when a patient apologetically came right up to her desk and requested that the fees be reduced.

'What fees?' she asked.

The patient explained, adding that he had been paying the 'fees' all along while it had been rising steadily, but the latest amount was a bit too steep for him to afford.

Dr Pai told the patient that KEM did not charge for what he was talking about, it was a free hospital.

'We all know it is a free hospital,' replied the man patiently, 'and we all also know that we have to unofficially pay some of the doctors to see us. We also know that the doctors share the money with their seniors, they tell us frankly upar tak dena padta hai. Since you are the doctor right at the top and the money has to come till you, I thought I would come to you directly for a small reduction in the fees.'

A mirthless smile curves dean Pai's mouth as she recalls another very recent incident. 'The by-pass project at the CVTC just would not take off. I kept wondering why until I found out, doctors were taking kickbacks from a private hospital for referring the patients to them. There was a time when medicine was an art of healing. We held the patient's hand, we spoke gently, we looked into the eyes of the person who had to be healed by us. Then it became a science of technology. And now it is commerce and trade.'

Dean Pai's son has just completed his medicine degree. She is very close to retirement, there are times when the pressure becomes far too much and she contemplates premature retirement. But it is still nothing compared with what she went through during the first few years of her taking over KEM as the dean. 'I constantly had someone below me talking to someone above me in the BMC, they would sandwich me, they would try and faze me. I kept coming up against vested interests, I almost resigned with the harassment. Then I was told that they were trying to transfer me because I was holding up their gravy train. That is when I dug in, and refused to get traumatized. Those terrible times are behind me, thank God.'

Retirement might mean practice in private hospitals, she has not really thought about it. But she is looking forward to her writing, Dr Pragnya Pai has written more than 160 articles in medical journals and as a paediatrician has authored five books in very simple Gujarati and Marathi on childbirth and subsequent child care. 'I have been,' she says reflectively, 'able to remain upright and uncompromising on my core principles during my career. This has been my biggest achievement personally and has earned me the largest number of enemies professionally. So be it.'

He has made time for memories. 'When the dean told me about the rape I was shattered,' Dr Sundeep Sardesai quietly recalls, drawing invisible lines with his forefinger on the desk. He is done for the day with his eight attachments at various hospitals, the

247

patients at his clinic have all been seen during the evening and spoken to calmly, they have left content that their doctor cares for them and not just the consultation fees they pay him.

His voice is still low, even, measured as he continues, 'The other day I read about a man whose wife was raped in front of him. What must have this man gone through while it was happening? In spite of such facts, movies glorify rape. Does it occur to no one, not even the censors, that the instigation of rape is as big a crime? The media, including women's magazines, report on rape in such a blase fashion these days, no one seems to be shocked by rape any more. Why, has it become an acceptable crime? Is it enough that if the woman is raped she should be successful in getting on with her life physically, mentally and financially? No, it is not okay to get raped even if you emerge victorious legally and emotionally at the end of it all. The mainstream Press should ask for the law to be made very severe when dealing with rapists.'

Yes, Dr Sardesai is aware that the sweeper did not get his sentence for rape. 'What can I offer as my answer? At that point in time it was not an area I was capable of handling at all. I was too far gone, there was too much that was terrible happening all at once. I was having a very bad time coping with as much as I could. It was important for me to try and act normal with myself, stick to my schedules and not give in to my pain, because I had to conserve my energies for my final exams and her treatment. When she opened her eyes, when she swallowed, hope flooded my being. I kept hoping against hope even when Ramdas and I went to see her at that convalescent home.'

Ramdas shifted to Bangalore with his wife after his father died, he is happy to be away from Bombay. His old distrust of allopathic drugs and the medical profession at large has been rekindled, he telephones his friend in Bombay, Dr Sundeep Sardesai, to check on all prescriptions which the Bangalore doctors write out for him.

Dr Sardesai has two sons, a good wife, a decent life. For the annual Ganapati festival he goes with his family to his village near Margao in Goa. Poojas are held here, among the bountiful land and the green fields and the slightly-swaying coconut trees. It is a time for the reaffirmation of family ties, for much happiness, some introspection, for gratitude to Ganesh for all this goodness.

Such contentment, it should be for every woman. It could also have been Aruna's.

Nirmala has found her kind of contentment. Her son Rakesh works in a bank, her younger son Rohit is completing college, her husband Ratnakar Shivrao Telang markets food colours and flavouring essences all over the country, her flat in Borivli has quadrupled in value from the time she moved in as a new bride.

Rakesh and Rohit Telang know about Aruna, their mother has told them a bit. Would they marry a girl who had been raped? 'That is a very difficult question to answer honestly,' says Rakesh after some thought. He has seen Aruna from afar when visiting with his mother and father a few years back. 'My mother kept talking to her in Konkani, she did not even know we were there.'

'I went several times,' says Nirmala. 'I would make my husband take me because I cannot manage the local trains on my own. Twice the hospital authorities would not even let me see her, once I managed to get them to unlock the door to her room. But I do not seem to exist for her anymore.'

Ratnakar Telang recalls the time he saw Aruna bustling around at his wedding with Nirmala. 'I was told that she had a fabulous horoscope, every astrologer had predicted the best for her. Not one of them mentioned even a mild accident to her, leave alone such a ghastly act. Ever since I saw, with my own eyes in the hospital, what had happened to her, I have preferred to keep my distance from astrologers.'

Nirmala breaks in, with distress in her voice, 'The sins of the forefathers visit the children, that is why Aruna is suffering so much. I wonder what I can do to help, I pray for her even though I know that poojas have been performed and the best in foreign medicine also procured for her by her fiance. I had told her not to shift to her sister's house, but she was so worried about saving money for his clinic. This would never have happened if she had continued to stay in the nurses hostel till her wedding day.'

Wouldn't it?

Ravi Ramakant does not like the prefix of doctor attached to his name. 'Do engineers or journalists announce their professions at the beginning of their names?' Sound logic this, so let it be said only once that Dr Ravi Ramakant is the head of the department of radiology at The King Edward VII Memorial Hospital. A dedicated KEM-ite since 1971, Ravi Ramakant is also known all over Bombay's medical fraternity for his interest in the kind of knowledge he can glean on his, and allied, subjects through the computer.

In the last few months, though, Ravi Ramakant has been trying to find out if there is another case like Aruna Shanbaug's anywhere else in the world. He has been working quite assiduously on the computer, logging in whenever he has had the spare time. He has gone through several existing files, checked for others, used powerful search engines, chatted internationally through the internet, posted a few notes. The response has mostly been about people connected to life support systems and euthanasia, starting with Karen Ann Quinlan whose parents waged a long battle in the American courts to let their daughter go peacefully. All very black and white cases, Aruna Shanbaug's is one of those which falls in the several shades of grey in between.

Somewhat like the soldier's in Delhi, shot in the spine and immobile in bed ever since. His brother continues to look after him at home, tending to his every need because all this man can do is blink of his own volition. Television journalist Nalini Singh, who resides in Delhi, recalls the time she went to see him, 'He was an army captain when this happened some decades back. Physically completely unable, he is mentally fully conscious and communicates his needs by blinking. It's like this, one blink for an A, twenty-six blinks for a Z, it takes him a while to complete spelling out a sentence. He was crying when he blinked this to me, "I want an end to this life".'

And then the army captain cried much more when he, yet again, realized that he could not wipe his own tears.

How many years can some people exist, before they are allowed to be free?

The textile merchant comes back, most unexpectedly, with a transistor cum tape-recorder for Aruna. This gives rise to a new problem, who

251

will ensure that this two-in-one does not get stolen?

Matron speaks with dean Pai on the telephone about it. 'The earlier transistor got stolen, I am told. You made some new nighties for Aruna recently, one disappeared straight from the washing-line. This lady journalist who wrote the article wants to get her packets of those readymade, disposable diapers. It would be very convenient for the nurses when changing Aruna but I don't know where to keep those because they will definitely vanish. Different nurses go to Aruna's room for her care, according to their shifts and schedules. Different cleaning women are also sent in there. It is difficult to keep track, this is why we are not keeping anything in her room. What would you like me to do with this tape-recorder, Dr Pai?'

A temporary solution is worked out so that Aruna can avail of someone's generosity and listen to that which she loved a quarter of a century ago. Everyone will do the best they can for Aruna Shanbaug, but the times are such that their best will just not be enough.

**30** January 1998. Twenty-four years have passed from this day in 1974 when staff nurse Aruna Shanbaug regained consciousness. That is, regained consciousness in the medical sense, she came out of her coma. Hindsight makes for perfect vision, 20-20, the question is now easily asked, which was the bigger tragedy? That she did not slip from coma into death? Or she survives with what makes life worth living irrevocably destroyed?

There were several at that time to help her regain consciousness. There are an entirely different set of people today who pray for her release, what other solution would be valid?

They are the same old answers still, much of the world continues to be anti-euthanasia. But is not the question slightly different in Aruna Shanbaug's case?

'Not for the law,' replies advocate Keshav Shridhar Sahasrabudhe. CID sub-inspector Sahasrabudhe retired as assistant commissioner of police, Crime Branch, Thane, on 31 October 1997, after thirty-seven and a half years in the police force. He is now on the other side of the law as an advocate. 'Not really the other side of the law,' he demurs with a smile. 'In fact, my experience should help put it all in the right perspective.'

Advocate Sahasrabudhe points out that two judges of the Supreme Court of India had some time ago decided that the Attempt To Commit Suicide law under Section 309 of the Indian Penal Code was violative of the provisions of the Constitution of India. 'But this decision was overturned by a larger bench with the result that Section 309 continues to be operative.' In other words, to try and commit suicide—obviously non-applicable if the attempt is successful—is a crime in this country.

Adds H.D. Shourie, director, Common Cause in New Delhi, and long-time speaker for the right to die with dignity, 'An Indian court is not yet geared to the concept of allowing a person to be assisted in suicide. I have been expressing that when a person has reached the terminal stage, medical technology should not try to prolong his dying. It will take a long time for our country to wake up to this type of proposition.'

The right to die, which country allows it in the world? Actually this is a bit of a misnomer, everybody has the right to die. The point is, the right to choose to die. The right to choose the time and manner of one's death, doctor assisted suicide, active euthanasia, mercy killing—it continues to be a difficult issue all over the world. As *The Economist*, in its always measured analysis on all subjects, once pointed out, 'Few laws have been drafted to regulate the delivery of death.'

The Netherlands is one country which is liberal towards mercy killings and even protects its doctors from prosecution if four guidelines are followed. One, the patient must clearly, voluntarily and repeatedly ask to die. Two, the patient's suffering should be both unbearable and non-relievable. Three, a second opinion should be sought. Four, the death should be reported to the coroner. Doctors not following any of these four guidelines can be prosecuted for murder.

The northern territory of Australia took some initiative but their 'Rights of the Terminally Ill' law was scrapped when voices were raised against it, although it was very strictly worded. The patient had to be over eighteen, suffering from an incurable illness, examined by three doctors, one of whom would be a psychiatrist, to see that the patient did not have a treatable depression, the patient would have to wait a week before signing a consent form and then wait another forty-eight hours before dying.

In 1994, the American state of Oregon passed a 'Death with Dignity' bill where the patient would have to make both an oral and a written request for lethal medication in the presence of two witnesses, one of whom was not to be related to the patient, not an inheritor to any of the patient's assets and was not connected in any way with the place where the patient was being treated. The patient would have to wait for at least forty-eight hours for death after making the written request.

The trouble with all anti-euthanasia arguments are that while being mostly valid they leave very sick, and dying, people with no choice but to remain in a state of perennial suffering. It is unlikely that any anti-euthanasiast would ever want to be in that patient's place.

In November 1996 the *New England Journal of Medicine*

closely examined how Netherlands had fared in 1995 and compared it with a similar review conducted five years earlier. There was only a slight increase in deaths from euthanasia with no particular evidence of careless decision-making on the part of the patient, doctor or relative. Yes, some euthanasia deaths were going unreported to the coroner but the system of supervision against any kind of abuse was getting more and more accurate. The review found that in 1990, doctors in the Netherlands received 8,900 requests for assistance in death and in 1995, 9,700 requests, most were from cancer patients between fifty-five and seventy-five years of age. But doctors were very careful in how they responded, among the total deaths in the country only 1.7 per cent in 1990 and 2.4 per cent in 1995 were from active voluntary euthanasia. Grey area deaths—that is, administering pain-killers in such large doses that the patient passes away in a drugged haze—were around nineteen per cent of the total deaths.

Is the Dutch data hiding anything? That doctors could be ending the patient's life without consent about the time of death—'She would have died a week later, I needed the bed now'? Abuse from relatives—a sick wife can either choose death or ill-treatment at the hands of a brutish husband? Death has become a treatment in itself?

Still these are no reasons to not continue an active debate on the right to choose to die. Additional safeguards can always be sought to be put into place, adding to the ones of the Netherlands, Oregon and Australia. And keeping in mind that it would take an extraordinary law that could ever disentangle, in each and every case, the motive of mercy from that of easy disposal.

1 May, 1998. The nurse looks at the empty bed in ward four and moves her chair to

it along with all the files. This gives her a chance to spread out all the patient files and work faster than on her tiny duty desk. She is young, she appears enthusiastic, she looks up with a smile when an equally young doctor walks up to her desk-bed and asks her the position on the patients in ward four.

He is on his rounds, obviously the first few of his fledgling career. The nurse and the doctor go through the patient charts together, he checks on some of the patients themselves. He dawdles again at the desk-bed, 'Anything else?' She goes through her list, 'Ah yes doctor, staff nurse Aruna Shanbaug, I wanted to check on whether her multi-vitamin tablet is to be continued.'

'Who?'

'That Aruna, the one who is inside there.'

'Oh her, unlucky number thirteen,' so saying the doctor loses interest, there is no starting thrill here.

Inside, number thirteen as this idiotic young man has just decided to rechristen her, looks unseeingly at a point on the wall. Her head with its white, short-cropped hair lolls to one side, the morning's tea and bread runs down from the side of her mouth to the pillow in a trickle of brown vomit. She will turn fifty years old exactly a month from this day.

Somewhere else in a world left far behind, a carefully framed picture of a pretty young girl with thick, dark hair hangs alongside those of gods, goddesses and departed relatives. Her bright eyes bore into the darkness of a locked house.

Video coaches with blaring music whoosh past on the National Highway 17 nearby, leaving dust in their wake.

# READ MORE IN PENGUIN

In every corner of the world, on every subject under the sun, Penguin represents quality and variety—the very best in publishing today.

For complete information about books available from Penguin—including Puffins, Penguin Classics and Arkana—and how to order them, write to us at the appropriate address below. Please note that for copyright reasons the selection of books varies from country to country.

**In India:** Please write to *Penguin Books India Pvt. Ltd. 11 Community Centre, Panchsheel Park, New Delhi 110017*

**In the United Kingdom:** Please write to *Dept JC, Penguin Books Ltd. Bath Road, Harmondsworth, West Drayton, Middlesex, UB7 ODA. UK*

**In the United States:** Please write to *Penguin USA Inc., 375 Hudson Street, New York, NY 10014*

**In Canada:** Please write to *Penguin Books Canada Ltd. 10 Alcorn Avenue, Suite 300, Toronto, Ontario M4V 3B2*

**In Australia:** Please write to *Penguin Books Australia Ltd. 487, Maroondah Highway, Ring Wood, Victoria 3134*

**In New Zealand:** Please write to *Penguin Books (NZ) Ltd. Private Bag, Takapuna, Auckland 9*

**In the Netherlands:** Please write to *Penguin Books Netherlands B.V., Keizersgracht 231 NL-1016 DV Amsterdom*

**In Germany :** Please write to *Penguin Books Deutschland GmbH, Metzlerstrasse 26, 60595 Frankfurt am Main, Germany*

**In Spain:** Please write to *Penguin Books S.A., Bravo Murillo, 19-1'B, E-28015 Madrid, Spain*

**In Italy:** Please write to *Penguin Italia s.r.l., Via Felice Casati 20, I-20104 Milano*

**In France:** Please write to *Penguin France S.A., 17 rue Lejeune, F-31000 Toulouse*

**In Japan:** Please write to *Penguin Books Japan. Ishikiribashi Building, 2-5-4, Suido, Tokyo 112*

**In Greece:** Please write to *Penguin Hellas Ltd, dimocritou 3, GR-106 71 Athens*

**In South Africa:** Please write to *Longman Penguin Books Southern Africa (Pty) Ltd, Private Bag X08, Bertsham 2013*